# Daniel n...

## soft warm hand

What he wanted to do was take that hand and put it against his heart to tell her how much he had hated leaving her so early this morning, how much he loved to touch her, have her touch him.

What he needed to do now was to keep his hands, his lips and everything else off her. She did not need his hang-ups in her life.

She looked away and instead focused on the documents in front of her. "Liam Bailey's account of maintaining law and order in the early eighteen hundreds is a combination of fascinating and dead dog boring."

"I don't suppose he built a tomb and walled a man up in it."

She sputtered out a laugh. "I hope not. He and his legend have messed me around enough."

"Remind me not to cross you."

"Oh, please, you have crossed me too many times to count."

He stopped studying the file in his hand and gave her a wry look.

"Okay. So some of the times you crossed me, I liked it."

Dear Reader,

Thank you so much to the readers of my books.

Come to Maine this time! Mia Parker has been out in the world, and she knows her small hometown of Bailey's Cove is rare and special. The people value friendship, family and the legend of their pirate founder—and his treasure. When Daniel MacCarey arrives here, his intentions are not to instigate a treasure hunt that may destroy the town, nor does he set out to break Mia Parker's heart—but will he do both?

I hope you enjoy Mia and Daniel's story as they each face their demons and search for their own treasure.

I'd love to hear from you. Visit my website at www.marybrady.net or write to me at mary@marybrady.net.

Enjoy the Harlequin Superromance authors blog at www.superauthors.com. Comment and you just might win great treasures.

Warmest regards,

Mary Brady

# MARY BRADY

—

## Better Than Gold

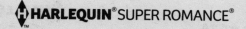

HARLEQUIN® SUPER ROMANCE®

Recycling programs
for this product may
not exist in your area.

ISBN-13: 978-0-373-71888-7

BETTER THAN GOLD

Copyright © 2013 by Mary L. Biebel

Printed in U.S.A.

www.Harlequin.com

## ABOUT THE AUTHOR

Mary Brady lives in the Midwest and considers road trips into the rest of the continent to be a necessary part of life. When she's not out exploring, she helps run a manufacturing company and has a great time living with her handsome husband, her super son and one cheeky little bird.

## Books by Mary Brady

### HARLEQUIN SUPERROMANCE

1561—HE CALLS HER DOC
1691—PROMISE TO A BOY
1730—WINNING OVER THE RANCHER

Other titles by this author available in ebook format.

To my husband and son, who are always there with love and encouragement. To my family of friends and fans, especially my siblings and cousins, who help fill my stories with real life and love.

And to good-hearted pirates everywhere. Argh!

## Acknowledgments

A heartfelt thank-you to the people of the state of Maine, where I have built a fictional town on their beautiful coast without so much as a by-your-leave.

# *CHAPTER ONE*

A STARTLING *THWACK* reached Mia Parker where she stood on an upended bright orange bucket, chipping away at eighty-year-old plaster.

"Holy crap. Oh, holy Jesus, save us!" Charlie Pinion's irreverent bellow buffeted her, and the pry bar she had been using clattered to the floor.

"Jesus, Mary and Joseph." This cry from another, the ordinarily sane member of her construction crew, concerned her more than the first.

"Hey, what's going on back there?" She hopped down onto the old wooden floor and headed from the storefront section of the building toward the rear of her future dining room. The two areas were divided by a twenty-foot-long, four-foot-thick wall with open doorways on each end. Storage closets were tucked into the ends of the dividing wall. An odd arrangement, but the building was two hundred years old, so many opinions and various needs had altered the floor plan over the years.

Mia stopped in what was left of the doorway and tugged the dust mask from her face.

Charlie stood, posed like a burly statue, raised sledgehammer still clutched in his pudgy fists. He gaped at something his large body blocked from her view. Beside him scrawny Rufus Boothby slowly drew down his mask to tuck it under his neat red goatee.

The workers had demolished most of one closet and stripped the plaster, lath and support frame from the far side of the dividing wall. In the middle where the closets terminated stood a column of gray granite. Another oddity. There should be no column in that wall.

"Charlie!" Stella LaBlanc's excited shout came from the direction of the newly installed Women's Room in the hallway past the kitchen area. "Charlie, you big creep, I told you to wait 'til I got back."

She rushed out tugging at the zipper of her jeans as she sped across the room. "The treasure! You found the treasure! I knew it had to be—"

The dark-haired woman threw up her arms as if to ward off something and skidded to a halt between the two men, her ponytail flipping forward over her shoulder. Then slowly she lowered her hands and leaned forward a bit. "Oh, wicked cool."

Mia tried not to get too excited about what this trio had found. Being their keeper, making sure they stayed on task, was practically a full-time job. Plus the residents of Bailey's Cove, Maine, had been searching for the treasure of the pirate Liam Bailey for two hundred years and no one had found a trace. She didn't expect that to change today.

Stepping up to the group, Mia followed their collective gape to the exposed column of rough granite, three feet wide and deep and taller than Charlie.

What the heck?

Then she saw the hole, waist high—and inhabited.

Mia blinked and blinked again. No matter how many times she closed her eyes and opened them, she didn't see anything but hollow eye sockets staring out from a foot-wide gap where Charlie had knocked away the stone with a sweep of the big hammer.

"Holy— Oh, my God. I can't believe it. You're right, Charlie. Holy—er—cow." Her words fell into the silence as she gawked with the rest of them at what she could not possibly be seeing.

A skull. Inside the hole. A human skull, not that she was any expert, but it didn't seem all that hard to assume at that moment in time.

Light from a naked ceiling bulb bathed the dull brown skull, highlighting the emptiness where someone's brain used to be. Mia closed her mouth and looked up at Charlie.

Charlie let out a shuddering sigh and the heavy hammer hit the dusty floor with a sharp crack.

"Hey, Charlie, you really know how to find 'em," Rufus said, slapping his impossibly thin thighs, sending up a puff of dust.

"You gonna run away like you did when you found that rat?" Stella teased the big man.

"Wait, let me get your skirt and frilly apron," Rufus tossed out.

"You can't make me be a wench," Charlie almost squeaked out.

"Charlie, nobody's going to make you dress up like a wench for the restaurant opening. And hush, you guys. Leave him alone." Mia wanted to glare at the pair of hecklers, but all she could do was stare at the skull, a bit horrified herself.

Slowly Mia closed the distance between her and the column of stone and crouched for a better view.

Rufus, named well because of all his red hair, hunkered down beside her. "Hey, boss, not much of a treasure, heh?"

"There's a body in the wall of my new restaurant."

"Seems appropriate for a place that's gonna be called Pirate's Roost. Nice and creepy," Stella added.

Creepy was right. Mia shrugged off the feeling.

"You suppose anyone wondered where he went when he didn't come home?" Rufus asked with a chuckle that sounded more like bravado than anything else.

"Come on. Somebody died. Let's have a little respect." Mia knew this skeleton was going to cause her all sorts of trouble with the remodeling, more delays, more cost, but it was a person, after all.

"Died a hundred years ago if you ask me," Rufus muttered, straightening and stepping away. "Wall's probably been here that long."

The building had been part of the frenzied construction that went on during Maine's early statehood and incomplete records had the building as a hotel. The only available plans for the building did not show this wall or the closets.

Mia looked from Rufus to Stella. "You two take Charlie and get out of here for a while."

"With pay?"

"We'll see."

"Good enough." Stella nodded back.

"We're gone," Rufus added, tugging Charlie away with Stella's help.

Murder? Mayhem? Death?

The skull looked old. Old bones were good, weren't they? She rubbed her plaster-coated hands on her dusty jeans.

"Rufus," she yelled after the fading voices of her workers, "call Chief Montcalm." The chief of police in Bailey's Cove for the last five years was a hands-on kind of guy, a real good law officer, and he'd want to know about this.

"Ah-yuh, boss" came the distant reply.

She stared into the hole.

*Are you just a skull or a whole skeleton?* If this was just a skull, maybe the column of rock was a sacred place, some beloved relative's shrine. *Please don't let it be some murdered guy.* She didn't have time for intrigue. She had a restaurant to open before the tourists began to head north; hungry tourists.

Inching closer, she leaned down again. Darkness filled the recess and made it impossible to tell if there was more than just the skull, and her flashlight didn't help much.

If she could just get a better look…

She tugged a small chunk of loosened rock away with the tip of one finger. A prickle up the back of her neck made her look over her shoulder, sure the chief would be standing there, fists on his hips. When she saw she was still alone, she extracted another of the pieces Charlie's hammer knocked loose.

Through the enlarged hole, she could see there were other bones in the confines of the stone-and-mortar coffin, more of the skeleton. The column was a crypt.

Carefully, she placed the chunk on the floor and straightened. "Sorry, buddy, whoever you are. I'm sorry you're in a wall. I hope it's just some kind of weird burial and that nothing evil happened to you."

Keep it simple. No muss. No fuss. Get the bones out. Get the demo finished. Get Pirate's Roost open and ready for the tourist flood in a few weeks—six and a half, if she had her way, the first week in June. If that happened, she'd keep her shirt and her house, too.

And maybe the town of Bailey's Cove could capture a few of those tourist dollars to help plump up the coffers of the failing small town, population fourteen thousand and shrinking.

She jumped as her phone began to chime from her pocket.

"Hello, Monique. How's your day going?"

Her best friend since, well, practically birth, half of M&M, sighed big before she answered.

"Mrs. Carmody just left the shop." Monique huffed. "She wants to sue us because we can't get the stains out of her fake Persian rug. How about yours?"

"Nothing special. I have a skeleton."

"Don't we all. I told her she should keep the cat out of that room or at least change its food." Monique continued her thread about one of the dry-cleaning business's customers.

Mia chuckled. "Mrs. Carmody's lonely. Maybe she feeds the cat that food so she can haul her rug back in to you. She likes you."

"She could spill chocolate on one of her wool blazers or something." Monique paused and then let out a small shriek.

Mia laughed.

"What do you mean you have a skeleton? Of course you have a skeleton, but that's not what you're talking about, is it?"

"Turns out there's a column of granite in that dividing wall in my future dining room."

"And?"

"And Charlie knocked a hole in the column."

"And he found a skeleton? A people skeleton?" Monique gasped exaggeratedly. "Who is it? How'd it get there?"

"I don't know any of that but it looks old. The granite's a crypt, a tomb, I guess."

"A tomb?" Monique swallowed loud enough for Mia to hear.

"Weird, huh?" Mia ambled out into the storefront area, lowered herself to sit in the dust and leaned back against the wall letting the sunshine filtering in through the dirty window warm her.

"You win," Monique said after a thoughtful pause. "I won't complain any more today. Any idea how he, she, it died? You find a musket ball or a hatchet or anything?"

"I don't even want to think about how this guy died. It's all too—"

"Spooky and gross," Monique said, concisely defining what Mia was feeling.

Mia rubbed at the dust on her forehead. "You probably called for a reason, Monique."

The sudden close blare of a siren wailed practically at the front door. Mia pushed up and brushed off her butt. "The chief is here."

"Don't hang up yet. I called because I wanted you to come over later. Granddad brought us a *lobsta*."

"I was planning to work until—"

"Six-thirty. Be here by six-thirty-five."

"I'll be there." Mia would have stayed every night until she couldn't lift a hand or the pry bar if her friend didn't look out for her.

"I want all the details tonight. You and the chief have fun, now."

"Thanks for the dinner invite."

"Somebody's gotta keep you alive. We're depending on you, ya know. Bye."

Mia said goodbye, wondering if the undertone of melancholy in her friend's voice was real or coming from her own panicked emotional filter.

A moment later, the police chief and two officers strode in and her three workers came stumbling after. One officer stayed at the front door, the other headed straight for the back of the old stone-and-clapboard building.

Chief Montcalm marched toward her, a purposeful expression on his face. He looked about fifty years old. Steel-gray hair, penetrating dark eyes with salt-and-pepper brows, almost creaseless forehead, nose slightly crooked. Fetching in a middle-aged sort of way and hadn't changed an iota in his nearly five years he'd been in Bailey's Cove.

"Ms. Parker?"

Mia straightened. His words felt like a command and she almost saluted, but tucked her curly shoulder-length light brown hair behind her ear instead.

"There's a skeleton in there." She pointed at the wall her crew had been demolishing.

The chief nodded as if he judged this source reliable,

then gestured toward Stella, Rufus and Charlie. "You three, wait outside on the benches, and don't be flagging down passersby on Church Street to yammer at them about this."

The workers' faces fell in unison and Mia had to keep a smile to herself. She knew each one of them wanted to rocket off to their personal corner of the town to tell anyone who would listen what they had found. She was equally sure the chief didn't want any more people tramping through here, and the townsfolk of Bailey's Cove would invite themselves in and do a whole lot of tramping if they thought there was something interesting to see.

"Has anyone touched anything since Charlie's hammer?"

"Um—er—" He knew. How'd he know? She dipped her chin. "I moved a few pieces of stone so I could get a better look, but nobody touched the bones."

Chief Montcalm nodded and motioned with one swipe of his hand for her to follow. She hurried after him, grateful he'd deal with this matter decisively, no dithering. That should save time. She'd have everybody back to work, possibly as soon as a few hours.

The chief strode to the hole in the wall, crouched, unclipped the flashlight from his belt and shined the beam in past the skull. After a moment, he stepped back and shook his head.

"What, Chief Montcalm?" Murder? Mayhem? Plague? She stopped her mind from rushing to the wild places.

"I know you're in a hurry to get this project completed, Ms. Parker, but I'm going to have to delay things until we have all we need from here."

"I—um. I understand." What could she say? This was a person in her wall. But how long would the delay be? A couple of hours? All day? She almost shuddered to think of what more work stoppage would do to the opening date. If she missed the first migration of tourists, she might never be able to keep the Roost open. If the Pirate's Roost didn't stay open, what would that say about Bailey's Cove as a place to visit. If the tourists didn't come, the town would continue to shrink and fade.

The chief stepped over to where she waited. "We can start processing the scene, but I want everybody out of the building while we get to work. We'll get you and your people back in here as soon as we can."

"Has the body been here a long time do you think?" Mia asked, almost afraid to hear the answer.

"Most likely a long time because whoever did this used granite and not brick. Brick if it were easily available would have been a lot less work. You probably know this building's history better than I do."

She doubted that, but she knew he wanted her take. "The building was first built as a hotel and restaurant in around 1818 by the town's founder. It has been many things including abandoned for about two decades from the mid 1970s until '95 then it was a political headquarters. Recently, it was, of course, the yarn and crafts store. I don't know how long this wall's been here."

The chief scribbled as she spoke, and then he looked up and gave her an even gaze. "I suppose we ought to let your crew go soon."

"Charlie at least. Before he bolts anyway. He found an occupied rat's nest last week. Took off across Church Street to Braven's for a beer in the middle of the afternoon and didn't come back. I had to coax him to work the next day with Pardee Jordan's donuts. Juvenile, ah-yuh, but that's Charlie."

Chief Montcalm lowered his eyebrows. She suspected he already knew everything she was babbling at him about, but he listened anyway. That's part of what made him a good police chief.

"My people will get statements from all of you," he

said when she shut up. "We'll check and see if there's any identification on the body."

"Do you think there might be? Even if it's really old?"

"I could see what is probably clothing remnants. Something to identify the remains could be in there. What's left of the clothing will at least give us a more accurate time frame."

A man in paper coveralls entered burdened with equipment, presumably to record the scene and gather clues. Chief Montcalm turned to face Mia. "I'm gonna have you wait out on the porch with the others."

"But I thought I'd stay and…"

Another of his crisp gestures and she turned to join the others on the porch.


IN A DIMLY lit room in St. Elizabeth's Manor nursing home in Portland, Maine, Daniel MacCarey pulled the chair up to the bedside of his elderly aunt. "I'm here, Aunt Margaret."

He took her delicate hand in his and pressed softly.

The quiet sounds of evening at the nursing home clanked and moaned as his great-aunt Margaret breathed softly. Her eyes fluttered open and then closed.

The flowers he had brought to brighten her room three days ago were beginning to fade. The faint smell from the lilies lingered in the air the way her Chantilly perfume had in her stately old home long after he had moved her to St. Elizabeth's. He had wanted someone to be with her all day and not just on Sunday afternoons, holidays and the rare evenings when he could get there to visit her before she fell asleep.

The nurse had called him an hour ago to come. "She says it's time."

The call hadn't been a surprise. Margaret Irene Mac-Carey was ninety-two. Three weeks ago she started looking tired, stopped attending activities with the other residents, eventually stopped leaving her room. A few days ago, they wanted to move her to the acute-care facility, but she had insisted they call for the hospice service to take over her care.

No one had argued.

"I'm sorry, I have to go, Daniel."

Margaret's feathery words came so softly he thought at first he had imagined them, until he saw her eyes open, a faint smile settled on her delicate features.

He brushed his fingertips across the back of her hand. "Is there anything I can do for you?"

She closed her eyes and when she didn't open them, Daniel found himself hoping for more time with her. He patted her hand.

She turned her hand over to squeeze his. "Scare you, did I?"

"You've been scaring me since I was a boy. Why should today be any different?"

Slowly, her eyelids lifted again. "You'll be fine, Daniel."

"Of course I will." His only living blood relative was about to let go of his hand for the last time. He leaned forward in his chair and repeated for both their sakes, "Of course I will."

"Funny. It never occurred to me until it was way too late—" she paused and took a breath "—that when I left, you might end up the last of us. Alone."

She breathed quietly for a minute and then continued. "I'm sorry. I always had your dad and then I had you. Couldn't you just find a woman who doesn't want children? Or even a man, for goodness sake."

"You're so progressive for such an old lady, Aunt Margaret."

"I'm serious about you finding somebody." She squeezed his hand again. "And I have to try one more time. Just because you won't be having any more children doesn't mean there isn't somebody out there who doesn't want to spend the rest of her life with you."

"I've got my work."

"You've got classrooms full of those transient college students." Her voice was weakening, becoming more breathy.

"I've got many things in the works," he said.

"You are so nice to try to let me leave in comfort."

"Don't worry about me."

"You're all I've got left to do. I've finished everything else." Her voice came out raspy and halting.

"Don't worry about me," he repeated.

"I've no worry left in me. I just see things more clearly these days." She paused and her gaze drifted to a photo on the shelf attached to the wall beyond the foot of her bed. The framed picture of a soldier with his arm around a beautiful young woman had kept vigil over his aunt for as long as Daniel could remember. The young woman was Margaret MacCarey in the 1940s with her fiancé, before an enemy bullet had immortalized the soldier at age twenty-four.

Margaret had lived a very long time with the pain of a broken heart in her eyes and sometimes, when she thought he wouldn't notice, on her face. Loving that much when it was futile and hadn't been good for him, either.

"So what they say about hindsight must be true."

She turned her head slowly to look at him. "Hathaway left me when I was almost twenty-two and it wasn't until a couple decades ago that I realized I wouldn't have had to find another love of my life. I could have been happy enough with a substitute, as long as the man loved me. I would have had a companion. You could have had a cousin or two. That is my only real regret."

The words came more and more slowly and Daniel found himself leaning closer and closer to hear them.

"Promise me and promise yourself, you will pursue your dream."

"I promise, Aunt Margaret and I will love you always," he whispered in the quiet left when she stopped speaking and barely breathed.

"Hathaway." Her eyes drifted closed and a moment later her breathing stopped.

Daniel had no doubt the man who had won and kept Margaret MacCarey's heart had just come and taken her hand to lead her away to eternal happiness and peace.

He smiled and swiped at his eyes with the back of his hand. She had always been a great lady. He'd miss her.

Daniel leaned back in the chair. In the quiet, he clenched and unclenched his fists. Several emotions fluttered in and out. Most seemed natural and even expected when a loved one passed, but the appearance of anger took him by surprise. He wasn't angry with his great-aunt Margaret, or fate, or even himself. The dark feelings were just inexplicably there.

He looked up to see the nurse in the doorway. She took a few seconds to gather that Margaret MacCarey had passed and came quietly into the room.

Gently she placed fingers on his aunt's wrist. "Are you all right?" she asked him.

"I am." He would be soon, after this knot in his gut went away.

"We loved her here, you know."

He nodded slowly. "Everybody loved Margaret Mac-Carey." He spoke carefully. This nurse did not deserve to feel his anger.

"You can stay as long as you like."

"Thank you. The arrangements are all made." He gave her a smile. "She saw to that. Said all she and I had to do was show up."

"Sounds like our Margaret. I'll make the phone calls to

get things started. You let me know if you need anything. Oh, wait. I have something for you." She reached into her pocket. "Miss MacCarey said you wouldn't know anything about this. Insisted when I came on shift that I keep it for you because she was going to be leaving. She said it would be up to you whether or not you kept the secret." The nurse shrugged and handed him a small worn velvet pouch tied with tattered ribbons.

"Secret?"

"She didn't explain and I figured you'd know." She glanced at Margaret's quiet form. "I'm so sorry."

"Thank you." He held the lavender velvet pouch for a moment. His aunt was always full of charm and warmth, but there was always a mysterious side to her, things she would almost say before stopping. He had assumed it had to be something about Hathaway. Now he wasn't so sure.

"Put on the call light if you need anything," the nurse said as she laid a hand on his forearm and then left him alone holding his aunt's last secret.

After another moment, he untied the frayed ribbon holding the small pouch closed. Inside was a note.

*My dear, Daniel, you will be getting a package from my attorney in the near future. Please, promise me you will live a long and fulfilling life as I did. Even in the darkest night, all is not lost.*

*Love,*

*Your Aunt Margaret*

He upended the pouch into the palm of his hand and out fell a ring, a woman's ring, gold with a large pale blue stone surrounded by diamonds.

Lustrous, expensive, the kind Great-Aunt Margaret would have happily worn, yet he had never seen the ring before this moment.

## CHAPTER TWO

"YOU'RE LATE."

At 6:42 p.m. Mia shed her old wool coat and shook the rain off on the porch to keep the hardwood floor of Monique Beaudin's foyer dry. The expression on her friend's delicate, oval face said worried friend, no trace of anger. That would be Monique, the M to her M. Mia wasn't sure she had ever truly seen her angry.

"Hey." Mia stepped inside and toed off her shoes. "I thought if I hung around, Chief Montcalm would eventually let me back in."

Monique raised her naturally perfect dark blond brows.

"Well, he didn't," Mia continued as she tucked her damp hair behind her ears. "He had a couple of his people put that yellow police tape across the doors and they all gave me the stink eye as if they thought I was going to break into my own place as soon as they drove away."

"So, did you?"

"I would have, but Chief Montcalm scares the bejeebers out of me."

"Well, relax." Monique took a deep breath and exhaled slowly, accompanying the breath with flowing hand movements.

"I wish I could relax, turn it off like you do. I wish I could."

"Practice. Practice and maybe a nice glass of sauvignon blanc will lighten the mood."

"What makes you think my mood needs lightening?" Mia stiffened her shoulders as if miffed, and then slouched.

Monique bubbled out a laugh and led the way to her neat, frilly living room. "Sit. You need it. I'll drop dinner into the pot and I've got everything else ready."

By the time they were finished drinking their second glass of wine, lobster shells and remnants of Monique's handmade bread lay strewn on the serving tray between them.

To pay the lobster its due and because they were both starving, most of the meal passed in silence broken by such things as "Oh, this is so wonderful" and the cracking of shells.

"So are they going to let you back in soon?" Monique asked as she placed her neatly folded napkin on the table.

"I hope so. Every hour the police lock me out, the more pitifully behind I get. I need my crew back in there tomorrow to have the place ready by next Monday because the finishing crew is due to start." Mia sat forward with her elbows on her knees. "What if all this is for nothing?"

"What do you mean?"

"What if we're too late to build the town up, to make a difference. Building Pirate's Cove will bring in a few tourists, but it's only a start. We need more motels and shops, even more restaurants. And it wouldn't hurt to have some boating business, sightseeing or something like that. If Pirate's Roost fails, especially before I get a good start, will the rest give up?"

"Funny you should mention boating." When Monique sank back against the cushions of the navy couch, Mia realized the usual spark in her friend's bubbly personality seemed to be dim tonight. It hadn't been her imagination earlier on the phone. "What's going on?"

Monique let out a sigh that sounded like defeat. "I hate

to bring it up because it's like an old broken record in my life."

"I'll get my Victrola," Mia said. "Come on out with it."

"Well, when Granddad stopped by to leave our dinner—" Monique gestured toward the remains on the table. "He told me he was moving south, before the snow flies next fall. Says too much of the town has gone so he might as well go, too."

Mia leaned forward, put her stockinged feet on the floor and clutched a frilly chartreuse throw pillow to her chest.

"What happened this time?" The threat Edwin Beaudin, a longtime widower, had been making since Monique's mother had died two years ago weighed heavily on his granddaughter.

"There's a for-sale sign on the Calvins' lobster boat. You can guess how it went after he saw that. Says he might as well give up *bee-un ah Main-ah*." Monique used her grandfather's heavy Maine accent. "I don't know what I'll do if he goes. I wish I still had Mom. He'd stay for her."

Mia's heart ached, but..." Maybe you and I will have to make him stay."

"You know my granddad. He's more stubborn than you are."

"That's what I'm depending on."

"You have an idea?" Monique's expression brightened and so did Mia's heart.

"I have a skeleton, and a crew that needs a nanny. What if he still felt like he was a necessary part of the Bailey's Cove community?" When Edwin Beaudin lost first his wife and then his daughter, he lost the will to battle the elements, pollution, poachers and the competition for the ever-dwindling supply of fish and lobster. "And I need the shoulder of a big strong man to lean on."

"You?" Monique laughed out loud. "Need a shoulder to lean on?"

"I'm glad I'm so amusing."

"Well, you're so 'I can do it myself' that I never thought I'd ever...ever...ever hear you say those words. Lean on someone, especially a man and especially after Rory."

"I'd like to think I've forgiven myself for agreeing to marry a guy who would give me a ring he paid for with my money and have the guts to ask for it back when he changed his mind."

"I'm sure you think you have, honey, but trust me, you still don't lean on anyone for anything."

"I lean on you."

"That's because I feed you."

"There is that." Mia put her elbows on her knees again. "But besides fishing or hauling in a big *lobsta* for his granddaughter and her friend, what does Edwin Beaudin like better than to rescue someone?"

"Nothing. He's been rescuing me my whole life." Monique's big blue eyes opened wider in dawning comprehension.

"Do you think he'd be interested in supervising those three workers for me, keeping Charlie out of the bar? I can't pay him much up front, but as a former boat captain, he can keep a crew in line."

"He might."

Mia felt some of the same tentative hope she heard in Monique's voice.

Monique's shoulders sagged again.

"What?"

"Granddad's right about so many of the old-timers leaving. What if he's right about getting out of town, building a life of some kind away from here? What if it is time to give up?"

"Giving up on Bailey's Cove means, giving up our hometown having a place in Maine's heritage. All we'd have left are the fading memories. No one would care or, after a while, even remember the folks who worked so hard to make this a viable town, your ancestors and mine. At least half the people in Bailey's Cove have a relative who settled somewhere around here."

"But do you think it's worth it to beat yourself up to get the restaurant finished? Wouldn't it be easier to leave it all behind?"

"I've been out there in the world and there is truly no place like home. No place like home." She clicked her stockinged heels together. "And I plan on fighting for it."

"I hope you're right."

"And I know for sure my workers need an overseer because I can't be there every minute. Finding a skeleton in the wall is not going to make them work more diligently. If it's okay with you, I'll ask your granddad."

"He'll clamor to help you, at least for a while."

"For a while is good enough for now. A Mainer stays in Maine unless there is a really compelling reason to leave. He's a *Main-ah* right through to his salty old core."

Monique pushed up from the chair and carried the tray to the kitchen. "I should be reassured by that, 'cause it's hard to imagine him on a golf course or a beach somewhere under a palm tree with an umbrella drink in his hand."

Monique returned with a bowl of grapes glistening with water and another bottle of wine. After pouring them each another glass, she plopped down on the couch and brushed her flowing blond locks back with the crook of her arm. "Why do I have to lose everybody in my life?"

"I came back."

"You did, and I love you for that." Monique held a grape in her mouth, making her cheek puff out. "Do you think Pirate's Cove will make enough of a difference?"

"A small one." One of the things Mia loved about Monique was her friend's penchant for asking the hard questions. "But we have to start, to invest time and sweat equity somewhere, to regrow our town. I'd say money, but right now it's the bank in Portland's money, not mine."

"Do you suppose the police'll call you tonight with any news?"

"I don't know what the procedure is. I don't know if they'll call me at all. If they don't, the chief will get a new desk ornament. Me."

"You're such a toughie." Monique plucked another grape from the bowl and ate it.

"And you're such a girly-girl." To make her point, Mia tossed a pillow with a beaded pink ruffle at her friend.

"What do you suppose will happen with the bones?"

"I don't know. I guess they have to determine how old they are before anything is decided. I just hope they get them out of my wall quickly."

Monique hugged the pillow and grinned. "I know what we need to take our minds off everything else."

Mia waved both hands in the air. "No. No. Not your favorite subject."

"Men!" Monique said and then gave an exaggerated sigh.

"Ha!" Mia leaned back and put her head against the crocheted doily draped over the back of the matching mauve chair. "Men. Had 'em, don't need 'em."

"You got robbed. That rat Rory should still be here."

"Yes. I did and he should. But since I had it all and lost it—twice—"

"I wonder—" Monique put a finger to her chin "—if you'd still say *that* if another good man came along and rang your bell."

"I'd ring his bell right back and send him from whence he came."

"Whence?"

Mia expelled an unenthusiastic huff. "I'm fine just the

way I am. Maybe if I want a man, I'll go after Chief Mont-calm."

"He's gotta be your dad's age."

"What about Rufus's baby brother? He's neither attached nor too old."

"He just left for college, so that'd make you a cradle robber."

Mia slapped the knee of the clean jeans she'd put on after her shower. "Well, that about exhausts the supply of men here in the Bailey's Cove area. I think that's why I moved back here. I wanted a peaceful life."

Monique snorted. "So, that seems to be going really well."

"Skeleton aside, in a few short weeks, I'm going to have the best restaurant for a hundred miles. I'll have tourists clamoring for a meal as they head north and then again when they head south and I'll have a nice cozy mortgage and a nice fat business loan to keep me warm."

"You'll get the chance to work even more hours in a day than you do now. You'll have even more employees to keep on their toes, and more—"

Monique's front doorbell gave its usual unenthusiastic *dong-dong*.

"Am I being saved by the bell?" Mia asked.

"That's gotta be for you," Monique said without any indication that she intended to get up. "Granddad's already safely perched on his barstool for the evening and you're here. That's the entire list of people who might want to talk to me this late on a Tuesday night."

"Won't be for me, either. They'd have called me if they'd wanted me." Mia patted the pocket where she kept her phone. The pocket was empty. "Or not. My phone's in my work jeans."

"How'd they find you here?"

"Because my social life is so grand as to have a total

of three options, the Pirate's Roost, my house or yours, and maybe because my kiwi-green SUV is parked in your driveway."

"And is likely to be there all night because you drink like a fish." Monique gave her a twitchy-faced smile and the bell rang again.

"*Your* doorbell is ringing." Mia smirked.

"You're closer." Monique tossed the pillow back.

"I guess since you provided the lobster dinner, I can answer your bell."

Mia got up, successfully taking a sip of wine as she went, and opened the door to find Officer Lenny Gardner on the stoop. One more for the short list of bachelors in Bailey's Cove. She looked him up and down. How could they have forgotten fastidious Lenny? Everybody in town knew he would take either of them as his wife, and having grown up with him, neither of them wanted a man that badly. But the boy had certainly grown up to be a well-built man.

"Hey, Lenny."

"Chief wants to talk to you," said the police officer who did everything he could to make himself attractive, including aftershave and a smartly pressed uniform and, holy cow, he must lift pickup trucks at the gym. The ploy might even work if he weren't so bossy.

"What did he find out?"

The cop eyeballed the wineglass in her hand. "I'll drive you."

She looked at the glass and then at him.

He shifted his gaze over her shoulder at Monique, who had come up behind her, and the expression on his face said her small ash-blond friend was Lenny's first choice.

"I'll drive you there and back," he promised when he turned his attention back to Mia, this time with the pursed lips of judgment. "We can't have you endangering the townsfolk."

She stifled a two-and-a-half-glass-of-wine grin, but she couldn't deny that he might be right.

Monique poked her in the back. When Mia turned, her friend tilted her head toward Lenny as if to ask, what about him?

Mia handed over the glass, made a deranged face and mouthed, "For you."

Monique made a "call me" sign with her pinky and thumb. Mia nodded, grabbed her coat from the hook behind the door and followed Lenny to the squad. The chill in the night air sobered her a bit.

Be good to me, Chief, she thought.

"Lenny, what did the chief find out?" she asked once they were in the squad and he couldn't dodge the question as easily this time.

"If Chief Montcalm wanted me to tell you, I'd have told you."

That couldn't be good. "No hints?"

Lenny kept his gaze straight ahead, both hands on the wheel and didn't comment. When they arrived at the police station, he escorted her inside with a hand in the middle of her back. If she hadn't known him long enough to have seen him tinkle in the sandbox when they were four, she might have pointed out just how politically incorrect that old-fashioned gesture was. For all she did not like about Lenny, he wasn't a chauvinist. He meant the gesture in the same polite and helpful way he would if she were his grandmother.

There was a lot to be said for homegrown Maine boys in today's world. Maybe Monique should snap him up.

"Ev'ning, Ms. Parker."

The chief greeted her plain-faced in the doorway of his office and gestured her to a visitor's chair in front of his desk. That couldn't be good, either. If he wanted her to sit down before he told her anything, he must be expecting an untoward reaction.

"Thanks for calling me in, Chief." She wondered if she sounded sober. She hoped so.

As she settled into the chair, she heard the door click shut behind her. Whatever he had to say, Mia was sure she didn't want to hear. But, let it rip, like a Band-Aid off tender flesh.

That was definitely the wine.

The chief sat down in his chair and placed his hands flat on the old-fashioned green blotter. "I thought you might like an update."

"Oh." She bunched her shoulders and then let them sag. "I'm ready, Chief Montcalm. Lay it on me."

"We've removed the body and brought it here to our small crime lab. There was no ID with the body, but we did determine from the clothing remnants the body has been there for a long time."

She almost stood. "If the body's gone, can I have my building back now?"

"I'm afraid not. The crypt and the surrounding area will need to be studied."

He tried to make his words sound kind and conciliatory, but she slumped in her chair.

The chief officially calling it a *crypt* somehow made things seem more creepy or maybe the wine was… She stopped the thought and brought her mind back and tried hard to listen, the way he did when she spoke.

"Since the circumstances are suspicious by nature of the body being in the wall, this has to remain a police matter. I called in the state's criminal investigation division."

More people, more time. She dropped her chin to her chest. Of course he called the CID and processing an old skeleton most likely moved slowly through the state system. So they would probably not be there tomorrow. Her brain buzzed with calculations of lost time and the impact delaying the work would have on getting the restaurant open, especially if the state investigators couldn't get here until, say, Monday.

She might have to cancel the finishing work set up for next week, go bankrupt, move to the poorhouse and let the town of Bailey's Cove be completely taken over by a population of non-Maine city dwellers seeking to escape on the weekends and for a week or two during the summer.

It wouldn't be so bad if these people were all lovely friendly people who wanted to visit a great small town and then go quietly away, but there was that ten percent who couldn't help leaving their mark by damaging what wasn't theirs. The town council had decided to take things slow and Mia agreed with them. If too many visitors arrived before the town's infrastructure was upgraded, Bailey's Cove wouldn't be able to protect itself and could turn into a place the natives would not recognize.

Then when the tide of visitors ebbed, the town's two-hundred-year-old structures like Braven's tavern, Pardee's Donut shop, the town founder's home overlooking the town from up on Sea Crest Hill, the boathouse, even the docks would all bear the marks of these visitors. No amount of tourist dollars would make up for that kind of damage. Meanwhile Edwin Beaudin would have packed up and left Pied Piper–like because townsfolk listened to Monique's granddad.

"Ms. Parker?"

She snapped her gaze up. Two glasses of wine next time and that would be it. She swiped the back of her hand over her forehead.

"I get it. More people, more time. Okay." But she didn't get it. She didn't get how she was going to do this. Her life wouldn't end but getting back on her feet could take half a lifetime and she'd have to do it away from Bailey's Cove, *out there* where life had definitely not been good to her. In Boston, where she had completed her college degree, she had been downsized from her job and lost the first love of her life. In Portland, her home state, she'd lost another job and gained a fiancé who eventually left her.

The chief gave her a look that spoke of an apology.

"What now?" she asked. She'd let the chief finish first, then she'd don her rags and go find a bridge to live under.

"Because of the age of the case, the CID expects to be here in two weeks, three at most."

Mia took a big gulp of panic. The partially demolished wall was the center of everything. Even if she were allowed to demo and build around the wall, the work would come to a disastrous halt by the end of two weeks for sure. "That long?"

"And I can't let you in the building until they give the okay."

The big darkness hovering in the background inside her head began to descend over her thoughts. "I can't go in at all? Not at all?"

"And they'll need the scene for at least a day or two after they get started."

She couldn't help fidgeting in the chair. She'd already spent her savings, dug deep into the bank loan, and the teeny tiny trust fund set up for the historic building's renovation would evaporate if the project failed.

Her fingernails suddenly looked too long and she had the urge to bite them all off. Something she hadn't done in over a decade.

"So do you have any idea who that is in the wall?" The chief's tone was quietly demanding.

She looked up. "Who it is? No. Should I?"

"You've done research on the building."

"I know some of the building's history, but I have no idea who might be in the wall. Do you?"

Chief Montcalm frowned. "It needs to be considered that this might be the remains of someone from very early in the town's history."

She snapped her gaze up to meet his. "How early?"

"I don't really know anything for sure, but I can ask the CID if they will allow me to call the university. The university might send someone here to check out the site sooner than two or three weeks."

"Call them!" She huffed out a breath and shrugged. "Sorry, if you call them, I might get those three workers off the street and back on the job sooner. Will the state let the university take over the site?"

He gave her a solemn nod. "If the university is interested, they could send a forensic anthropologist."

"And the state will agree?" Some of the two-to-three-weeks darkness started to lift.

"An anthropologist would most likely be called in on the case anyway and someone could be here as early as tomorrow, most likely Monday."

"So, this anthropologist might come and go before the CID could even get here."

He leaned forward over the top of his big wooden desk. "There is always the chance the anthropologist could be here longer. They like to be thorough, but they would definitely start sooner."

"And you want my input?" Her wine addled input.

"You have the most at stake and obviously, the sooner I get your input…"

"Call them. Please call and see if they'll allow the university to send someone."

"Are you sure?"

"I'm feeling very sober now, sir, and I'd be very grateful if you called. The least that might happen is Bailey's

Cove would learn more of its history. More history might mean we could bump up the flow of tourists a bit." She stopped talking when she realized she was speaking uncensored thoughts. "I'm sorry. If you made the call, I would be grateful."

"First thing in the morning then."

The chief might be Mr. Inscrutable, but the little twitch in his temple told her he had more to tell her. "Is there something else?"

"Yes, and I thought it was only fair to warn you so you wouldn't be caught off guard, and things got out of control."

She tucked her fingers under her thighs. "Out of control how?"

"I don't know who the person in your wall is, but I do know this town. I doubt anything less than a forensic analysis will convince them the body hasn't been in there… for…say…"

She gasped. "…the full two hundred years."

"See how easy it is to jump there?"

"But what if it is?" Too many thoughts buzzed in her head. "Two hundred years? You don't think that might be the man himself."

A glint of a smile showed in Chief Montcalm's eyes. "It's best we leave any conjecture out until the university people gather the facts."

Having a part of Maine's history in her wall would be radically good for the long-term value of her restaurant, as long as treasure-hunting frenzy, as happened in the past, didn't tear the town apart first. A murdered man from long ago. So long ago…

"Liam Bailey? In my wall? A town founder? The pirate in my wall?" She quickly put a hand to her mouth. "Sorry, sir. You're right. It's so easy to go there."

## CHAPTER THREE

DANIEL DOWNSHIFTED and turned off the highway onto the road leading to the small town of Bailey's Cove. Monday morning hadn't dawned early enough to suit him. Sleep had been nearly impossible since last week when his aunt had died.

Anger was the last thing he expected at her death, but that's what he got and it hadn't gone away.

When he had closed his eyes, the nights had been no match for the darkness of these feelings and he paced or put on his athletic shoes and ran on the deserted campus.

Any rational person would do as his aunt suggested, go out and find someone to share a good life with, but it had been four and a half years since he had been a totally rational person.

Today he'd hurried out of his condo and left in the dark for the two-hour drive and his morning appointment with the chief of police in the old coastal town.

He edged his hybrid into the gawker's pull-out overlooking the small town and got out. Still too early to meet the chief of police, he leaned against the warm hood, arms folded over his chest, and watched the foggy pink dawn progress.

He felt different, indefinably changed since Margaret MacCarey had died, as though he had been perched on the edge of something for these last few years and her death pushed him over into unknown territory.

Even the clothes he now wore were out of his usual

style. No open-at-the-throat button-down shirt, no casually unzipped polar fleece vest or even khakis. Just a natty
old gray sweater he hadn't worn for years and a pair of
jeans with holes as old as most of the students he taught.
Instead of his professorish-type Rockport Walkers, he wore
a pair of hand-sewn leather boots his aunt had given him
the first time he told her he wanted to become an anthropologist and *to see where people came from.* By now the
soles had worn down and were so smooth and thin that
he might as well have been wearing moccasins. Someday
he'd get them repaired.

He snorted softly. He was so far off the track he had
planned to be on by the age of thirty. No tenure in his near
future, not even a hint of a major project now or down the
road. And here he was in this small coastal town assigned
to another, at best, unremarkable cataloging of some small
point in the history of Maine. That it was necessary and
someone had to do it didn't make it better.

The anger tried to swell but he took control and brought
it back down to a simmer. The university had been and
still was being infinitely patient with him, giving him
time off when he needed to be with his wife and son and
then his aunt.

He was grateful for their kindness.

The cool dawn breeze of early April brushed against his
face with a fan of salty moisture. The cold and the town
awakening under a mottled shroud of morning mist gave
him a feeling of agitated contemplation. Whoever this was
found in the wall, he was eager to get started and finished.

His department chair had wisely reassigned Daniel's
classes as of today. "You'll get a call soon. And pack a
bag," his boss had said last week. "We need to get you out
of here for a while."

He had gotten the call in the form of a succinct voice
mail. *"Dr. MacCarey, this is Police Chief Montcalm from*

*Bailey's Cove. During some remodeling of a building, human remains where found in a wall. Since you have consulted on previous archeological finds in the state of Maine, the head of your department referred me to you, and the state crime lab has authorized you to assess the scene."*

A follow-up phone call had set today's appointment.

Daniel looked at his watch. Twenty minutes until his appointment with the chief. He might as well spend the time inspecting the site. A look at physical evidence could do more than two days of futile browsing for information about Bailey's Cove. All he knew was Archibald Fletcher had founded the town in the early 1800s, the population of the coastal town was just over fourteen thousand and the average temperature this time of year got up as high as fifty degrees.

Not very helpful.

He pulled the car out onto the road and coasted down the hill into town. As the road's descent into town flattened out somewhat, he passed two gas stations, one across the street from the other, and a hardware store with a pair of moose antlers mounted under the peek of the gable. A combination law and accounting office, a few abandoned buildings came next and then, flanked by pine trees, a small but proud-looking old wooden church that now lodged the Bailey's Cove Museum.

The church and the other buildings to his left had the gray-blue of the foggy harbor as backdrop. The ocean, the livelihood for many Mainers, would appear beyond when more of the fog lifted.

As he continued, the buildings leading to the town center were of varying age, some painted white, some redbrick and one pink tattoo shop. Most of them sat shoulder to shoulder lined up along clean streets that seemed to speak of a town that cared about its appearance. As he entered the middle of the town, one motley brown dog sniffed at something in front of the white-painted wooden building that housed Pardee Jordan's Best Ever Donuts and then moved next door to investigate the front door of an old wood-and-redbrick tavern called Braven's.

This was the kind of downtown that might someday support ornate lampposts, brick sidewalks with trees and flowers in planters. None of which would look out of place and all of which might wipe out the true character of the old town.

To Daniel's right and across the street from Braven's tavern stood the building he was looking for, an old three-story structure with a white-painted facade.

Chief Montcalm had been correct. The building wasn't hard to find. It was the only one in the small downtown with police tape crisscrossed over the door. Or it had been crisscrossed. The end of one piece flapped in the morning breeze.

Bay windows flanked the glass-and-wood front door. Five wood-framed windows sat evenly spaced across the span of each of the building's second and third floors. Benches sat on the sidewalk on either side of the two-stepped stoop.

He parked and got out. With the tape disrupted, the chief must already be there. Good. The sooner he got started, the sooner he'd get to work and then be gone. Going down to Boston and spending time alone seemed like a wise idea right now. Much better than inflicting the surliness he couldn't seem to shake on a town of unsuspecting people.

He ducked under the remaining police tape and stepped inside the building. The ceiling had been stripped, part of one wall had been torn down. The partially demolished wall divided the large front room from the back area, and was likely the place where the body had been found.

No chief, only silence.

A door on the far left wall probably led to a stairwell, and if this had been a hotel, there was likely a matching stairway in the back room for the staff to use. A single lightbulb hung from the ceiling by a cord, shedding feeble light in the large open space.

There was nothing in this room except an upended orange bucket with loose plaster and a pry bar lying on the floor nearby.

He moved quietly across the open area. On the other side of the wall was another large room with ladders and tools scattered around. Two boxes crossed with police evidence tape sat near one of the ladders, which meant the chief had done as he'd said he would and returned the remains to the scene. This room had the same dim lighting as the other room, and...

Bent over and leaning toward a column of granite that must have been behind the demolished wall was a woman with a flashlight in one hand. Her short blue peacoat hung open and draped over her hunkered form. Her brown hair looked as if it was streaked with honey and fell forward so he couldn't see her face. What he could see was her peering into a hole that had been knocked in the granite. The hole that had to be the one that had held the skeleton.

Slowly, she reached a hand up as if she was afraid something inside would bite her. What she might do is to contaminate the site. He didn't need any more of that than had already been done.

"Please, don't touch that."

STARTLED, MIA YANKED her hand back and tried—too fast—to stand up. She lost her balance, flailed her arms in a desperate attempt for control, but stumbled and plopped backward onto the dusty floor, her flashlight skittering out of reach.

From the floor, she said a brief silent thanks that who-ever this was, it was not Chief Montcalm.

"Who are you?" She tried to make her words sound like a demand, as if she stood face-to-face with the intruder and wasn't looking up at him from such a disadvantageous position.

"Daniel MacCarey," he replied with a speculative expression on his face lit by the harsh light from the ceiling bulb. This had to be the man Chief Montcalm said was coming from the university.

"The chief's not here yet. You can wait outside," she said because she didn't want him to witness the indignity of her having to get up and clean off her butt.

He didn't respond nor did he go away.

"You're early." She worked hard to remain pleasant, because she certainly wasn't getting any nice back from this guy.

"And you're tampering with evidence."

"Old evidence." She kept her tone even.

"Tampering with a protected archeological site." When he walked toward her, the bulb hanging from the ceiling spread better light on his face, his scowling face.

Scowl or not, it was a great face. Rugged. Two or three days' worth of very dark beard growth. Hair a bit too neat for her liking, but tousled by the morning's wind. Dark brown, almost black eyes, if the light coming from above gave a true indication.

He stopped in front of her, tall and lean, and relaxing his frown he held out his hand.

She studied him a second longer. Warm, comfortable in an old gray sweater and jeans with holes. Shoes of good leather, scuffed on the toes. Monique would like this one. Heck, she liked the look of this one herself, and she didn't like many.

He frowned again and started to pull his hand away, but

she reached out and grabbed hold. His warm palm met hers
and his fingers wrapped securely around her hand. Indeed,
strong. He pulled her from the floor as if she weighed as
little as her twenty-year-old-waif self, not her current self
with eight more years of growth. There had to be muscles under those raggedy clothes. Maybe even a six-pack.
Ooooh. She hadn't seen one of those in a while. Maybe
she wouldn't even let Monique meet this one.

*...for crying out loud...*

She steadied herself, let go and stepped back. This was
the guy who could let her get her people back to work,
maybe as early as this afternoon, so she gave him her
brightest smile and resisted the urge to pat the dust off
her butt.

"When the chief told me the university was sending a
professor from the anthropology department, I...well...
I sort of thought more gray hair and possibly a larger
waistline. Guess I should have taken the time to visit the
website." She wanted to wink. Heck, she wanted to wolf
whistle. She just smiled harder.

He frowned. "What are you doing in here?"

So much for making light of an awkward situation. "I'm
waiting for Chief Montcalm. He should be here anytime
now."

"Waiting with your hand in the hole?"

"Yes. You caught me with—" Deciding not to be part of
the let's-be-grumpy game, she refused to look at his scowling face and softened her tone. "If anyone has reason to be
annoyed, it's the guy in the wall—er—boxes. He's been
waiting a very long time to be discovered."

"Did you move anything or touch anything?"

Now she looked up at him. "I wanted to. I wanted to
tear the whole wall down and put in a dining room, but
I've been waiting, I think rather patiently, doing everything I possibly could that didn't involve actually doing

the work in here that has to be done. I have a business I'm trying to get up and running." All right, maybe she would play grumpy.

"And I have to decide whether or not there is historical significance to this site." He didn't look very pleased with the prospect.

She eyed him for an *a-ha* moment. "You drew the short straw." She raised her eyebrows to make the statement a question.

This made his face relax. Made him handsome.

A hint of a smile curled his sharply carved masculine lips. "You're right. It's not your fault they sent me to..."

"...a town the world seems to have forgotten?" she finished for him.

"I don't really mind being here. It looks to be a charming place."

She tried to gauge his sincerity and couldn't decide. "It could be a charming town again, will be, if we can make some changes."

He held out his hand toward her, this time in greeting. "I'm Dr. Daniel MacCarey. I teach anthropology at the university."

She took his hand readily and shook firmly. His handshake was a genuine palm-to-palm and not the fingertips she often got, and strong.

"Mia Parker. I'm trying my best to help build up Bailey's Cove, make it, if not a destination, at least a stopping place on the central Maine coast." She winced as her words came out sounding like the pitch she had given to the town council when she was seeking permission to renovate the historic building.

"Good, the introductions are all finished. We can get started right away." Chief Montcalm strode into the back room and gave them each a nod of greeting. He shook

Mia's hand and then Dr. MacCarey's, giving each of them
a direct and steady look in the eyes.

Mia held in a grin at seeing Dr. MacCarey stand up a
little straighter, pull his shoulders back a bit. The chief had
that effect on people.

The dark-blue-uniformed chief stopped at the cardboard
boxes containing the remains removed from the hole. She'd
seen the contents of the boxes already, at the police station. They gave her the creeps.

"Everything we removed from the site is in these evidence boxes. After the initial incursion..." He stopped
and looked at Mia.

"As far as I know—" She held up her hands. "No one
has touched a thing since your team took the skeleton and
clothing away. I haven't let my workers back in after they
first made the hole and—" she glanced over at Daniel
"—no one that I know of has been in the building until I
came in this morning."

Chief Montcalm glanced at her flashlight, its beam
shining a spotlight on the door of the back-room stairwell.
She walked over, plucked it up and flicked off the beam.

"Everything seems to be in order," Dr. MacCarey said
as he gave Mia another glance.

The chief seem satisfied and shifted his gaze to Dr.
MacCarey. "Strict crime scene protocol has been followed,
so there should be little that would compromise your investigation. Any questions?"

"Not at the present," Daniel answered. "I might have
some after I check out the site."

When the chief glanced at her, Mia shook her head.

He handed Dr. MacCarey a small portable data-storage
device. "This is all the photographs and information we
have. I assume you will be taking the boxes of evidence
with you when you leave."

Dr. MacCarey nodded and pocketed the thumb drive

he most likely thought of as quaint, like the rest of the
village was going to seem to him. Quaint. Old-fashioned.
Out of date. Used up.

Not if she could help it.

"Then I'll leave you to it." Chief Montcalm secured his
hat on his head in preparation to face the wind again. "If
you need anything, you have my number."

He turned to Mia and said, "Put the tape back in place
when you're finished. The natives are restless and it might
help keep them out for a day or two longer."

A blink later, the chief's back, as he was hurrying
around the dividing wall, was all there was to be seen of
him, and another moment later, the squad car's engine
started up.

"Succinct sort of guy, isn't he, Dr. MacCarey?"

"Direct and to the point, and call me Daniel if you don't
mind." He studied her as he made the request. "What were
you looking for when you were peeking in the hole?"

She snorted. She had prepared herself for the ax to fall.
What he offered instead was curiosity. "Thanks for not
ratting me out to the chief."

"I would have if I thought you had disturbed anything."

"Fair enough." Was that what she had been doing? Until
she had peered into the hole this morning, she had tried
not to think about sticking her fingers in where they didn't
belong. "Well, I was—um—looking for treasure I guess."

"That would be why Chief Montcalm said the natives
are getting restless? Treasure?"

She wasn't sure she should tell him the town's closely
guarded obsession. Muddying the waters, when they didn't
need to be mucked up. "Like the chief said last week, the
university would be looking for facts, not wishful thinking."

"And?"

The one word was a snippy demand and she wanted to

grab it and toss it back. Instead she took a deep breath. "Most people from outside the town are not aware of the fixation the folks around here have with the story of our town founder Liam Bailey."

Daniel drew his brows together before he spoke.

"Bailey? I thought the town's founder was Archibald Fletcher."

"And the people around here are more than happy to let the world believe that."

"Bailey must have been quite the figure for them to have kept him alive, so to speak, for all this time."

"You really don't know the legend?"

He shook his head slowly as if replaying the information he had on the town and its occupants past and present.

"Well…" Mia hedged. "I know a little about the town, but I don't want to—"

"—skew the data with hearsay."

"That'd be about it. If the chief didn't tell you, maybe I shouldn't say anything." She wondered how long her nose had grown with that one. Though it wasn't an out-and-out lie. She worried that telling him about Liam Bailey now might delay things. But not telling Dr. MacCarey was sure to make things take longer, because if or when he found out the guy in the wall could have been a pirate, he might have to redo some of his work based on new information.

And it would be dishonest to deliberately leave out what might be a significant detail.

"I'll find out eventually." He seemed to be able to see the war going on inside her head. "I can probably ask a few of the townsfolk. Someone is bound to know in a place this small."

"If they haven't made the leap yet because the chief hasn't spilled the beans, they might now that you're here. So unless you can prove conclusively it's not, the town is going to think these old bones belong to one of the town's earliest settlers."

"Why would they think that?"

"Because that's what they so desperately want to believe…but they would never have told you. You're an outsider and he's our most, I'm going to say treasured, missing person, the person any one of them would give a month's lobster take to find."

"Wouldn't they want the mystery solved as to who this is?"

"It's not really about the mystery. It's about the man and his legend. His life and his fate are the fodder for lively conversation after two or three beers."

She could almost see the gears turning. He was thinking this might not just be your average citizen who got boxed up in the wall. His face lost more of its tightness and took on the look of anticipation. Grumpy was much better for her time line. Chief Montcalm said forensic anthropologists liked to be thorough. This one had switched from mostly disinterested to almost eager. Thorough was sure to follow.

"So do you think this could be a historical figure?"

She looked up at him for a long moment and almost reached out a hand toward him. This time she wanted to snatch back every word she'd said since he had frightened the flashlight out of her hand

She pressed her lips together for a moment before she replied, "I hope not."

He turned away and surveyed the area, the partially torn-down dividing wall, large open space, doors on either end of the room, one to the stairway and one to the kitchen, a hallway leading past the kitchen to the restrooms, a back door leading to an alley.

"I had planned to take pictures, inventory everything, box it up and be gone." He seemed to speak to himself, as if thinking all this would have to change.

Her chest squeezed harder and she breathed to try to make the feelings of dread go away. The pressure did not ease.

"You could still do that," she said, trying to feel some hope.

His dark brows came together. "Why don't we start with you telling me about the man you suspect this might be?"

"I—um—don't suspect anything." Which was mostly true. Other people suspected Liam Bailey, the pirate who had helped found the town of Bailey's Cove, never left, never ran away as the official records seemed to say. She wanted to bite her fingernails, but took a deep breath instead.

"What is your guess?"

"I didn't think people like you worked on guesses."

"Like me?" He rubbed at the neck of his shabby sweater.

"Anthropologists. Um—university—er—types."

The corner of his mouth turned up and a different type of clenching started, this time in her lower belly. He was even better-looking when he smiled.

"Then let's call it a hunch." He stared steadily at her. Thorough seemed to be taking over. "What's your hunch? Tell me all you know about this early settler."

He used his gaze to pin her to the spot, but she wiggled free and retreated to the middle of the room where there seemed to be more air.

"I don't do hunches very well, either. My hunch that I should build a restaurant in a historic building because it might attract tourists is turning out to be a less-than-stellar idea."

He reached a hand toward her. "May I borrow your flashlight, please?"

She flipped it to him. He flicked on the beam and shined it in the hole.

She couldn't stop the pirate thoughts as they buzzed

through her head. Maybe it was Liam Bailey who had been in that hole, crypt, tomb, whatever it should be called. Becoming part of the legend, having the pirate in her wall, would be grand for the long-term value of her restaurant, but at the same time devastating to the construction project, and the project would have to be finished to gain any benefit. And if treasure hunters overran the town as they had in the past...well, she didn't want to go there.

"People died from various causes back then," Daniel said as he continued to shine the light in all directions in the foot-wide gap knocked open by Charlie's sledgehammer blow. "Trauma and disease mostly, and a few from old age. The records, such as they were, when paper and ink were scarce and made fragile by time, will most likely be few."

He stood and handed the flashlight back to her.

"So what are you saying? We might never know who this is for sure?" Relief and disappointment?

"Too early to know. I'll start with the archives at the Bailey's Cove Museum. They will probably have more information than the university has."

"No." She grabbed his forearm. If she sent him away she'd only make things worse. This guy had to know what the people of the town would think, would do.

He stopped and looked at where she held his arm and she dropped her hand and let out a long breath. He needed to know if he stirred up the town, he'd have to fend off the treasure hunters.

"Is that coffee?" He pointed to the thermal carafe on the floor, one cup upended on top of the pot's lid.

She nodded. "Fresh. I brought it with me in case I got to go back to work this morning."

"Do you have another cup?"

"Yes, sorry, and I have manners, truly I do. Would you join me for a cup of coffee?"

"I'd like that." He smiled full-on bright and swooning came to mind.

...*as if*...

She headed for a closed door of the someday kitchen, glad to have a place to hide for a second to regain some of her decorum.

"Mia."

She stopped and turned. "Yes?"

"You might want to…" He mimed brushing off his butt.

Decorum, yeah, right. "Thanks."

She hurried through the door and made sure it closed before she began cleaning off the seat of her jeans and the back of her coat. She so-o-o should not be distracting herself with the hot professor, no matter how great his smile was, not when life as she knew it might soon be tossed into the Dumpster outside the back door, along with all the rest of the useless debris.

She leaned against the old sink, pressing her hands against the cold porcelain. If she gave him all the information she had, he could take his boxes and leave. No, he'd investigate the site *thoroughly* first.

She pushed off. *Get back out there*. Nothing would happen until she did. A smile. It was just a smile, she told herself and brought her guard back up.

Several ceramic coffee mugs rested in the dish rack. She grabbed one, shoved a handful of cream and sugar packets into the pocket of her coat and headed back out to face fate or the enemy or whoever this guy turned out to be.

He stood, pensively staring at the gap in the wall. When he turned to face her, she shook her head at the flash of warmth that she could not stop as it spread through her.

"Let's go outside," she said as she approached. "It'll be warming up some by now."

With the carafe and cup in his hand, Daniel followed

her out to where benches on the old sidewalk flanked the front doorway.

"You can see the harbor better from that one." She pointed at the bench to the right of the doorway.

"Very nice. Very Maine," he said as he sat down on the far end of the white-painted bench where he could see the boats, gulls and Mainers doing what Mainers did every day.

She sat on the other end and held out her cup as he loosened the lid of the carafe and poured.

"Cream or sugar?" She reached into her pocket and then held out her hand with the packets on her palm.

"Black."

She wasn't surprised.

He sat back and as he gazed out over the harbor, she studied him. His profile, with well-defined nose, sharply defined upper lip and full soft bottom lip, looked good in the morning sun. Who was she kidding? He probably looked good in just about every light—or maybe very little light—like maybe that of a bedside lamp.

Hmm. She put her coffee on the bench near where he'd placed the carafe and folded her arms over her chest. These were things she definitely shouldn't be thinking about when her future was at stake.

She turned her attention to the endlessly changing but always wonderful view five blocks or so away on the docks at the end of Treacher Avenue. The water of the bay sparkled dark blue, and the fishermen and those who serviced the boats hurried around in their morning scurry, some starting their day, some already well into it.

A woman with a baby stroller stopped as she waved to someone on a boat in the water, but the boats were too far off to see who waved back. The town's stray brown dog stopped and sat beside her until she moved on and then so did he.

His cup sat beside hers and he had leaned forward with his elbows on his knees. "It's like an artsy movie."

"Evidence that life does go on even in a small town the world has never really noticed. I don't ever get tired of it," Mia said as she relaxed into the view.

"One of my fondest characteristics of people from Maine. They appreciate where they are." Dr. MacCarey, Daniel, looked more relaxed, seemed to have forgotten he was in a hurry to get the job done and get out of town.

"Would it be so bad if we never knew who the man in the wall was?" *And everybody's lives could return to normal?*

She had stirred up more than she had ever planned. She had to get this guy to let things go. To get out of town no matter who was in that wall.

She could hear the little angel on her shoulder reproaching her even as she had the thoughts. *Integrity! You've got nothing if you don't have integrity.*

Phooey.

## CHAPTER FOUR

MIA RUBBED HER shoulder and asked Daniel, "Do your records mention Liam Bailey?"

"He was an early landowner. The assumption is made that the town was renamed after him, but there is no record as to why." Dr. MacCarey, Daniel, withdrew his gaze from the harbor and turned it on her. His eyes were definitely that deep dark earthy brown, the kind created to hold sensuality and mystery at the same time, and right now they held a keen kind of interest.

"Anything else?" The words croaked a bit when she spoke, so she picked up her coffee cup to break eye contact.

"The library at the university has some factual information, but it's pretty—" he paused "—bare-bones."

She sputtered coffee and had to wipe her mouth on the back of her hand to keep from dripping on the front of her coat. "Bare-bones. I can't believe you said that."

He held her gaze again as he spoke. "Even anthropologists use humor—from time to time."

She shouldn't have looked at him again. His face was definitely much more relaxed than when he'd first arrived. He looked more accessible.

"I tried to find information about Liam Bailey." She turned away and forced herself to search the harbor for something to latch on to. After only a moment, she spotted what she knew, even from this distance, to be the Calvins' boat, the *Lady Luck,* the one with the for-sale sign. So much for luck.

"There doesn't seem to be any information out there, not about our Liam Bailey anyway," she continued, and then realized she had a white-knuckle grip on her coffee cup.

"It's hard to find specifics about someone from two hundred years ago." He sounded pensive. "Unless they were famous or notorious."

Famous or notorious. If he never found out Archibald Fletcher was a usurper and not the original founder, he'd have no reason to suspect this body was anything more than a minor mystery, just a minor player sealed up in a wall, and Dr. MacCarey would leave out of boredom. Archibald Fletcher had a gravesite, after all, and had never gone missing. Liam Bailey, the ship's captain who originally started the settlement and called it South Harbor, had a story, a legend.

It wasn't boredom that made the townsfolk leave. It was desperate circumstances. The Calvin brothers weren't just selling the boat. They were selling their traps, their federal permit, their livelihood, and diminishing Bailey's Cove by yet another good family.

Mia quietly sipped her cooling coffee.

"Does your museum have more information?"

This time when he brought up the museum, she looked into his eyes to see if she could read what might be in his heart. He matched her gaze beat for beat with the deep earthy color that seemed to warm her soul and body. She snapped her gaze away—again—before she embarrassed herself. Drooling would not be good.

"The museum does have a little information, but much has been lost to time and the salty air."

She should just send him there, not tell him the secrets of the town. Heather Loch, who ran the museum, would not tell him tell more than a few facts and maybe he'd be satisfied with that.

"But you know. Don't you?" His tone grew soft, seductive.

…and she was such a sucker.

"It's much more interesting when one thinks of Liam Bailey as…the town's founder, and not Archibald Fletcher." She sighed. "And as…"

"As?"

She didn't dare so much as a look at him right now. "As a privateer."

"A privateer in the early 1800s was usually a—"

"Pirate," she finished.

He laughed out loud. As much as she hated it, she liked the sound. He had a nice laugh, friendly, with a touch of boisterous.

"I know. I know." She grimaced.

"So the town's secret is a pirate's treasure?"

"I feel like such a traitor."

"You don't think I would have found out?" His voice carried a teasing lilt now.

"Maybe, but it would have taken you a couple of years to pry enough information out of the folks around here to be able to put things together and come up with pirate's treasure."

"Why do I get the feeling you have much more to tell me about this pirate?"

"Because you're smart."

"That's true."

When she chanced a glance, there was a hint of a smile in his eyes. "And humble."

"So my Aunt Margaret used to say." The corners of his mouth turned up again.

"I need to know you understand, the more I tell you, the more I feel my remodeling project slipping away. The more I hold off telling, the more dishonest I feel, but right now it's no longer a matter of betraying a town's trust. If this town doesn't survive, there will be no one to betray."

He looked at her for a long time, as if measuring her, and then said, "Mia, I will be judicious with what you tell me."

She dipped her chin in acknowledgment. "That Liam Bailey founded the town of Bailey's Cove, and that he had been a privateer, seem to be anchored in truth, as far as the people of Bailey's Cove know it. What has been passed down through the generations is that there was a young woman in whom Bailey showed a particular interest, and she in him. Some say he was paid off by the young woman's disapproving father, Archibald Fletcher, and with the cash in his pocket couldn't get out of town fast enough. He was never heard from again. The story goes, Fletcher maintained Bailey went back to sea and some say he went west to find gold."

"You don't think that's what happened?"

She gave a sharp laugh. "I have no idea. The other side of the story is the girl's father started the rumor that all Bailey wanted was her substantial inheritance, and what really happened was the man had Bailey killed. It isn't much of a leap to get from that to Liam Bailey being entombed in the wall of the hotel he built as part of the settlement's initial push to become a town. Ironic."

She held up her coffee cup in a sweeping motion and continued. "As you can see, Bailey's Cove hasn't grown too terribly much since that time, so we can't blame the world for ignoring us."

He poured more coffee. "And the treasure?"

"Ah, the treasure. It's custom here in Bailey's Cove, like prayers before a meal or removing your hat before entering someone's home. You don't tell outsiders about Liam Bailey and especially not his treasure."

He gave her an honest and open look of interest.

"The chief said he knew that when the university showed up, tongues would start flapping. Well, he actually used the term 'troublesome gossip.' That your arrival would give folks ideas about digging for treasure...again, and that didn't turn out so well for the town last time."

"So if the pirate buried his treasure and then was killed before he could dig it up..."

"Bingo. Until now, it was just a body in the wall. Chief Montcalm asked me not to talk to anyone about it, which I didn't, well, mostly I didn't. He made my workers quake in their boots, so I'm sure they only told a couple dozen people what they saw." Something about this man made her want to spill her guts, to bare all. Oh, for pity's sake. "Since the place hasn't been raided, I believe official word has not leaked out from the chief's department. The chief's people say the bones are old. Will you be able to tell how old the remains are with carbon dating?"

"Without a doubt."

"Oh, wow. That might be very helpful."

"I'll be able to tell the age of the body to within a couple hundred years." He shot a disarming grin at her and some unseen barrier between them seemed to fall away. "Carbon dating so touted in the media is much more accurate when dating eras—when it's confined to thousands of years. Some archeologists believe it's been fine-tuned to be able to pinpoint up to within a few hundred years, but it's always under scrutiny. Telling how old a person was at the time of death is relatively easy nowadays, but the decade or even the century gets dicier. Though finding pirate's treasure might help."

"Oh, please, don't. Please, don't." She was absolutely sure she didn't want to hear his answer, but she had to ask the next logical question. "If you suspect this is Liam Bailey, will you bring in a team of people?"

"I could, but usually the more people, the more time spent processing a site, and more confusion."

"So you might still be able to get what you need and leave today?"

"The more I hear about Bailey, the more complicated this investigation is getting."

Mia blew out a breath. "Of course it is."

She might have to gag that angel on her shoulder.

WHEN DANIEL GLANCED at the woman beside him on the bench, she looked deflated, as if she were tired of shouldering the bravado necessary to keep a project this size on schedule.

"Was it something I said?" he asked quietly.

"Yes, it was." Her light blue eyes reflected the morning sky and for an instant he thought he might be able to gaze into them over a cup of coffee or even a glass of wine. Something he never thought he'd do again—stare into a woman's eyes.

He quickly changed his thoughts. "I think I said something like, the more I hear, the more complicated this whole investigation is getting."

"That's the gist."

"Wouldn't finding out a pirate was buried here be beneficial for the town, a tourist attraction?"

"Yeeees," she drew out the word. "The town needs the monetary boost tourists will bring. Skeletons were not part of the timeline for—well—for profitability."

He watched her closely, trying to figure out if there was something else behind her words. On the surface they seemed self-serving, but there was also an almost bleak tone to her voice, which made him suspect there was much more. "Earlier, you mentioned a dining room. A restaurant?"

"That's my goal."

"Are you a chef?"

"Oh, no. Creating food takes more imagination and certainly more skill than I have. I'm a businesswoman. Can't you tell?" She gestured to her demolition attire. "Hotel and restaurant management."

"Does the place have a name?"

She gave a soft snort. "I chose it before all this got started and now I'm a bit mortified. I thought I'd be clever and call it Pirate's Roost."

Her smile, though embarrassed, shined bright like the sun off the water. It was clear to see she was proud of what she was doing here, had great hopes for success.

"So a pirate in your wall would complicate things?"

She brushed the toe of her shoe against the concrete of the sidewalk. "I'm on a tight timeline. There have already been so many delays, and if the Roost is not finished in time to draw tourists this season it will be hard to keep things going over the winter. Plus things can get a little sketchy around here when the hopes of treasure stirs things up."

"So if I got out of the way, the Pirate's Roost might have a chance to stay on schedule."

"It would help a lot."

"I'll check out the crypt. I might only need a few days with the site, a week at the most." She might have masked a gasp with a cough, but he wasn't sure. "I'll need to get the contents of the boxes examined to see what the remains can tell me."

He sat back and watched the goings-on in the harbor. Sometimes gathering information on a site meant letting the indigenous population say what they needed to say. He let silence ask the next question.

"I really need to get the demo and remodeling finished as soon as possible."

He nodded.

A dingy bounced against the hull of one of the fishing boats as someone on board worked to secure it to the side of the boat.

"In a way," she continued, "the town's survival depends on getting the village brought up to the twenty-first century. This is, we hope, the first of many projects."

"And if this turns out to be a pirate who hid a treasure?" He glanced at her. "Will the whole town turn up?"

She leaned her chin in the palms of her hands. The sun glistened golden in her hair and the wind blew the loose curling locks across her cheek, made pink by the morning breeze. He wanted to tuck the hair behind her ear. He wanted to tell her everything would be all right, but he knew he did not have that power anymore, in fact never had that power.

"Not all of the folks here are crazed by pirate lore, but enough to make my life difficult, and maybe yours." She nodded across the street at the two teenagers with their heads together. Their glances kept turning to where he and Mia Parker sat on the bench.

"You'd like to toss me out of town, wouldn't you?"

She snapped her eyes to his face. "Yes."

He laughed at her honesty. "Then I'd better get started on finding out about what went on in there."

"Please do." She picked up the empty coffee cups and carafe and stood.

"I need to do the preliminary examine by myself." And then, so there could be no misunderstanding, he added, "I'd like it if you left for a half hour or so."

There was a time in his life when she would have been just the type of woman he would have sought out. She didn't have to give him any information he had not found at the university, but she did. She could have been bitchy about wanting him to get in and get out, but she wasn't.

Yet, if she had come into his life years ago, he would have hurt her, too, just as he had Mandy.

"I have a few things to do. I'll be back in thirty minutes...or so. My phone number is inside, on the back wall."

He notched an eyebrow.

"That way my workers have no excuse not to call me when they need me."

She walked quickly away and he wondered how much she had invested in this project, and even more, how valuable a historical site this might turn out to be. The more significant each of these factors, the greater their problems would be.

With a toss of her head, she flicked the hair from her face and climbed into a small green SUV.

He wondered how she'd feel about him and the guy in the wall if she knew the state had given the university, and therefore him, the power to keep her site for as long as he deemed necessary. How she'd react if the university asserted its right to the Power of Eminent Domain. With that power, they could buy her building at fair market price, which in this depressed town would pay her only a fraction of what she had already invested in the remodeling.

She wasn't even a part of his life and already he could do her harm, he thought, as he went back inside the building. Flashes of old memories, the smiling face of a little boy, the feeling of proud parents when the child was born. And the pain when it all fell apart.

# CHAPTER FIVE

MIA PLUCKED HER keys from under the seat and was about to start her SUV when a shadow blocked the sun coming in the side window. Mickey Thompson, one of the teenagers who had been loitering across the street, grinned in at her, one of those half ogle, half goofy kid grins only a fourteen-year-old could manage.

She lowered the window. "Mickey, why aren't you in school?"

"We got a late start today and the bell don't ring for another ten minutes."

Which meant he'd be late and didn't much care. "What can I do for you?"

"Can we go in now that the cops have taken the police tape down?"

"The building is private property. You don't get to go in without an invitation."

"Who do we have to ask?"

"Me."

"So can we go in?"

"You can go to school."

Another shadow joined Mickey's. Between Mickey and his friend Tim O'Donnell, they had nearly a bushel of shaggy brown hair.

"What'd she say?" the other teen asked.

"She said to go to school."

"Now," Mia said, and as the teens moved off slowly, they balefully eyed the building with secrets they weren't being allowed to poke around in. The trickle before the flood.

Right now, she had to get away from Daniel MacCarey and the destruction he could cause in her life, and she needed to marshal her mental troops before she dived back into a pirate-infested pool.

One person in town would sympathize with her.

Apex Cleaners, where Monique worked, shared an old aluminum-sided strip mall with the Cove Real Estate Agency, a pharmacy, three other small businesses and two empty stores. As Mia approached, the front door of the cleaners popped open. Mrs. Carmody, the lonely cat lady, emerged and streaked to her car, leaving Monique standing in the doorway holding the rug.

Mia waved and Monique rolled her eyes.

"Hey, I heard he's good-looking. Is that true?" Monique asked as she led Mia into the dry cleaners after putting the rug in Mrs. Carmody's trunk.

"If by him, you mean Dr. MacCarey, the answer is yes."

"Dr. MacCarey, eh?"

"Anthropologist," Mia said as she leaned her elbows on the service counter.

"Good enough."

"Good enough for what?"

Monique stood on the other side of the counter and took up what she must have been doing before Mrs. Carmody arrived, shoving incoming laundry into bags and labeling them.

"Good enough for you," she said as she gave a couple of shirts an extra hard shove. A harsh gesture for Monique, who was usually a gentle soul.

"You are not talking about what I think you're talking about."

"You bet I am. If you don't want him, I'll take a crack at him."

"No, you wouldn't. And what's going on with you?"

"Oh, nothing, really, nothing." Monique made dismissive circles in the air with her hands.

"Monique." Mia stilled her friend's hands.

"Okay, I thought I got a new regular customer, but... Never mind."

"Never mind it's not important, or never mind you don't want to talk about him right now."

"Can we just do *never mind* for a while?" Monique's eyes held a pleading look.

"Okay."

"Did you hear Mac and Sally are engaged?" Monique asked over-brightly.

"Does that mean he's done saying he's sorry for taking you on the worst date ever?"

"What do you mean? You thought getting champagne up my nose was a bad time?" Monique shoved more laundry in a bag.

"I thought running out of gas and having to be rescued in the middle of the harbor was the best part."

"Mia, what if it could happen for me? After all this time, I find a guy right here in Bailey's Cove? I get to marry, live happily ever after right here at home." Monique got all dreamy-faced. "I still believe, you know."

Mia shrugged and smiled. "Who knows? Your heart may wander right into bliss."

"So what are you doing here instead of being over there with him? Hiding so *you* won't fall in love?"

"Hiding so I won't commit murder and then brick the wall back up with an anthropologist inside."

"You are so totally bad."

"I wish." Mia leaned her elbows on the counter. "I wish."

"Ms. Parker, *I* wish you'd at least help Ms. Beaudin when you're here," Mr. Wetherbee, the shop owner, said as he appeared between the beaded strands of the curtained doorway leading to the back room. "If I had both of you to do the job, I might get a good day's work done around here for the money I pay this little slacker."

Monique tossed a lightweight laundry bag at the shop-keeper's head in reply.

Mr. Wetherbee haha-ed good-naturedly and continued out the front door, leaving the bag where it had fallen.

"You don't need him," Mia said, still leaning on her elbows.

"Except he owns the store."

"Minor detail."

"I suspect he pays me so much because he wants me to have enough money to buy the store from him someday." She tossed another filled bag into the canvas cart of waiting laundry and turned on Mia with a long sigh. "So back to you. You wanna kill a guy that cute. Must be a really good reason."

"I made it clear to him about how important it is for me to get back in there and get the job done, but he's so…so…"

"Ah, anthropologist-y?"

"I think I hate him."

Monique looked up from the label she was scribbling out. "'Cuz he wants to get things right?"

"Maybe, but maybe because he's good-looking and he's funny."

"A bone-and-pot-shard guy is funny? Since when do you not like funny?"

"Oh, please." Mia clapped her hands to her cheeks and squeezed her face into distorted horror.

"Would he be just exactly the kind of person you'd want if you ever looked for another man?"

Monique sighed again and Mia knew she was hiding something, but played along anyway.

"Yes." Now she threw her hands up imitating her friend. "Right. Fine!"

"And the kind you'd like to hop in the sack with."

"No. No. No. I don't want to go there."

"Until hell freezes. I know." Monique shook her head. "So why are you here if it's not for my advice on how to land the big one?"

Mia sighed. "Moral support and he threw me out. I'm getting a complex—about being asked to leave my own place."

"Maybe you should go across the street and talk to Delainey Talbot at Morrison and Morrison. She could probably get you in to see one of the attorneys today or tomorrow. They might help you get him out sooner."

"I hope I don't need an attorney and I certainly can't afford those guys."

"You want me to come over to the Roost…" Monique hunched her shoulders and flexed "…and tell that guy how it's gonna be?"

Mia snorted. "No."

"Then why don't you go back and seduce that hunk right out of town?"

"Because I'm not sure you're all right. Is it your grand-dad?"

"No, it's not, and I'm fine." Monique leaned on the counter across from Mia so their noses almost touched. "And don't fall in love with your anthropologist, and if you do, don't get your heart broken."

Monique's last words seemed as if they were personal. A guy? Monique and a guy? Why didn't she know?

Mia put a hand on Monique's. "Be good to yourself, my friend." *Don't get your heart broken, either,* Mia thought as the door rattled shut behind her.

She crossed Church Street, passed the redbrick build-ing with a stately facade that housed the town's most successful attorneys and walked north to Treacher Avenue. Daniel's car still sat parked in front of the Roost, which made her frown as she continued.

From the corner of Church down Treacher to the harbor were the most colorful five blocks in town and her favorite to contemplate. The Three Sisters, three Victorian-style homes, sat in varying stages of neglect. Built for the daughters of a long-gone shipping magnate they sat side by side on Treacher Avenue not far from the docks. Each was a prime candidate to be turned into a bed-and-breakfast or a boutique by someone who had enough faith.

Next door to them was an artist's studio still closed for the season and surrounded by pine trees and low-growing junipers. After that came an old shed falling into disrepair, languishing because of a disputed estate.

All the time as she walked, her thoughts bounced between the man at the Roost and Monique. She hoped her friend wasn't dabbling in long-haul truck drivers again. That had not gone well for her in the past. And she hoped Daniel MacCarey would just plain go away.

When she reached the docks, Mr. Calvin the elder gave her a wan smile. She could tell he didn't want to sell the family boat, either. Two other fishermen and the woman from the Marina gave her speculative looks making her wonder if the truant teenagers Mickey and Tim had been down here spouting tales of yo-ho-ho instead of being in school.

Everyone else gave her smiles and waves, lending her the encouragement she needed for when it was time to start back up the hill and get to work on Dr. MacCarey, if not on the demolition.

Although, what would do her really and truly good was if she got back to the Pirate's Roost and Daniel MacCarey's hybrid was gone. Maybe she could resume the special kind of lunacy she called her life, where the only workers she could find were slightly off balance, piles of bills were expected and she had teenagers drooling to enter the premises where a skeleton had resided for who knew how long.

The two women who had moved their yarn and craft shop from the building she was now renovating to be closer to the docks stood in the doorway of their shop. Pins and Needles sat directly across from the Three Sisters, positioned well if the Sisters were ever renovated.

"How's it going, Mia?" one of them asked.

"I'm making good progress." Mia used her standard answer to the question because Monique told her using *marginally crappy* would be off-putting to many people.

"I see you have company today." Translation: *Did you find out who the skeleton from your wall is yet, and if not when?* Or: *Who is this guy and is he married?*

"I do." Mia went on to ask about their week and they answered they had all the new inventory ordered for the spring tourist trade, hoping this year there would be better crowds than last year.

Mia waved and moved off before they could ask more about Daniel MacCarey. "Have a nice day, ladies."

When she reached the corner of Treacher Avenue and Church Street, she scrunched her face at the sight of the professor's hybrid still hugging the curb in front of her building.

She was sure she didn't want to leave him alone with her future any longer and ducked under the single piece of tape still in place.

The air inside hung still with the musty smell of old building. The ax-strike marks on the exposed beams in the ceiling made the building look its age, as did the wide planks of the floorboards. It would be a charming place when she got it finished and there could be no ifs about it. She would get it finished.

It was quiet, almost spooky quiet.

"Hello?" Mia called into the silence.

She rounded the partially torn-down wall, and the room beyond was as quiet as— No, not a grave, not creepy quiet. Hushed as the eye of a storm, that hair-raising kind of stillness where the excitement and anticipation of a wild ride lived.

She ran a hand down the back of her neck to chase away the feeling giving her a chill.

A clinking sound put her in a dead stop.

A delicate tapping came from—

The basement.

She had been down there only twice.

Every chain saw massacre and Halloween movie played in her head as she gripped her flashlight. The hollowed out basement dug into the dirt and blasted into the stone was eerie and repugnant and would still be even if her pitiful flashlight became a host of floodlights.

The basement door at the far side of the old and soon-to-be-renewed pantry squeaked obligingly as she tugged it open. She shrugged that off, too.

Lights! Yes, the lights were on. Daniel was down there.

The smell of the old, dank, partial dirt-floor basement wafted insults at her nose as she started down. Vegetables and wine had most likely been stored here when the building was a functioning hotel.

She stopped halfway down and listened. "Daniel?" she called more timidly than she had intended.

The shrieking sound from the movie *Psycho* screeched loudly in her head.

*Oh, shut up!* she said to herself and continued down.

The light at the bottom of the stairs did a pitifully meager job of keeping the darkness at bay, and the tapping restarted.

"Hello?" she called tentatively. *Chicken,* she chided herself. "Daniel, are you down here?"

The tapping stopped. So did she, on the third step from the bottom. As quiet footsteps approached she couldn't help the urge to flee.

Then Daniel stepped into the light shed from the ceiling bulb at the bottom of the steps and looked up at her. "Hello again."

Shadows from the dim bulb deepened the contrasting planes of his face and the light danced in his dark hair. Feelings stirred inside her, things she hadn't felt in a very long time.

She rubbed a hand on the thigh of her jeans.

"What are you doing down here?" she asked.

His expression grew more serious and he held up what she supposed were archeology tools. "Exploring to see if there are any other areas that might need excavating."

"I hope not."

"And why are *you* down here?"

"I just wanted to see if there is anything I can do to help…" *Get you the heck out of my building.*

"Have you done much exploring on this level?" His tone told her this was a hedge, an opening gambit.

"No." Already she didn't like the way this was going. "Just a couple of quick inspections. Why?"

"There's a section of the floor that's been dug up."

Mia thought back to when she had toured the basement the second time to make sure it could be used for storage.

"One of the previous owners was doing something in the furnace room, but I have no idea what." Or nothing she'd admit to—digging for treasure. Mia descended the last three stairs, and the smell of old dirt and mustiness grew stronger, until she stopped beside him. Then it smelled like—*mmm*—man.

"Not in the furnace room." When he spoke she realized she might have zoned out a bit because he took a step away from her.

"Somewhere else? Oh, not rats. The digging didn't look rodentlike, did it?"

His expression lightened and she knew she must be wearing what Monique called her hilarious horrified gape. She closed her mouth.

"In the old cold storage room, where the floor is still dirt and not concrete. Dug up with a shovel and probably a pickax. The dirt in that floor has been packed down by a couple centuries of use and neglect, so dug up by a very determined digger."

"Freshly dug, I suppose." She knew she should go inspect the hole, but she liked being just where she was. Maybe she even wanted to step closer, to take back that step he had taken away.

"Yes, and then someone tried to refill it, but you can imagine how that went. Ten pounds in a five-pound bag."

Treasure hunters. She wondered if the trickle was already a full running stream. Or maybe just her three workers.

"I guess I should take a look."

She envisioned Charlie, Rufus and Stella each with a pickax in their hands, or maybe it was Mickey and Tim. Smiling politely she stepped calmly around her guest. Was he just a friendly visitor? Or was he an enemy?

The old storage room, an erstwhile hold for potatoes, apples, turnips and anything that would keep in the earth-chilled room for the winter had previously had only stone walls, a dirt floor and a couple of old crates, no hole.

When she entered the back room, a shiver ran down her body. There was no mistaking the disturbance.

"Someone digging for treasure?" He sounded amused from behind her.

She wanted to punch him for that. Good thing she only had violent thoughts and not actions. *Someone digging for treasure.* There were already so many suspects.

Slowly, turning to face him, she said, "Please, don't
mention digging for treasure in this town. The people
around here do not need any encouragement."

He nodded. "You won't get any argument from an anthropologist. Treasure hunters are a bane for any—er—
archeological site."

She laughed. "Thanks for not saying *dig*."

"I'm finished down here for now if you'd like to go up
where it's warmer."

"Warmer would be good."

She put her flashlight in her pocket and they marched
in silence across the old floor and up the steps. Halfway
up she wondered if Daniel was watching her butt. She was
a warm-blooded woman; she'd be watching his. What if
he wasn't watching? She wanted in the worst way to catch
him in the act, whichever it was, but she trudged on wondering if her jeans were too tight.

Speaking of jeans. The more she saw how well this guy
wore his holey ones, the more she liked them, and his raggedy sweater, as well. His slumming clothes. She couldn't
imagine his teaching clothes would look this good.

In fact, he probably looked really, really good with no
clothes at all.

He followed her to the front room, where the morning
light filtered in through the windows. She tried not to in-
hale too noticeably as he stopped beside her. Apparently,
nothing could dampen her suddenly awakened sense of
the male side of the planet. Unless, maybe, he decided to
tell her he'd come to ruin her life completely.

"I have given a cursory check of the contents of the
boxes. Are you interested in having a look?"

When she glanced at him, there was an unmistakable
light of excitement in his dark eyes. Damn.

No, she didn't want to see that light and she certainly
did not want to see what was in the boxes. She wanted him

to take those bones and rags and go. She wanted to move forward with her funky little life, finish the restaurant so the chef she had hired didn't give up on her, so the banks to whom she promised payment didn't come demanding what little she had. "Look at old bones and raggedy clothing?"

He grinned and his eagerness brightened. "That's about the size of it."

"Yes." Okay, so she wanted to see them, get his opinion.

"I'll bring the boxes out where the light is better."

His gaze rested on her face. His eyes searching and... like expensive dark chocolate, like the moment of shadow just as the sun sets—they stopped the air moving in and out of her lungs.

She tore her attention away and took a gulp of air. "I'll help."

He picked up a box and moved away. She followed his lead and they carried the remains out and placed them on the floor in front of the window.

He had a very good backside.

"So I would guess people outside your department usually blow you off when you ask them to come look at your bone and rag collections," she said. Maybe old bones would shock her back into sanity.

"Gave up long ago. Most prefer museum replicas."

"That'd be my first choice. The woman who runs the museum here claims to be a descendent of Liam Bailey." *Shut up. Shut up. Shut up. Don't pique his interest.*

He pulled on a pair of disposable gloves, hunkered down and flipped open the lid of one of the boxes.

The light flared again in the professor's eyes. He loved this, the hunt for antiquities, even if they were only old bones and tattered cloth.

"We could be looking in on a pirate."

She hunkered down beside him. "I can see you on the deck of a two-masted schooner, long dark hair flowing in the wind, shirtsleeves billowing." She touched his arm as if touching that sexy sleeve.

He leaned away from her touch and reached under the top layers of bags to pull out a large plastic bag containing remnants of brown fabric.

The bag and the sudden look of all business on Dr. MacCarey's face dispelled all the visions in her head of the romance of pirates.

The dead man's clothes. The man in her wall's clothes. The answers to many of her questions and maybe enough of Daniel's.

Or maybe they would raise too many more questions, and Dr. MacCarey wouldn't leave for a month—maybe he'd stay and look for the treasure while Pirate's Roost became just a memory.

# CHAPTER SIX

MIA WATCHED DANIEL take on the persona of college professor as he hand-measured the weight of the bag of clothing remnants. "The cloth is substantial in weight when compared with much twenty-first-century clothing, some noted exceptions being denim and felted wool."

"I keep trying not to envision a fully dressed human," Mia said, but leaned forward anyway.

The creases beside Daniel's mouth became visible through the darkness of his trendy stubble. As a teacher of young adults, he must have practiced this look of stern concentration many times before today.

"Clothing allows one to envision a living breathing person."

"That's my problem," she replied as she studied him.

Whatever measure of rapport the two of them had was diminished to instructor and student. The change felt like a loss, so she smiled.

"There isn't much left of this specimen's clothes, except the type and content of the cloth and dye. Any remaining structure will help determine the cut, style and time frame in which he lived."

"Is the cloth brown because it's brown cloth or because it spent time in the wall with a—um—dead man?" She found she couldn't call him a specimen.

"That's a very good question. The lighter-weight cloth is most likely part of his shirt." The anthropology professor turned the bag over so she could see the remnants of what was a mottled-brown ruffled collar or cuff. "The heavier cloth was pants and jacket. Most likely that cloth was brown before the body went into the wall."

She kneeled down beside the box and ran her fingertip across the plastic-covered ruffle. "What about his shoes? Wouldn't they tell you a lot about what time period he came from?"

"The shoes weren't in the crypt."

She peered into his dark, teacher-mode eyes. Something else lurked there. Something dark and sad.

"You know I would love for you to take your boxes and release my site."

He held her gaze, giving her one of those *I hate to tell you this, but...* looks. "Sometimes the disposition of a site is not up to the people closely involved. The importance of the find determines whether or not the site is quarantined."

"*Quarantined* scares me, but it won't deter treasure seekers." She thought of the two high schoolers, the men at the docks and the shop owners. "It's started already, you know."

"What has started?"

"It's not just someone digging in my basement. Have you ever seen mayhem before?" She stood, putting her hands on her hips because she never knew what to do with them when she was anxious, and right now she was very anxious.

"I'm not sure what you mean." His dark eyes did not move from hers.

"Nice normal people behaving like crazed—um— What are those nocturnal rodent things in the desert that steal shiny stuff?" She broke the gaze between them to stop herself from putting a hand on his cheek and testing his stubble for its degree of softness.

"Wood rats, pack rats."

"Yes, those, but these rats have big pickaxes and shovels, and they know no boundaries. I'm going to have to sleep here." She clasped her hands together and twisted them into submission. "Unless, you find this is just a specimen, a man from, say, fifty years ago, who was afraid of being buried in the ground, so they put him here, in my wall."

This anthropologist, this hot guy, this man who couldn't hide that he had secrets of his own, held her fate in his hands.

She intended to wrench it back.

He shook his head, but he didn't look as regretful as he should look if he was going to crush her hopes to dust. "At least as long ago as the beginning of the twentieth century."

"How do you know?"

"No zipper in his pants, what was left of the pants."

"No zipper? Oh, so how old is the zipper?"

"First patented in 1851 by the man who invented the sewing machine but not used much until the 1930s."

She worked hard to listen to his words and not the drumming inside her head telling her *this is it*. He was in full professor mode talking about zippers and the body being older. The drumming grew loud.

He stopped, slid his gloves off, and gave her an apologetic look. "Sorry, when you weren't taking notes, it occurred to me we weren't in the lecture hall."

"No problem." The noise subsided.

The corners of his mouth turned up. Daniel had returned and Dr. MacCarey had again dropped into the background.

"So the body could be from the late 1800s or early 1900s then." She wanted so badly to believe that so she could collapse in a heap of relief.

She gestured toward the remains in the box. "Tell me this is a body from the last century."

He reached for her hand and curled his fingers around

hers for a moment. Then he let go, cleared his throat again and stepped away. "I wish I could."

His reaction to touching her interested her. What was that about? Secrets. Maybe some mystery.

"At any rate," he continued, "all things have to be considered."

"Considered? As in studied for a few days or considered as in a couple weeks?" Months, years? She walked over to the grimy window and directed her stare out at the street.

The shivers of dread began to skitter across her skin again and she knew why.

Hot live man. Old dead man. And one man who a few months ago pulled up stakes because she wasn't good enough. Well, this was all a great reminder, any kind of man was not a good idea in her life right now, or maybe ever.

"So what do you think?" he asked.

When she turned to face him, he raised one dark eyebrow.

"About what? About having an old guy in my wall? About treasure hunters already in my basement?" *About you and me, baby?*

"You said you might have to sleep here. Where are you going to set up your cot?"

She laughed out loud in spite of everything and shook her head. "I don't know why I'm laughing. If this guy in my wall turns out to be a founder of the town, if he is the privateer Liam Bailey, I'm…"

"Hey." He reached toward her but then must have thought better of it and dropped his hands to his side. "It's too early to tell much except he's probably pre-1930. I'm going to do some research into the building. I'll start at the museum. When I have anything, I'll let you know. I'll also take these remains to the university and get some of the more eager students started on inventory and examination."

That spark of anticipation flared in his eyes again. He was lusting after an anthropological find the way she was lusting after demolition.

Heaven help them.

"Yeah, that'd be great." She'd just go wait some more, go over the blueprints again, check the vendor lists one more time, count the pile of bills to see if she'd broken a hundred yet, listen to her mom's voice mails about her latest club meeting and how Mia should join. Worse, her mom's messages could be to enumerate her dad's faults.

She picked up a box and he picked up the other.

"Tell me about the woman at the museum, the one who claims to be related to Liam Bailey." He followed her out into the bright sunshine.

"Her name is Heather Loch. She comes from a long line of Mainers, or so she says, including Bailey. We don't really know much about her."

Mia placed her box in the trunk of Daniel's car and he put his in beside hers. "No one believes any of her claims to Bailey because it's believed he died without offspring. Her family money did rehab the exterior of the old wooden church and for that we're all grateful."

She wondered if she should warn him about Heather, but quickly decided Ms. Loch was something a person needed to learn about on their own. "Tell her I sent you. She might be—um—more to the point."

"Thank you, for all your help." He held out his hand.

She took hold of his outstretched hand and pressed her palm firmly to his as she tried to read whatever was in his face. "Daniel."

"Yes, Mia."

She ignored the flush spreading through her as she held on to his hand.

"I don't want you to break the hearts of the people around here, and I fear it won't take much. All they will need to get their hopes up is for you to hint that any one of their fantasies might be real. No one has any proof that Liam Bailey ever had treasure to bury, but if they think he died here and didn't go off and spend his wealth...who knows. So please, be careful."

She let go of his hand and stood and watched as he drove away.

DANIEL HAD SEEN the old church on the way into town and headed back that way. As he drove, he found his thoughts turning to the soft smoothness of Mia Parker's hand, the sparkle in her blue eyes, his reaction to her, as though he had some right to start anything with her or any woman.

He'd keep his guard up. Keep his hands to himself. He knew very well how to play the distant, observer role.

When thoughts of Mia faded, anger surfaced, and he forced himself to pay attention to the town instead. There were more residents out now. A man and a woman each pushing a baby stroller. Two middle-aged women in jogging suits strolled casually off onto a side street.

A redbrick building sandwiched between two white-painted wooden buildings appeared to be an upholstery shop and one of the white buildings, a small grocery store. The other white building seemed currently unused.

Apparently, pink was out because equipment had been set up and was blasting the peeling pink paint from the tattoo parlor, exposing the brick below.

At the church, he parked in the gravel lot, got out of the car and shoved his fists deeply into his pockets. When he touched the old velvet pouch with his aunt's last secret, it did not lift the darkness.

He hadn't taken the beautiful old ring out of the pouch since the evening at the nursing home. Maybe in the dim light of the room he had made it all up. For all he knew the ring was a glass bauble set in brass.

No. It was real.

Walking around the perimeter of the old church some of the anger abated, leaving an empty ache in its place.

The old church stood unpainted, facing the elements naked. Modern updates like concrete steps and replacement wooden siding probably spoiled things for the purist, but if the Loch family money had preserved the artifact, they should be applauded. Preserving history belonged to everyone.

As a breeze of the warming day brushed his face, he squeezed the pouch in his pocket. Margaret MacCarey had left a secret as her legacy. A secret he'd have to discover, someday, when it felt easier to probe into the history of the very dear woman.

Mia's image floated into his thoughts, and when he concentrated on her beautiful face, a little of the darkness faded.

He knew he could face Heather Loch now and she might help him find what he needed to free up Mia's building. He pulled his hands from his pockets and headed back toward the entrance.

Gulls pecking at something on the sidewalk squawked and flew away as he approached the front entrance, where the sign above the door read, simply, Bailey's Cove Museum.

Below the sign were a pair of weathered but well cared for doors of exotic wood in an arched doorway, most likely mahogany. They looked out of place in a church so small and so old and had probably been imported, perhaps as an offering by a rich church member who had sinned badly or a dowry of sorts by the establishing clergy.

Suddenly, one of the peaked doors swung open and a

done with the site on Friday and she and her crew could prep on the weekend.

"Hi, this is Mia."

"Mia, this is Jennifer at Markham Construction."

Mrs. Markham. She didn't call often. "Hi, Jennifer. Are you calling about next week?" She played through her head the begging and pleading she'd have to do to get Rufus, Stella and Charlie to work on the weekend, but she knew she could get at least two of them. She'd just do the rest. Heck. She didn't need sleep.

"I am. We've heard you've stopped work on Pirate's Roost again. We're sorry to hear that."

Fate twisted painfully in her chest. How had they found out? That's right. Markham's brother is married to a woman who used to live in Bailey's Cove.

"We should be able to get back in soon."

"I'm sorry. We can't take that chance. We need to re-schedule." Jennifer's tone was sympathetic but firm, that's why they had her make this kind of call.

"No, Jennifer, I can get the place ready."

"You know we've done this before a couple of times. The last time, we ended up laying off a few people. We need to move on to the next job."

"Can you wait a day or two and then cancel my job if we need to then?"

"I'm sorry, Mia, I really am."

"Mrs. Markham, can you give a tentative to the next job and keep mine on the schedule?"

There was a long pause. "I can try to do that. Although, if there are any difficulties, I'll have to call you back."

Mia flopped into her car and tossed the phone on the passenger seat. She banged her head on the headrest a few times and then started her car and headed for the Bailey's Cove police station.

## CHAPTER SEVEN

As IT TURNED out, Mia wasn't able to be squeezed into Chief Montcalm's schedule until two o'clock the next day. To fill her time, she'd spent Monday afternoon talking with the bankers in person and generally trying her best not make herself crazier than she already was. The bankers, at least, seemed willing to give her the leeway she needed, mostly because they were only postponing the draw on the lines of credit.

After she and Monique returned from their shopping trip late in the evening, they drove past Pirate's Roost just to check on things. The building was fine.

In bed, when she had finally banished pirates, bills and bankers from her mind, the image of Daniel MacCarey seeped into her head and would not leave. His handsome face, his quirky humor that so meshed with hers, the dark shadows of past wounds in his eyes.

When she couldn't sleep, she tried scolding herself. The two of them were passing ships, after all—no matter how sexy his lips were, how beautiful his eyes were, how much more he could make her feel with a look than Rory ever had with his whole arsenal.

She'd spent Tuesday morning with the useless minutiae that had seemed so vital to her construction project a week ago, and she hoped dearly would be important again. A lunch of pineapple and plain yogurt because they were all she could get down, and the time had finally arrived to leave for the police station.

None too soon. The teens, Mickey and Tim, had been loitering again that morning on her drive-by. She wanted to padlock them to their desks at school, but she remembered what it was like to be inside when spring warmed things up, and this day was a peach.

The police station was on the opposite end of town from the old church and the site of Pirate's Cove stood almost at the midpoint between the two. The "new" section of town, built in the 1950s, included the police station, the town hall, the new church and the town's most popular café, Mandrel's, along with a motel and several shops.

"Chief Montcalm has somebody in there, Mia, but he should be finished any minute," Melissa, the receptionist said when Mia arrived at the station. "He said he's glad you're here, he has something to discuss with you also."

Melissa Long had been several years ahead of Mia at South Harbor high school. Her naturally flaming-red hair and starkly pale skin had made her the most popular cheerleader, prom queen, student council president, et cetera, in the school's history. She had married one of the Long "boys" whose family owned the grocery store down near the upholstery shop.

"Thanks, I'll be in the waiting room," Mia said after she finished filling in and signing the logbook.

The woman nodded and smiled. Melissa had a sad smile these days, as if she had been expecting more out of life and hadn't gotten it. That was the kind of look that seemed to precede people's deciding to move away from Bailey's Cove. "Missy" had been an artist and her yearbook said she wanted to own her own studio. Maybe she would someday, right here in Bailey's Cove. Prosperous small towns could use more than one of almost anything.

As she approached the six-chair waiting room, Mia could smell the burnt coffee. She helped herself anyway and poured in a hefty dose of powdered creamer.

"Pour two if you don't mind."

She nodded at the chief's words and upturned a second cup.

"White stuff?" she asked as she looked over her shoulder. He seemed to fill the doorway even though he wasn't a big guy.

"Black. Please."

He took the cup from her and nodded his thanks. "Let's go to my office."

She followed him across the waiting room and the lobby, feeling as though she were scurrying after his measured stride.

In his office, she and the chief took up their usual positions on opposite sides of the old desk. Mia remained silent. Chief Montcalm had something to say and she wanted to find out what it was before she started to run off at the mouth, as Monique said, and forgot to listen.

"How are things going with Dr. MacCarey?"

"We sort of have this understanding right now. He knows what I need. And I know he's doing what the site requires based on the significance that the person in my wall played in history. I assure you, Chief, there have been no fisticuffs—yet."

The chief gave a faint smile and Mia realized she had just jabbered. She closed her mouth and folded her hands in her lap.

Chief Montcalm took his cue. "You wanted to see me and there is always a good reason."

"I'm worried about people inviting themselves into my building, worried about the burial site."

He nodded and jotted something down before he looked up and said, "I have read the reports of what happened here during the last treasure frenzy, so I have an idea where your fear is grounded."

"My dad was a kid," Mia said as she leaned forward in

her chair. "He remembers the fires and the crowds. Says the thing he remembers most is being afraid. Do you think it could happen again?"

"It would be easy to say no, but today's communication capabilities might help or hinder. It's hard to say. We have already increased coverage in the area of your building, but please let me know if you need anything more."

"I'm very grateful, Chief, because thanks to social media, I can see the information about treasure in Bailey's Cove splashed across the world in seconds and having a come-one-come-all effect."

"Speaking of the media, I have some old records dating back to the earliest era of the town, which you will not have seen."

"You've got records? Accurate records of what went on around here when the town was established?"

"I suspect old doesn't necessarily mean accurate. They are whatever the person writing them needed them to be at the time."

"But I thought all the records were burned in that fire in the fifties."

"The official records did get destroyed. These are private logs akin to a diary. They have been maintained and handed down from one person to the next among the highest-ranking law enforcement authorities in the town at the time. These records might have information germane to the remains in your wall."

"Do they tell what happened to Liam Bailey?"

"Liam Bailey initiated the log."

"No-o-o." Mia snapped forward in her chair in disbelief. "Not the man himself, dead two hundred years. Wow."

She watched Chief Montcalm's face for any hint the man was kidding—as if—and continued. "It makes a kind of sense. He must have been used to keeping a log. He had been a ship's captain for somewhere around a decade. Why didn't I know about these records?"

"The tradition has been for the records to be held close and passed on when the next person in line is deemed fit to be the keeper."

"So they didn't burn up with the official records." The wheels in her head began to spin wildly. "What's in them? Can I read them?" *Stop.* "Sorry. Please go on."

"Many kept the records in their homes, so when the town hall and the police station buildings burned, these records were safe. You are the first person I've told about them."

"I'm honored." By now about a million thoughts had flooded in and she wanted to voice them all so her head wouldn't explode, but she kept her mouth shut and waited for him to continue.

"I've had them almost three years. They haven't been a priority until now. I've scanned them, but I have not been able to give them the time they deserve. I'd appreciate if someone could look through them and find out if there is anything that any of us needs to know."

"I'll do it. How many are there?"

"Thirty-two boxes and because there are so many and they are of historical value I've called in someone to help."

"I'm looking forward to reading them." Who? she thought.

"Last week I had them put into a storage unit here in the police station. Building codes are much better now and I thought them valuable enough to use the town's resources to safeguard them."

Mia leaned back and the chair squeaked. "I thought I knew this town's secrets."

The intercom on the chief's desk blinked.

"Excuse me," he said to Mia as he picked up the handset. "Yes."

He listened for a moment.

"Send him in, please." The chief looked up at Mia. "Dr. MacCarey is joining us."

A sudden thrill shot through her, making her heart beat faster and her whole body tense with anticipation at the thought of seeing Daniel MacCarey again. She measured her breaths and stood because the chief did.

Daniel appeared in the doorway every bit as good-looking as she had led herself to believe. He was dressed as he was yesterday, but the sweater was a lighter color today. His dark eyes met hers and held, stopping her breath altogether. She looked away and sidestepped to the other chair.

Somehow, she needed to get a grip.

THE SIGHT OF Mia standing beside the desk in the chief's office sent crazy thoughts rushing through Daniel's head, and if he had to be honest…more.

He had not slept any better last night than he had most others, but last night his reasons were different. He'd spent the time trying not to think about Mia Parker. Seeing her bright and beautiful this afternoon had him thinking he'd like to see her every day, every morning.

Those kinds of thoughts would not benefit either of them, and yet, when the chief called and asked him to come to the station to meet with Ms. Parker and him, he could not get there fast enough.

Now she was standing in front of him, her blue pea coat hanging open, and today she had a green stone hanging on a fine gold chain around her neck. The chain disappeared under her red scarf and he found himself wanting to trace its golden path with his fingertip.

"Please sit." Chief Montcalm snapped the spell.

Before he sat, Daniel pulled the chair out at a better angle, so he could see the chief and Mia as they spoke.

"Dr. MacCarey, Ms. Parker and I have been discussing a

set of files that have been maintained by law enforcement officers since the early days of Bailey's Cove."

"Private files? Secret records?" The idea did more to capture his interest than the morning he'd spent teaching the three best students in the anthropology program how to examine and catalogue the remains he had taken to the university. They definitely sounded better than the time he spent in the company of Heather Loch. He'd have to discuss that particular interaction with Ms. Parker.

"Secret is a term that would most likely be applied using modern standards. They are closely guarded. I've glanced through the files and I believe the contributors kept them private for their own reasons and for the sake of the town."

"Did they talk about treasure?" Mia asked.

"Although I found no specific reference to treasure, some of the information, even in the modern files, could incite treasure hunting. In today's world, widespread speculation about the presence of treasure in Bailey's Cove could—" He paused for a moment. "I'm going to quote... 'lead to an invasion of people bent on destruction that could rip out the heart of the town.'"

Mia sat up straighter and then moved forward on her chair. "Isn't that—um—harsh, Chief? I always thought as long as a few of us remained we could prevent complete— er—death and destruction." Her voice held a note of distress, but her face remained a practiced calm.

"The words were quoted by the chief of police only eight years ago, and first written by a sheriff in 1869."

"Around the time the citizens voted to change the name of the town," Daniel said. He had at least gotten the name-change time frame from the museum.

The chief folded his hands on the desk's green blotter. "I'm a newcomer, an outsider, but through the records I reviewed and talking to folks like Ms. Parker, I've been able to see some of what makes this town live and breathe.

And I might add cautions of death and destruction in the log myself."

Daniel glanced at Mia to see her eyes widen.

"Do you really think things could get that bad?" she asked.

"Even if that never happened—" Chief Montcalm paused and looked at each of them. "The town's heart is slowly dying."

Mia nodded.

"And you think I—we—can help?" Daniel asked.

"The best I can offer is access to the records for the two of you."

"When can we start?" she asked.

"You can begin anytime you want."

"Now would be good for me." She stood, as did both men.

"Melissa will show you where the records are stored." The chief leaned forward and placed his hands on the desk. "She does not know what they are and I'd like you to share the contents only when you deem it necessary. And please confine your time in the records room to the day shift, eight to four-thirty. It's best to keep civilians confined to the public rooms during the off shifts."

"We understand," Mia said.

"Yes, of course, and thank you, Chief Montcalm." Daniel leaned forward to shake hands with the chief.

"Thank you, Chief." Mia took his strong handshake, as well.

The chief walked them out to the reception desk where he handed a key to Mia and instructed Melissa to show them where to find the special storage room.

Melissa gave Daniel a longer once-over than she had when he'd arrived in answer to Chief Montcalm's summons and then she gave Mia a look that Mia reacted to by pursing her lips and shaking her head.

Daniel thought he might like the people of this town.

Florescent light fixtures lined the dingy ceiling of the basement hallway. The walls were an institutional shade of green tiles. Scuffed black and old white linoleum covered the floor.

"Thanks, Melissa," Mia said as she inserted a key into the lock of a door labeled No Admittance and reached in to turn on the lights.

Melissa craned around Mia to see into the room and was clearly disappointed by what she saw. The twelve-by-ten-foot room had the same green walls and black-and-white tile as the hallway, though the room's floor tiles were brighter.

One small table with two chairs sat to the right of the door. On the table were two pads of paper, a pair of sharpened pencils, a magnifying glass and two boxes of gloves, one large and one small, and a gooseneck lamp. A floor lamp stood across the room near several stacked plastic boxes. "We can take it from here, Melissa, and thank you," Daniel said to the lingering secretary.

Melissa's smile drooped but she tossed her red hair and sauntered away. He got the feeling people often acquiesced to what she wanted.

"Would it bother you if we closed the door?" Daniel asked, even though being closed in a room with Mia Parker might not be the best idea.

"She'll find a reason to come back, you know, and she'll probably tell everyone we're down here. Fairly soon we can expect a parade of the curious." Mia stepped around him, looked directly at him, a challenge he thought, as she closed the door and turned the lock.

Her expression made him suspect this woman was keeping her fires banked and waiting in case she needed to run ahead of a storm, whatever storm these records could bring. The chief seemed to know her well, to trust her.

She continued to study his face, as if trying to figure him out. He let his gaze wander. The way her wavy, light brown hair fell on her shoulders, it seemed to beg to be picked up by the handful and pushed back away from her face, so her jaw, her ear, her neck could be kissed.

"How much does the chief know about me by now?" he asked to make his mind go someplace besides kissing Mia Parker.

She nodded and smiled. "You're very quick, Dr. Mac-Carey. You are right to think he knows. He knows everything from public sources, private sources and a few sources you won't even think of. Scary, huh?"

"A bit intimidating."

"He does what he needs to do to help keep the citizens of the town safe, like having us examine these records even though they are his and his alone." She moved over to the table and chairs. "I suspect he chose you and me because we have a stake in not blabbing what we find to anyone who will listen."

"I promise not to blab."

She grinned with the tip of her pink tongue between her white teeth and he wondered if she knew what that did to him.

"Mock me if you must," she said, "but the chief knows everything. Though, he won't share his information—unless necessary."

"I'm reassured."

She made him want to smile. This made it even worse that he had to tell her his boss had ordered more limitations on the site. "Before we start, I need to say something."

"Will it make me ecstatically happy?"

"No."

"Do I need to know it right now?"

"Also no."

"Would you be so kind as to tell me later?"

When he nodded, she asked, "Do you have any preferences on how we do these records?"

As she spoke, she removed her coat and placed it on the back of a chair. The dark blue, long-sleeved T-shirt she wore clung to her thin shoulders and small waist, and her jeans snugged against her hips. The gold chain lay against her neck and he had to force himself not to step forward and touch her where it lay.

Now he wondered if he needed to open the door no matter who might come snooping. No, all he had to do was remember the past or fear the future. "Sort them in chronological order as we go is the way I'd do them."

She rubbed her hands together. "Let's do it."

The passion inside her glittered in her eyes. Her cheeks flushed, amplifying her clean, fresh beauty. He considered whether or not he could inspire her other passions, as well.

He cleared his throat. Clearing his head might well be hopeless, but he sure as hell needed to try. "You'd make a good anthropologist."

"I'll keep that in mind if being a restaurateur fails me."

She stopped and put a hand on his arm as she locked her blue eyes to his. "Are we ready for this?"

"Are you?" He scooped up her hand and somehow found the strength not to kiss each fingertip.

"Well, you know. I told the chief I'd do this. If you want to go up and tell him you wimped out…" She shrugged and stepped away. "Please do."

"You're still trying to get rid of me."

"Yes, though I'm starting to think you might not be so bad." Her mouth curved as she put gloves on and picked up a box of files from one of the stacks. "Which means I need to try harder to get rid of you."

"Anthropologists are difficult to get rid of."

"And thorough, Chief Montcalm said." She puffed out a quick breath and sat down on the tile floor, scooting the box between her legs. "What I should want is to burn these, all of them, in case they destroy the Roost's chances, but I can't think of them as anything but a colossal prize for the town."

Her hair tumbled down into her face as she peered into the box and took out a file. When she opened the folder he wanted to move her hair out of the way so he could see her face. More than reading files, more than an anthropological find, he wanted to put his hands in that hair.

His colleagues at the university could be right. He might need a keeper, but not for the reasons they all thought.

She moved closer to the lamp and he grabbed a box of his own.

After they had been working for a while, Daniel opened his third box and found files from 1917 through 1920 written by a Chief Francis Reagan. The man seemed rather pleased to have seen the rest of the country finally come to its senses and pass prohibition laws because the State of Maine had been a leader in that social battle.

Getting lost in some of the files was irresistible and was going to make getting through them take a lot longer than it should. Mia didn't seem to mind and neither did he. Though sometimes he found himself absorbed in watching her read files, like now.

She glanced up and smiled at him and it went right to his gut and places lower. "Nineteen twenties?" he asked indicating the box he had.

"Over here." She pointed to a row near the table and when he got up, came over and slid a box in the line of ascension ahead of his. "You know, a museum might find these files very interesting."

When she looked at him with big blue innocence, he chuffed instead of answering.

"You didn't find our museum interesting?" Mischief played on her face.

"You could have warned me."

"Ah-yuh, I could have, but what would have been the point? After all I've said about you getting in and getting out of town quickly, you'd have thought I was trying to hide something from you."

"I would—"

"—have." She grinned a dare at him.

"I would have doubted you."

They studied each other with the smiles stuck on their faces. He realized he didn't just like her smiles, he liked being the reason she smiled.

"So I saved you some time by letting you get the visit out of the way." She sauntered over to him and emphasized her point by pressing the tip of her finger into his shoulder. Her eyes never left his. "We could have argued first and then you would have gone anyway."

"All the same." He retaliated with a shoulder prod of his own, a place he thought would be safe, but he was wrong. The attraction he had tried to squelch erupted and he had to step away. He grabbed a box and retreated.

"Wouldn't you say Heather Loch and her museum need to be experienced at least once?" she asked as she casually bent over and retrieved another box.

"She's certainly one of a kind."

Heather Loch had demanded to know why he hadn't delved more deeply into his own past, extolling the virtues of research and asking tough, frank questions. He hadn't given her a reason.

"To be fair, if Heather'd just leave a person alone to browse, there are some facts in the museum," she said, her head bent over the box of files. He wondered if she was being more deliberate than her casual manner indicated and forced himself not to watch.

"And the building is well kept," he said. "That says

something good about Bailey's Cove that the church wasn't torn down long before Ms. Loch took it over."

"See you have been learning about our fine town. We are rooted deeply in history here." She spoke the words lovingly. Her dedication to Bailey's Cove made her even more attractive.

"She didn't tell me anything about her being related to Liam Bailey, which surprised me."

Mia looked at him and raised her eyebrows. "She doesn't trust you yet."

"I'm a good guy, really I am."

"I'm sure that's what pirates say about themselves, too." She challenged him as she spoke and he wanted to cross the space between them and kiss her parted lips.

*Work,* he reminded himself. He delved into his own box, but couldn't help but wonder how much more there was to know. "Why did they change the name of the town from South Harbor to Bailey's Cove when they did?"

"It's never been clear exactly why the name was changed. But I was thinking, wouldn't it be the biggest joke—" she held the file aloft her hair falling away from her face "—if they tore the town apart and the treasure of Bailey's Cove turned out to be thirty-two boxes of paper?"

Her expression suddenly got more thoughtful, sad, and she looked away because either she wanted to retrieve another file or to keep him from seeing her face, he wasn't really sure.

## CHAPTER EIGHT

DANIEL LOWERED HIMSELF to the floor next to Mia, facing her. "Mia, what we're doing here could ruin things for you."

She moved closer to him, close enough for her body heat to seep into his and she tried to smile. Her sadness shined through, a beacon of dread. "I just need to get the restaurant launched in time."

He could see in her eyes she was not playing him. This was more than a business enterprise to her.

"I get that it's important." He pushed her hair behind her ear so he could see her face. The softness of her skin beneath his fingertip sent a demand through him. He wanted her, wrong as it was.

"The town's historical significance is dying a slow death. We're losing the folks who know the lore, the heart of South Harbor, of Bailey's Cove." She looked at him with too much trust. "I'd like to think finding a pirate's treasure would sustain the town, but it's easy to see in this world, it would be a flash flood leaving destruction in its wake and no genuine future for us. I wouldn't want the entirety of Bailey's Cove to be reduced to a hokey tourist attraction."

Passion ran deep in her, hidden by the layers life had forced her to create. He found himself inhaling as much of her scent as he could, absorbing her. "Is there anything you can do in the meantime?"

"I can't stop it. I don't even know if I can slow it down." She sat up suddenly and plucked a folder from the box. "I can't think of a reasonable and rational way to steer the ship in this rising storm. And even if I had the power to keep everything under wraps, I can't make that decision for the entire town and I'm afraid to mention anything to the Mayor or the town council. I'm afraid they might take up shovels themselves." She stopped and looked up at him. "Daniel, what do I do?"

He could tell by the look on her face that she regretted the question as soon as she asked it, and that she didn't ignore her misgivings said more about her strength than anything.

He took the folder from her hand and put it back in the box, and her blue eyes flashed at him.

She leaned into him, drawing him toward her until their lips were almost touching. The smell of her filled him and her blue eyes sparkled up at him. The sadness had lifted, replaced by smoke.

"Action...sometimes you just need to take action." His words came out breathy as she shifted closer. Then her eager mouth moved over his, as his reservations silently imploded until he could barely remember them.

When he put a hand behind her head to deepen their kiss, she came to him, encircling his neck with her arms. He pulled her onto his lap, pressing her softness into him, his mouth testing, tasting. She met his tongue with hers and...

...she broke the kiss as suddenly as it had started and moved carefully off his lap and back onto the floor. "This is—um—wonderful, but the chief probably didn't consider that we might get along *this* nicely."

"I suppose not." Cold reality came back swiftly when he realized he had lost control. "I'm—"

"Don't you dare apologize."

"I might be sorry—"

"No." She covered her ears.

He felt the laughter rising easily inside him. "I might be

sorry we met under these circumstances." He spoke with his mouth very near her hand so she couldn't help but hear him, nudging her fingers with his lips until she wiggled them in protest. "Or that I have to delay your project, but I'm not sorry I kissed you. You taste like a morning after a spring rain."

"Oh, thank you."

He smiled because that's what she did to him, made him smile, and she managed to look sexy with her hands still pressed to her ears.

"Are you finished?" she asked.

"Yes." He leaned in and took another taste, which she readily gave to him. Her mouth explored his as she moved her hands from her ears to his chest. When she curled her fingers under the hem of his sweater, he snatched them up in his.

It didn't stop her. As her lips explored his face, her other hand reached under his sweater and found flesh. Her touch distorted reason like some crazy spell, stirring things inside him he'd never felt.

He placed a kiss on the soft skin where the gold chain lay on the nape of her neck and then raised her chin until she had to look into his eyes. "The last thing I want to do is to lead you to believe I have anything to offer you. I don't and that's not you, it's me."

She stared at him for a moment, any uncertainty completely gone from her clear expression. "Chivalry is not dead." She resumed her exploration, taking inventory of the muscles in his abdomen, and then her expression changed to a dare as she flattened her palm against his belly and moved lower.

"In fact, chivalry might be dead and gone if you keep that up." His voice was nearly a growl.

She slid her hand back up to safer territory. "It is alive and well in an anthropologist come to study my bones."

He touched a fingertip to the angle of her jaw. "They are great bones."

She leaned toward him again, and he stroked the soft skin of her neck. Then he reached into her thick, soft hair and luxuriated in the opulence as the silkiness slid and tumbled through his fingers—and he felt control begin to slip again.

"Hey, aren't we supposed to be reading records to see what we might find about those old bones?" he said against her ear and then left a kiss.

She moved away. That was a shame because having her close enough to touch, smell and taste seemed right.

"You're right." She took her phone from her pocket and looked at the screen. "No signal. I'm—um—going upstairs to check for messages."

With Mia gone, the room seemed dimmer, maybe even smaller. The light feeling in his heart receded, and the anger seeped back inside him.

Was he crazy?

He needed to think with a smarter part of his body... because his heart could get him in trouble, worse, it could get someone else's into trouble if he let things go too far.

He pushed the boxes into their proper order. If he couldn't fix himself, he for sure should not harm Mia any more than the consequences of that skeleton dictated.

A few minutes later, she hurried back into the room, tossed the room keys to him and grabbed her coat. "There's a problem at the site."

She ran out the door.

MIA RACED HER small SUV up Church Street. The sun hung much lower in the sky than she imagined it would. They had been in the records room longer than she thought, kissing, touching. And it had been wonderful. Full-on fantasy stuff.

But reality had returned quickly and succinctly.

A squad car sat out in front of Pirate's Roost and when she got inside, two police officers stood in the doorway to the back room.

"Hello, Officer Gardner." She greeted Lenny and then she turned to the other officer. "Hello, Officer Doyle."

"Hello, Ms. Parker." The older police officer turned away and stepped into the back room.

What was there? What did they find? Fear struck hard and she had to make her feet move forward.

Beyond the doorway, violent destruction had spread granite out across the floor.

"Oh, no."

Chunks, pieces that hadn't been there before, lay strewn about as if an explosion had taken place.

Her stomach twisted at the sight of the sledgehammer's handle resting against the wall.

"Whoever did this was careful not to break through the plaster of the front wall so no passersby or patrol squads out on Church Street could see what they were doing," Lenny said, looking at her less sternly than usual.

"How did you know anything happened?"

"The Sergeant told us to come by more often," Officer Doyle added. "We checked in the back and the door was open, it might have been jimmied, but the thing is really old, so it's hard to tell. Sorry, Ms. Parker."

There was no mystery left in the burial chamber. If there had been anything hidden inside, it was gone. "It will be hard to undo this."

"Do you think anything of value was taken?" Doyle asked as Lenny prowled, checking the other rooms and windows.

"Just the integrity of the crypt. They didn't even take the stupid hammer."

"We'll ask around the neighborhood and find out if anyone saw anything. Do you know if the back door was left unlatched?"

"Are you kidding?" She made a conciliatory gesture toward Officer Doyle. "Sorry. Since the chief told me on that first day I needed to be vigilant, I have been."

"We'll take the hammer and dust it and the door for prints. There isn't much else we can do," Lenny said as he reentered the back room.

"I think we have to check with Dr. MacCarey also. He's in town and should be here soon," she said.

As she studied the debris, she noticed some of the granite pieces were streaked with brown. She wondered if the lines were random or purposeful. She sucked in a breath.

"Are you all right?" Lenny moved to her side.

"I'm fine. I'm fine." She smiled to cover any alarm. Was the brown someone's blood?

Lenny's radio squawked something Mia couldn't make out. He turned away and answered the call.

"Is he coming?"

It took Mia a moment to realize the other officer was speaking to her. "Who? Oh, Dr. MacCarey. I'm sure he is. I can have him call you, if you need to leave."

"Are you all right here by yourself?" Lenny asked.

"I'm good."

"Then we'll be back to take your statements when we can," Lenny said and then executed a crisp turn and was gone, Officer Doyle hurrying to catch up, carefully carrying the big hammer sheathed in plastic over his arm.

"No problem. I'll let Dr. MacCarey know," she said aloud with only herself as an audience. The officers had gone to deal with lawbreakers elsewhere, and Daniel would be here unless he ran away because he had been kissing the enemy.

Too bad on many accounts if he ran. She had been looking forward to reading the records with an anthropologist whose experience might offer insight—and she wanted him.

Hunkering down over a larger piece of stone, she looked more closely. Clearly demarcated brown wavy lines stretched across the gray. The lines could be random. They could also have been put there by someone. Maybe they were some kind of old paint, not blood.

What if it was blood?

She had seen no markings on the outside of the crypt.

What if the man had been alive when he was placed in the wall? What if he were trying to leave a last message? Even a dreaded pirate did not deserve that fate.

Horror washed over her until she began to tremble and almost fell back into the dust and rubble.

At the sound of footsteps she stood and moved away.

"What's going on?" Daniel demanded and then quickly raised a conciliatory hand. "I'm sorry. What happened?"

When she didn't answer, he took hold of her arm and turned her gently to face him. "What's wrong, other than the obvious?"

She shrugged a shoulder, wondering where the prickly side of this man came from, but let it drop and pointed a finger toward the largest chunk of granite. The patterns in the discoloration seemed easier to see now. Even in the dim light of the dangling bulb the markings looked purposeful.

He bent down beside the debris and shined the beam of his flashlight across the stones until it landed on the large one. "The markings don't look random."

"There's another one." She pointed across the scattered pieces to a similarly large piece with more brown lines.

"Random or not, it makes a difference until we know for sure," Daniel said as he continued to scrutinize the debris.

"I'm so sorry this happened, Daniel."

He stepped over debris until he stood at her side. Then

he tugged her chin up until he could see into her eyes. "Are you all right?"

"I'm good."

He ran his thumb across her lips. "That response sounded automatic."

All she could think now was, *Touch me, touch all of me.*

"I'm afraid the instant answer is almost always the one I give these days." She moved away before she stepped up and demanded he put his arms around her.

"Do you suppose the man was still alive when he was walled up?" she asked as another shiver of horror swept through her.

"I'll have to take a closer look at all the pieces before I can make any sense of the discoloration."

She heaved her shoulders and sighed. "I just wanted to sell great seafood and a passable hamburger to the tourists."

He was already absorbed in the scene and might not have heard her sad lament. Just as well.

She left him to assess the damage and went to stand in the front window to be sad alone. Falling night brought out twinkling lights in the harbor and in the town.

It all looked so peaceful, so normal, and she loved every brick, boat and brown dog in the town.

As the reassuring thoughts filtered through her head, it occurred to her she should be rejoicing. Some of the questions the site had raised had been answered by several swipes of the big hammer. There was nothing else in the crypt. There was no treasure buried there.

Was it so terrible to want things to be normal?

She wasn't even sure she knew what normal was supposed to look like. It certainly couldn't be finding the man in her wall had been buried alive.

Normal certainly wasn't being attracted to the man who had swooped in, helped trash her world and would sail out again as soon as he finished with Pirate's Roost.

When she reentered the back room, Daniel was studying one of the pieces of granite. He looked up at her as if he had something he needed to tell her.

"Did you find answers?"

"No, but I still have something I need to tell you."

Oh, that thing he tried to tell her in the records room.

"Okay. I'm ready. Tell me."

"This morning I spoke with my boss."

"That old fuddy-duddy of an interfering man?" Mia paused. "Sorry, I don't know your boss."

"He's a medium fuddy-duddy of an interfering man."

Nervous energy made her laugh at his response, but she was sure she was not going to like what the *duddy* had to say.

"He wants me to forbid—"

She barked a not-amused laugh. "Forbid? He wants you to forbid?" Did this ever get better?

She started forward and he grabbed her and put his arms around her.

"*Forbid* anyone from entering the building until it is decided whether or not this is a town founder."

She rested her chin on his chest and looking up at him with a grin, said, "You are so doing a terrible, horrible job. Just look at how many people have been in here."

He grinned down and kissed the tip of her nose. "Maybe you should charge admission."

She started to laugh. "If the duddy fires you, you can come and wash dishes in my— Wait!" She put her hands on his shoulders and pushed back to look into his face. "In my kitchen at home because I won't have a restaurant kitchen."

"The university sent me here because anyone with half a brain could do this job."

"Your problem is you have a whole brain, but that's nothing. Banks lent me a whole boatload of money to build a restaurant on this spot."

"That seems to be going quite well."

She patted his chest and moved away. "You can come with me when I go apply at a big-box store for a job."

She laughed at all the ridiculous things in her life and then she laughed again because it was all she had.

"What's going on?" Lenny stood in the doorway, looking most fastidious shifting his gaze between the two of them.

"Just the usual, Officer Gardner," she responded.

Lenny looked at Daniel and frowned. "I'm Daniel Mac-Carey. The university sent me to check out the site."

"With a hammer?" Lenny asked in a serious voice.

"He didn't do it, Lenny," Mia interjected. "Someone broke in after Dr. MacCarey and I left yesterday afternoon, sometime during the night. I'd guess."

Lenny gave a single nod. "I'm Officer Gardner." Lenny stepped forward for a formal handshake with Daniel. "Dr. MacCarey, since the university has jurisdiction over the site for now, Chief Montcalm said we were to defer to whatever you say as far as how the site is to be handled. I'd like to check out the rest of the property if that's all right with you."

"The granite from the crypt may have significant markings on it and I'd like to handle the pieces myself," said Daniel, pointing to the chunks and shards of granite.

"Whatever you say, Dr. MacCarey."

Lenny's radio squawked again and when he was finished talking he made arrangements to meet them at the station to get their statements.

"Thank you, Lenny," Mia said when the officers were ready to leave. "I, we, appreciate the police department's help."

"We do our best, ma'am," Officer Doyle added as they departed.

Mia hoped with all her might their *best* would be enough.

DANIEL DROVE UP the curving road, past the gawker's pull-out and away from Bailey's Cove. The lights of the small town faded fast, and his world seemed to shrink down to the two hundred feet of roadway lit by his headlamps. Uncertainty seemed to lurk out there just out of sight in the eerie darkness.

So much had changed since the sun had come up over the cove yesterday morning.

Tonight, by the time the police had taken Mia's and his statements, four hours had passed. A spate of petty crime, auto accidents and a domestic disturbance kept the officers on duty busy, and it was clear the scene at Mia's restaurant would need to be left until morning.

Officer Gardner suggested Mia and Daniel go home for the night.

Daniel headed from the coast toward the highway. The closer he got to the interstate, the more he thought about the cold emptiness at his condo. He usually didn't let his brain go there because in almost every quiet place he felt the same feeling of loss and emptiness.

Except for Bailey's Cove.

He supposed it was impossible to watch your family fall completely apart and not have your heart regard most of the world as bleak and empty. "It's not that I don't love you, Danny, but every time I see your face, I see Sammy's," his wife had told him two years ago as she stood in the middle of the living room in their family home, suitcase in hand.

Now, in the span of less than forty-eight hours, the fragile, uncertain path of his life had crystal clear options. The call from his boss had been about more than protecting the site.

What he hadn't told Mia was that their two futures were linked. Successfully proving the remains were Liam Bailey's would put Daniel solidly on tenure track and negatively impact Mia's chances of getting Pirate's Roost up and running in time for the northerly trek of the tourists.

Worse, if he backed away, chose oblivion for his career, the university would send the newest PhD candidate, Elliot Smith. Smith would not care at all who was harmed in the handling of the scene. At least this way, Daniel might have a chance of getting the time schedule accelerated for Mia.

When he reached the highway intersection, he headed away from the university and from his condo. A motel or an inn had to be better than what he tried to call home, where he had paced the floors most of last night and where most of his memories seemed to have followed him.

At the highway's next major crossroad, major for this part of Maine, the highway sign gave him a choice of an inn or a chain motel. He chose the inn because "some rooms with fireplaces" seemed like what he could use right now. Once he arrived at the inn, however, even a fireplace didn't seem like enough to fix the emptiness.

At the memory of Mia Parker's bright smile and warm lips he knew he'd rather spend the night in Bailey's Cove than any place else. He parked in the inn's lot, and called the number he had taken from the back wall at Mia's building. In the dark he listened as the phone rang.

"Promise me and promise yourself, you will pursue your dream," his aunt had said to him and he had promised.

"This is Mia," she answered and by her voice he could tell she wasn't sleepy, either.

"It's Daniel."

## CHAPTER NINE

"DANIEL, IS THERE anything the matter?"

The sound of Mia's voice washed over him and he imagined the look of concern on her face. He knew he had made the right decision for this night. *Go to Bailey's Cove.*

"I was driving and I realized it might be best to stay someplace local tonight. Can you recommend somewhere?"

"Come here."

"I can't do that."

"Because?"

"Because I'd be putting you out."

"I have a fire in the fireplace."

He gave a soft snort. "I've been feeling cold."

"I have a bottle of red wine I opened and plan on drinking by myself in a half hour or so."

He thought he heard some sort of muffled protest in the background. She wasn't alone. "I like red wine, but if you have company, never mind."

"Come. I don't really want to drink it alone."

There wasn't even a peep of a protest this time. "Where do you live?"

She gave him her address and added, "Halfway between Pirate's Roost and the police station and six blocks up the hill on Blueberry Avenue."

"I can find that. I'll be there in about forty-five minutes."

MIA TOOK HER hand away from Monique's mouth and said, "Get out."

"Was that him?"

Mia nodded and Monique shrieked.

The excitement of seeing Daniel again had started her heart racing the moment she heard his voice.

"How soon?"

"He said forty-five minutes."

"Plenty of time for you to change."

"What's wrong with what I'm wearing?" She had donned a clean, button-front cotton Henley and her most comfortable jeans after a shower.

"Oh, please tell me you're not wearing one of your ugly sports bras."

Mia tugged the neckline of her shirt and looked inside. "They are not ugly. In fact, this one is a lovely shade of navy blue."

"Faded navy blue. That makes it muddy blue. If I weren't two cup sizes bigger than you, I'd take mine off right now and make you put it on. Sexy, fiery red, with lace edges and a front closure for easy access. And there isn't even a man to see it tonight, or well any night, but I'm hoping soon."

"Do you wear red lace all the time?"

"Red, pink, apricot, I vary the color with each day, yesterday I wore blue, but lace, pretty lace, not that stretchy stuff that gets those clinging fuzz balls."

"It's highly possible, you know, that I will be the only one ever to see my bra." Mia laughed.

"You invited him to come here, to your home."

"Because he sounded like he needs a glass of wine and a warm place. A couple glasses of wine and I'll send him off to the Harbor Inn."

Monique laughed and pinched Mia's cheeks. "You're so cute when you lie."

"You are a very naughty woman. Does Lenny know?"

"Not yet, but I think he might be hoping."

"Did he kiss you yet?"

"Last night after he got off work. We had coffee. And a very nice kiss it was, too. He's like a throwback, a gentleman from a hundred years ago."

"I think that makes you very lucky, Monique."

"Yeah, all reserved and polite on the outside, and I suspect hot as a smithy's forge on the inside."

Mia smiled. "What if he is the one?"

"You know, every time I see him, I can't help wonder the same thing. I think I'm ready to go sit at Mandrel's and wait for him to come in for a late coffee. Give the gossips some new juice."

"I think we both know Lenny is ready."

"I hope so."

"You're a catch, Monique. Over and above your cup size."

"Haha! Well, I'm leaving. I have a counter stool to occupy."

"Don't have the pie." Mia gave her the usual warning about the almost irresistible pie at Mandrel's.

"It's only for lookin'. And I'm outta here."

"Keep me posted."

"Back at ya."

Monique slid on her short leather jacket and hurried away.

Mia picked up the things that wouldn't bother her if family and friends saw them, but seemed too messy for a real guest. She polished the two wineglasses she and Monique were going to use, brought more wood in, brushed her teeth because she had the time and wished she had some lace to put on instead of muddy blue.

Maybe it wouldn't matter. They had gotten carried away

earlier today. Maybe the mood would be totally different now.

The doorbell rang.

It had taken only thirty-nine minutes.

Mia rubbed her palms down the thighs of her jeans and put on her best not-nervous welcome face, and pulled open the door.

Monique thrust a handful of condoms at her and fled back down the sidewalk.

"Thanks," Mia called after her friend.

Monique gave her a thumbs-up, dove into her car and peeled off down the hill.

Mia laughed when she opened her palm and looked at what Monique had brought. Flavored, extra sensation and added pleasure.

She hurried up to her bedroom with them, and then thought better of putting all of them up there. She came back downstairs and put a couple in the drawer of the table near the couch.

When they had been prudently distributed, she checked her hair in the hall mirror and smiled at what she saw. Wild hair. She felt a little wild.

This time when the doorbell rang, she opened it to see Daniel MacCarey standing on her porch. His whiskers were turning into a beard, but they did not hide the deep distress carved into his face. His strong shoulders slumped and his eyes were red with fatigue.

She stepped back so he could come inside her foyer. "You look terrible."

After she closed the door, she reached inside the jacket he had put on over his ratty sweater and pulled him to her for a hug.

A moment later he lifted her chin and found her mouth with his as he backed her up against the wall and kissed her lips, her face, her neck. His whiskers were long enough to be almost soft but made his kisses seem more urgent.

When his insistent lips crushed hers again, she brought her hands up under his sweater and curled her fingers over his hard shoulders so she could lift herself higher and on tiptoes press herself closer. From here, she could have her way with his neck, his ears, his mouth.

The world suddenly became about him and the fire he lit within her.

Daniel MacCarey stood her up in her own foyer and plumbed the depths in her no one else had ever even stirred.

He was hard. And from being pressed up against the wall, she could tell all of him was hard.

When he put his arms around her and lifted her, she wrapped her legs around him, kissing, licking, nibbling whatever felt best at the time.

He somehow had the key to her passion and she couldn't seem to get enough of him.

If this was a dream, it was a good one.

He carried her into the living room and leaned over the sofa with her still clinging to him. When she let go and dropped onto the soft throw cover, he sat down on the edge beside her and she pushed up to face him. With her hands free, she stripped off his jacket and tossed it aside. He did the same with her Henley top. She reciprocated with his sweater.

She looked up at him. "Damn."

"What's wrong?"

"My friend said I should always wear a lacy bra that opens in the front." She looked down at her sports bra that was no way going to fall off easily.

The fatigue lifted from his face as he smiled and slid his fingers under the edge of her bra. She gasped when his thumbs brushed across her nipples. As she raised her arms, her bra followed the path the rest of their clothes had taken—somewhere else.

"Good?" he asked as he touched her collarbone and then skimmed his fingertips down to her breast.

She grinned. "It's getting that way."

Scooting her back down on the couch, he gently lowered his weight until they were chest-to-chest, heat-to-heat. She arched for more and reveled when he slid his arm beneath her and molded their bodies together.

She had not expected such a quick and fierce response from her body. There was magic between this man and her and she wanted to experience all of its bliss.

He ran his hand down and up her thigh, teasing her sensitive skin. He smiled as he then cupped her breast, gently caressing and massaging until she moaned. Slowly, maddeningly slowly, he leaned over her breast, finally taking her nipple into his mouth. She let out a small cry as his tongue danced over the erect tip.

"You do such nice things with your mouth," she said as she kissed his hair and traced the smooth skin of his shoulders and back.

He lifted his head and she thought he was about to fulfill her wish of nakedness, but he switched to her other breast and she almost forgot what her wish was. Her breasts had never felt so well made love to and when he brought his hand up between her legs and stroked her, she knew all of her was going to eventually feel the glory.

"Daniel, this is wonderful."

"It is." He lifted his head and watched her steadily as he unzipped her jeans.

When she smiled, he removed her jeans and then her panties.

He held the panties up on one finger. "These are lace."

"Thank you for noticing."

She plucked them off the tip of his finger and tossed

them. All she wanted, and she wanted it right now, was to have all of him.

When he didn't strip off his jeans, she realized he hadn't thought this out any more than she had. Thank goodness for a good friend.

She pointed over her head to the end table. "Top drawer."

He reached in the drawer, pulled out a condom and put it aside.

"Oh." She was so ready to use the condom, so ready she could have cried, until he started kissing her again, her lips, her neck, her breasts, over and over.

She panted, as happiness seemed to be the only emotion she could find, and then opened her eyes to find him studying her.

He smiled and continued to gently stroke her with his fingertips.

She gave a few more luxurious shudders. "That feels good."

"Yes, it does." He tenderly kissed her mouth and kissed where the chain lay against her neck.

"Am I having all the fun?"

In answer, he stood and stripped down his jeans and shorts as a unit and when he was totally naked, she grinned up at him. "Magnificent."

He laughed and donned the condom. Then he carefully lowered himself down on her and into her in one fluid movement.

The wave of pleasure hit her and instantly the world went away. There was nothing but the two of them.

"Yeah, magnificent," he said as she took all of him inside her.

Slowly, relentlessly, he pushed her up the peak, nudging her with his body, his hands, his kisses until, at the top, pleasure burst within her again.

He followed her and she knew for sure she wasn't the only one having a good time.

"Mia, that was amazing." He held her close, nuzzling at her neck.

"Exactly what I was thinking, Daniel."

He kissed her long and soft and she felt their bodies respond again.

A HALF HOUR or thirty seconds or whatever later, after they had used a second condom, he propped himself up on his elbow and looked down at her.

"What?" she demanded after he had been staring at her for several seconds.

"I keep wanting to say thank you, but I don't want to push my luck."

She pushed up and kissed his lips and then his whiskered chin. "Thank *you*. Though, I do know what you mean. Since we're supposed to be on opposing teams, enemies, and since I just had the greatest sex I've ever had, I'm thinking it's appropriate."

"The greatest ever, heh?" He licked below her ear. She hadn't realized until that moment how sensitive that spot was and she shivered.

"Call me sheltered, but greatest by far."

"Okay, Miss Sheltered, I am honored and pleased to have been a part of that action."

She ran her hand from his hip, across the ridges of his belly and up to his well-defined chest. "I wasn't kidding about the magnificent comment. You have taken very good care of your body. For that alone, I say thank you."

He chuckled and she realized what a nice, soft wonderful sound that was—intimate, unguarded and for the moment all for her.

"And you are even more lovely than I imagined."

A stomach growled loudly and she laughed. "Well, that puts all things into perspective."

"Mine or yours?" he asked.

"Maybe it was both of us." She massaged his shoulder. "Let me up."

Chilly, she scampered for the stairs. Her robe seemed more appropriate than putting her jeans back on.

"There's a bathroom off the kitchen," she called over her shoulder.

She donned her warm robe and slippers and then dug for a wrapped Christmas present from the back of her closet.

When the water was still running in the downstairs bathroom, she smiled and tapped on the door. After a moment, she opened the door a crack and stuck the present inside.

"And I didn't get you anything," he said, taking the box.

In the kitchen, Mia loaded up a tray with bowls and flatware and bread and butter, Daniel came out of the bathroom wearing a brand-new robe and slippers. "I don't know who he was, but tell him thank you for me."

"He is currently and forever relegated to the category of nobody." Mia realized she meant those words and the realization brought a kind of freedom with it.

She opened her robe and then his and reached inside to press their naked bodies together. He leaned down and kissed her long and hard as he reached around her and pulled them closer together.

When he lifted his mouth from hers, he asked, "How many condoms do you have?"

She laughed and pulled away to tie both of their robes. "I'd hate to faint. I need some nourishment."

He picked up the tray. "Dining room or living room."

"Near the fire in the living room, please."

By the time she had stirred the pot on the stove to make sure it was still warm enough and had gotten into the living room with the open bottle of wine and two glasses, he had moved the coffee table and stoked the fire. On the floor between the table and the fire he had spread a quilt and put out the two large wedge pillows she kept stored in the corner. He had even taken a placemat off the pile for each of them and spaced them on the table with a bowl, knife and spoon on each.

"Aren't you handy." She held out the bottle and glasses and when he took them, she leaned in for a lingering kiss.

"Pour. I'll be right back."

She brought in the steaming pot of Lobster bisque.

They ate all they could, moved the table out of the way, drank the last of the wine and then lay on the floor, shoulder to shoulder with their feet toward the crackling fire.

"So whose dinner did I just eat? I hope it was the guy who's going to get a used robe and slippers. Though there seems to be something extremely survival-of-the-fittest about something like that."

"No such luck, tough guy. It was my friend Monique's dinner."

"That's a good friend."

"You have no idea." She thought of the remaining condoms now in the pocket of her robe and hoped there would be enough for the night.

"Now you can tell me, if you want to, why you looked so miserable when you got here." She brushed at the hair that was almost long enough to lop onto his forehead.

He put his hand on her thigh and smiled. "Did anyone ever tell you you're a frank person?"

"I'm not always. You bring that out in me, and, hey, was that a dodge?"

"It might have been."

"Okay, new subject. Concerning you and me."

He looked at her curiously but didn't say anything.

"As far as I'm concerned, whatever is between us is just

between us. If it's a night, a week, a millennium, each of us gets to decide for ourselves. You don't want anything long-term and that's your stuff. I, on the other hand, just love to have my heart broken, and I can't do that without falling for someone first. That silly habit of mine, in fact, netted you a robe and slippers for the evening."

"A very comfortable robe and slippers, too," he said, and then his brows drew together in concern. "I don't want to break your heart."

"I did this to myself. I wanted you, Daniel. I wanted you badly, and I got you." She squeezed his hand. "I guess breaking my own heart is, I don't know, just one of the things I do. Lets me know I'm alive."

He squeezed back. "You don't need to break your heart. You are one of the most alive people I've ever met. You're so alive, you'd scare the hell out of most of the staff in my department."

"Do I scare you?"

He pulled her into his arms and kissed her on the mouth, a lovely lingering kiss. "You scare me silly."

"But you don't mind."

"You're like skydiving."

"And you like screaming all the way down?"

"So much that I want to go up again."

She turned on her side. "I can help you with that."

He got up and put another log on the fire and closed the glass doors.

"I have something I need to tell you," he said when he was finished with the fire and came back to the quilt.

"We've already got the 'I can't get involved' and 'the university rules my fate' stuff behind us, so let's have it."

He laughed.

"Oh, good, it's funny."

"No, it's not funny at all. I should have told you when I first got here tonight."

"I think the entire conversation between us when you first got here tonight was *You look terrible.* Pretty hard to squeeze any more in between the lines there."

DANIEL REACHED OUT and played with one soft wisp of Mia's hair.

Propped up on one elbow with the neck of her robe gaping open in such a tantalizing way, one breast sloping down until the edge of her nipple showed was almost enough for him to push her on her back and take her again, well and without mercy.

But he needed to get this out.

"I told you my department head wanted me to keep everyone away from the site until a determination was made." What a hideous contrast to speak about his boss when he wanted to make love to Mia until the sun came up. He'd never seen such ecstasy before and he wanted to see it again and again.

"Go on."

"What?"

"You seemed to get lost somewhere."

"Yeah, I guess I did. My boss also told me, if this is Liam Bailey, and if I take my time, get all the evidence, I can put myself back on the tenure track. I got diverted from the track several years ago."

She stayed up on her elbow and watched him. There was no anger in her face, not even disappointment.

"I should have said something before we had sex. Heck, I should have said something before I kissed you the first time."

"Listen, Daniel." She rolled onto her back. "I do appreciate that you are telling me now. I can see where it might get difficult between us. There was a time in my life when I would have been really mad at you."

He suddenly wondered what she knew about him. How much had the chief told her? "And now?"

"I have learned to deal with more in the past two years than I ever dreamed I'd have to put up with—"

He frowned in concern.

When she said nothing, he took a hold of the collar of his robe and raised his eyebrows.

"Yeah, that guy would be one of them."

"I'm making things harder for you."

"Not tonight you aren't, but I get the feeling we are— You are—" she turned her head and looked up him "—dancing around something, something dark."

Grief socked him so hard in the midsection he almost gasped and the harder he tried to push it down, the more it streamed forward around his barricades. Tears sprang to his eyes and trailed down the side of his face.

He tried to stem the flow.

No one, absolutely no one since Mandy had seen him cry, and she had not seen his tears since he had held his son in his arms the last time. Yet here he was, in the home of a woman he barely knew and whose life he could ruin and he was practically bawling.

She leaned over and dabbed at the corner of his eyes and the sides of his face. "It's okay. These are old tears." She spoke softly. She understood. "They need to be shed."

He couldn't form the words. Couldn't talk about a child who had been cursed with the genes of his father, cursed until death at the age of thirty months. Couldn't talk about the woman who loved them both and who had been decimated by that love until she had to flee just to survive.

Mia gathered him into her arms. "Thank you for sharing these tears with me."

He pulled her to him and hugged her for her compassion. She returned the hug and put her quilt over both of them.

If there were ever another woman he could love, it would be Mia Parker.

After a while, she opened his robe and put her hands on his chest, exploring. She kissed his neck, his chest and down his belly.

# CHAPTER TEN

"HOW'D IT GO?"

On Wednesday morning, eight days and counting, minus a little change, since the find in her wall, Mia sat in Monique's small neat kitchen sipping lapsang souchong tea and trying to behave as if all were fine with the world.

"Well. Very well," she responded.

"Details!"

"No." Mia plunked her teacup down on the old wooden table, shined to the limit of its patina.

"All right." Monique scrunched up her forehead and if Mia knew her friend well, she was looking for an end run around *no.*

"No and no," Mia said to ward off any attempt at getting details about the night. And she didn't want to think about this morning—at all.

"Awright, a'right, a'right, just answer me one thing. How many of those condoms I brought to you did you use?"

Maybe a bit of the truth might just shut her friend up.

"All of them."

"All of them?" Monique pounded her fists on the tabletop, slopping tea, and in an almost continuous motion fetched the dishrag to clean it up.

Mia raised her chin and did the slow nod of smug.

"Oh, my God, you, you, what's female for dawg?"

"What was I supposed to do? He has a six-pack." Mia

pointed to her abdomen and moved her hand up and down to illustrate she was not talking about beer.

"I would have thought getting it that many times would make you much less grumpy. Wait, where is he? Why are you here?"

"I got the morning-note thing."

"Ah." Monique refilled their cups before she sat back down in the chair. "How bad was it?"

"Said he left because he needed to get to the university and make sure the students were on top of things."

"The cad. Doing his job. How could he even dare?"

"He could have woke me up to tell me."

Monique grabbed her sides and laughed out loud. "You are kidding me, right? Wake you up from a deep sleep? A parade of elephants could march through your bedroom and you'd just dream on."

Mia slumped and took another gulp of her smoky tea. She knew this was true or at least her parents, her friend and others she no longer considered important had told her.

"Daniel's excuse is a reasonable one."

"Plus we ran out of condoms at 3:00 a.m."

Monique started counting hours on her fingers and Mia was sure she was about to compare the results to the number of condoms.

"Stop it."

"Wow. So you didn't take that as a demonstration that he likes you?"

"I guess I'm bummed because he likes me."

"Oh, yeah." Monique huffed disbelief. "Explain that one."

"Daniel made it very clear there could be nothing long-term between us."

"Because he has a wife? He's really an alien from an invisible planet circling Alpha Centauri? What?"

"He doesn't have a wife, but he might be an alien be-

cause I've never had anyone like him. He made me insatia-
ble." Mia swirled her tea. "I don't know what's the matter,
but he made a point of telling me right after we kissed at
the police station there could be nothing between us, so
there could be no confusion later."

Monique held her counting fingers up again. "Meet on
Monday. Police station kissing on Tuesday. Wow. Sometime after two. Wow. Condoms gone by Wednesday. I
might have to go to the yarn shop and see if they're gos-
siping about you yet."

"Shut up."

"Okay. Soon. So, a fiancée somewhere or he's got a
fatal disease."

"I don't know, Monique, and I didn't think I cared, but
I've never felt like this with anyone before, anyone, ever.
I didn't even know him a day and I wanted to kiss him.
Okay, ten minutes. What does that make me?"

"Picky. Nothing wrong with that. You picked. I mean
you really picked. You connected with this guy, you knew
it and you acted on it. That is wicked good."

"It does feel so...right, so very right."

"Maybe you can find out what his roadblock is and give
it a nudge, or maybe a blast."

"I don't know. I got the feeling whatever it is it's something scary. Maybe you're right. Maybe he has a fiancé in a
long-term coma somewhere. That would make me selfish."

"Yeah, the woman who came home to save a town.
Selfish."

"So, you want to tell me why you had a bunch of condoms?"

"Bought out Portland on that shopping trip yesterday.
Once I started thinking about Lenny as a possibility, I
really put my heart into it. He trusts me to get his laundry
processed according to his standards. That's a big deal for
him. He looked around my house as if—"

"Wait. When was he here?"

"Last night after he got off work. We sat and talked and kissed. Now, I gotta admit, it was nothing like you and Dr. Lovemachine, but we had fun. I had fun."

Mia spotted the clock on Monique's microwave. "Oh, no. I'm so sorry. It's almost eight o'clock. I gotta go. I'm doing something for the chief and I don't want him to think I'm not interested."

Mia tossed her red scarf around her neck and yanked on her coat.

"Call me later if you have time," Monique said.

Mia grabbed her friend in a quick fierce hug and then fled the kitchen.

At the police station, she flipped on the lights in the basement storage room, hung her coat on a chair and pulled out the box she thought might contain the oldest files.

The room was cold and lonely without Daniel.

Deal. She'd deal. She always did.

She tried to get excited about the files as she donned gloves, sat down on the floor and pulled the box close to her. Liam Bailey's logbook was at the front of the box. She stopped for a moment, contemplating what the pirate Bailey might have to say. Would he talk of treasure, of his great love? Funny, a two-hundred-year-dead man could ruin her life.

*Deal.*

The book had unlined pages, and he wrote in an uneven scrawl, faded and difficult to read. Someone had made longhand copies because of the fading ink and filled in their version of what he might have said.

He had logged in as simply Liam Bailey, not captain. He might have wanted to leave that part of his life behind. After she had read for a while she thought, too bad this was a record of law and order and not a bawdy pirate's tale. It seemed law and order wasn't all that exciting. Theft, brawls, treatment of women that made her want to go back there and tell them to grow up.

Though every word held historic interest, conveyed the difficulty of establishing a town in such a remote area, about building the hotel, there wasn't anything enlightening as to what happened to him. There was very little personal information at all, and when the log ended abruptly, it spoke to her of a man interrupted.

Interrupted by being dead or by getting paid by daddy to leave town? she wondered.

The record keeper second in line, whose notes began May 16, 1820, was a Woodrow Harriman who was appointed a commissioner of sorts by the first governor of the State of Maine. Harriman was to oversee the budding towns on Maine's central coast until some formal system of government was established. As she read on, Mia realized Liam Bailey did not quite finish the hotel before he disappeared. According to Harriman's file, Bailey hadn't finished the outside steps or the balcony—which if ever built was now gone. No mention was made of the wall.

The hotel, which Bailey had called the Sea Rose Inn, was not occupied for the first two years due to some kind of ownership dispute. That would explain how a body could reside there during decomposition and no one suspected anything.

The person responsible for the final disposition of the property was a man named Archibald Fletcher. The man seemed to own most of the land around Bailey's Cove that Liam Bailey did not own. He claimed Bailey owed him money and ended up with Liam Bailey's hotel and much of his land.

"Whoa!" She backed up and reread Harriman's next passage. "The home Mr. Liam Bailey built on Sea Crest Hill was also taken over by Mr. Archibald Fletcher, as it was insisted by his daughter that he install her and her new husband, a man named McClure, in the residence."

Mia knew that home, undoubtedly a mansion during the time of Liam Bailey, on the hill overlooking town. The home still sat there, mostly empty because a local man who now lived as a tycoon in Boston owned it.

Chief Montcalm was right. There was information in these records that should not be released without first considering the consequences.

Mr. Harriman didn't speak of what became of Liam Bailey at all, to say if he went west or back to sea. No mention was made of anyone paying Bailey off, although, in Mia's thinking, Mr. Archibald Fletcher would have been a prime candidate to have the wherewithal to buy off a pirate to save his daughter from a disastrous relationship as legend had it.

Mia found herself eager to search out more information about Mr. Fletcher, about his daughter.

She sat on the floor and leaned up against the wall. The dashing pirate Bailey may have used his stash to build the hotel, trying to prove to the father of his ladylove that he was worthy husband material. Then he built a lovely home on a hill overlooking town, a place to raise a family.

And then he walked away. Mia didn't believe it. No matter how many men had walked away from her, she didn't want to believe it.

By lunchtime she had made it through the first ten years of life in Bailey's Cove. She had also made it through the entire morning without leaving to see if Daniel had come back. What if he never came back? Ridiculous, he had felt the same things she had felt last night.

Then why was a tear trickling down the side of her face?

When there was a knock on the door to the records room, Mia swiped at her eyes and put on a big smile. The chief would see right through her anyway, but she could fool Melissa.

She opened the door to her mother's smiling face.

"I've found you at last," said five-foot-six, one-hundred-and-twenty-pounds-exactly Marianne Parker.

"Hi, Mom, you look great." And she did, always. Perfect blond hair, short knit jacket that matched her knit slacks, scooped-necked blouse in a lighter but matching shade.

"I've come to take you out to lunch." She looked Mia up and down and Mia forced a smile because she knew no matter how hard she tried, she felt as if she was letting her mother down in some way. Her hair might be parted on the wrong side, her black suit jacket not perfectly matching her black skirt. There was always something.

"Hang on a minute, Mom, I'll get my coat."

"Can't I come in?" Her mother craned around her to see into the room.

"Sorry, Mom. Chief Montcalm asked me not to let anyone in here."

Mia grabbed her coat and pressed the corners of her eyes to get rid of the moisture. Apparently, her heart had hoped Daniel would be at the door. Silly thing.

She smiled apologetically at her mother. "Sorry, I forgot we were having lunch today."

"Your phone must not work in the basement," her mom said as they climbed the stairs.

"And you found me anyway. Thanks. I would have felt bad if I missed you."

"It was easier to find you when you were always working on that building."

She squeezed her mom in a quick hug.

"I forgot why you're off today?" Mia asked as they crossed the street to Mandrel's Café.

"We surpassed our quota of home sales for last month, and believe me, that hasn't happened in a long time, so they gave us today off. Wednesdays can be slow, so it was a good day."

"How's dad?" Mia asked when they were seated at Mandrel's in her mother's favorite spot.

"Your father is always the same."

Her mother sounded sad when she spoke and that troubled Mia. Mia also knew better than to probe for details. Marianne Parker didn't respond well to personal questions from her daughter. "I feel like you're judging me," her mother would say.

Mia ordered her usual, oatmeal pancakes with maple syrup, and got her mother's usual response. "I don't see why you can't eat normal lunch food."

"Because I like pancakes and the oatmeal is good for me."

Her mother tsk'd as she dug into her chef's salad.

Lunch had to be cut short. Her mother had a meeting of the herb society to run to and Mia had records to read, not to mention, when she'd arrived that morning at the station, word was the police might be finished with the Roost this afternoon. Not that it would mean much for her if she still wasn't allowed to work on the remodeling, but she could always hope. With the crypt demolished, Daniel might be able to release the building to her.

And be gone.

Her steps faltered. By the time she put the key in the lock she wished she was anywhere but there. Reading records by herself might have its moments, but it was not much fun.

She swung open the door and sitting on the floor beside the boxes was Daniel.

He looked up. His eyes were tired and his face more drawn, as if he hadn't slept since she saw him last.

She stopped. What was she supposed to say? She felt her smile desert her as she closed the door behind her.

He leaped to his feet and was standing right in front of her in a blink. He searched her face and then drew her into his arms.

The warmth of relief swept through her followed closely by heat.

"It's good to see you," she said as she put her cheek against his chest. He smelled good, like shower and shaving cream.

She pushed back to look at him.

"You shaved." She reached her hand up and stroked the softness of his cheek.

"Disappointed?" He smiled at her.

She shook her head, her eyes glued to his face. He was good-looking before, but now... She swallowed. "Um—no."

"I needed to be at the university this morning to go over the processing techniques again with the students. They're good, but need a lot of guidance."

She plucked at the sleeve of his pale blue oxford shirt and then looked down at unholey jeans and professor-ish shoes, definitely a departure from worn leather boots. "So, Mr. Indiana Jones, do new students fall in love with you every term?"

"All the time, but I make it a point not to fall back."

"I missed you this morning."

"I'm sorry about the note. I tried to wake you, but you were in too deep. Maybe we worked too hard." With that he leaned in and kissed her hard on the mouth and just as quickly broke away. From arm's length he said, "If I start that, I won't get any work done."

She grinned and felt happiness wash down her body and settle as warmth in her heart. "Sometimes I think work is overrated."

He slid his hand into hers. "Come and do some over-rated with me."

DANIEL MADE HIMSELF let go of Mia's hand. What he wanted to do was take that hand and put it against his heart to tell her how much he had hated leaving her so early this morning, how much he loved to touch her, have her touch him.

What he needed to do now was to keep his hands off her, his hands, his lips and everything else. She did not need his problems in her life.

"I saw you finished with the first box." *And I see your heart in your eyes right now.* He knew what he saw there because he felt the same longing. Their connection was strong and undeniable, but he had to keep telling himself that it could not matter.

"Liam Bailey's account of maintaining law and order in the early 1800s is a combination of fascinating and mind-numbing."

"I don't suppose he built a tomb and walled a man up in it."

She sputtered out a laugh. "I'll kill him if he did. He has messed with me enough."

"Remind me not to cross you."

"Oh, please, you have crossed me too many times to count."

He quit paging through the file in his hand.

"Okay, so some of the times you crossed me, I liked it."

She grinned at him and he wanted to make love to her right there under Chief Montcalm's nose. Instead, he studied the file.

She told him eagerly about Bailey and Fletcher and Fletcher's daughter, about the Sea Rose Inn and the mansion on Sea Crest Hill, and about there being no hint about what happened to Bailey.

Then she continued with reading the nineteenth century and he started in the middle of the twentieth. They read to the shuffling of paper, the sound of the clicking clock and the vibration humming between them. When he came across a file from 1956 he read until he knew he had to share the information.

He held out the file toward her. "There is something in this one I think you might want to see."

"Read it to me." She gazed steadily at him as she made the request.

"It's from the 1950s. The name on the record is Chief of Police Buddy Knox. *'The town is restless. An outsider has come to claim the treasure of Liam Bailey. She says it is buried in a building of much importance to the town.'* The next day he says: *'Henrietta Loch has destroyed us.'*"

Her eyes were wide with alarm. "Loch. L-O-C-H?"

He nodded.

"Do you suppose that Loch is the same Loch family as Heather? Do you suppose that's why Heather came here and turned the church into a museum in the first place? I mean, she has always claimed to be a descendent of the pirate. She wouldn't have broken into the Roost, I mean, I've never had any reason to suspect her of anything so nefarious as to break in and destroy someone's property."

He wondered if she knew how beautiful she was with excitement gleaming in her eyes.

A crisp knock got their attention and she jumped to her feet.

"Hello, Chief Montcalm," she said as she opened the door. "You have arrived just when we had something to show you."

"I have some information for you, too. The preliminary investigation of the break in and damage to your property has been completed, Ms. Parker. We have some persons of interest, but no arrest warrants."

"Thank you, Chief. I appreciate everything your department has already done."

"We'll continue to keep an eye on the place and if we find out anything else, we'll let you know."

"We have a couple of things that might interest you, Chief. The house on Sea Crest hill was originally built by Liam Bailey."

"That one should stay under wraps for now." This was, of course, an order from the chief, not a request.

Daniel handed over the report from Chief Knox. "The page of interest is on top."

The chief scanned the document and handed it back. "If either of you has any questions, please feel free to call me. I expect you'll wrap up by four-thirty," he said as he nodded at the clock, which said four-fifteen. "Dr. MacCarey, if you'd come up to my office, I need to speak with you in private."

The chief marched away, closing the door softly, leaving Mia and him alone in the room. They stood facing each other, no boxes separating them.

He wanted to pull her into his arms again and kiss her, give her everything a man should give a woman, love, respect, himself. All he had to give Mia were promises he couldn't keep. He broke away from her questioning gaze and moved toward the door. "I'd best go see what the chief wants."

As he climbed from the basement to the first floor, the daylight got brighter and his thoughts darker.

Chief Montcalm motioned him into the office when he arrived. "I don't have anything more to tell you, but I need to ask. Do you want Ms. Parker kept away from the site?"

"Do you know something I don't about Mia?"

"I doubt it."

"Then she can have free access."

The chief gave a half nod.

"Have a good day, Dr. MacCarey."

Daniel's phone rang.

"Please, take the call here. I have business elsewhere in the building." With that the chief left.

Daniel looked at the screen. It was his department chair, Dr. Donovan.

"Dr. MacCarey, congratulations are in order for you."

"Thank you. What did I do?"

"That find of yours in that little town is going to get you a chance to take a big leap forward."

"I'm listening." This already sounded like good news that was very bad news for the little town and one of its entrepreneurs.

"We have a donor family that is just itching to get behind what you are doing. All you have to do is prove that's Liam Bailey you have in your lab and this family is willing to fund a pirate dog and pony show and launch your career with it."

*A pirate dog and pony show...* And ruin the charm and uniqueness of the town? As well as destroy Mia's chances with Pirate's Roost? "Sir, this sounds very interesting. Great for the university, but...do we know these people?"

"What we know, Dr. MacCarey, is that they are very rich, a husband and wife each with family money to give away, and you are correct if you think this is a boon. Do this and you will have brought in a huge donation to the university, to our department more specifically, and that kind of thing counts more and more these days. And I haven't even gotten to the best part for you."

He heard an ax fall somewhere in the back of his mind.

"The best part," his boss continued, "they will fund your work for two years with the option for three more if they see what they like. And if this comes off, I have to tell you your name goes to the top of the list for the next big project." The older man coughed his decades-of-cigar-smoking cough. "I know I don't have to remind you how long it has been since you were in that position. I wanted to tell you myself so you would understand how important this is to the department and the university and to you."

"What if it's not Bailey?"

His boss ignored the question and went on and on about how beneficial this would be for the university and how precarious the money for good projects was these days. Daniel replied, "Yes, sir," several times until he just let his boss continue uninterrupted.

"So come through for us, Dr. MacCarey. We're counting on you."

The phone in his hand went silent and Daniel knew he was alone again. His boss hadn't waited for a final "yes, sir."

The person who could change his fate with the stroke of a pen had just laid out his future in a crystal clear either/or. Notoriety or anonymity. Destroy or be destroyed.

He pushed up from the chair at the chief's desk.

If it were just between Mia and him, the choice would be easy. Mia's livelihood depended on getting the Pirate's Roost launched.

If he turned his back on this pirate show, he'd be turning his back on the dollars to keep people working on projects that really mattered to the study of humans on earth. The money for the serious work sometimes came from donors who wanted to be associated with something splashy, like pirates. Where humans really came from, and how we got where we are, often took a backseat unless a good spin could be added. The Blackbeard type of pirates had been good for spin for a hundred years.

The most important factors weighed on his mind and to the man's credit, his department head had not once mentioned the huge debt Daniel owed the university. For three years the university supported him, kept him on, gave him anything in their power to give while his life and his family fell apart. That was not a debt Daniel took lightly, and his boss had just called in a whole fistful of those markers at Mia's expense.

He left the chief's office, said good-night to the evening dispatcher and stepped outside. At five forty-five, Mia would be long gone. He wondered where she went, who she was with, and wished it was him.

The fresh, salty air took him by surprise. He'd forgotten how good it felt to breathe the sea air. He looked around as the lights of the town blinked on one by one.

He hated himself for allowing things to go too far with Mia. She'd hate him for it soon enough and rightly so.

In two hours he was staring out the window of his condo wondering if his life would ever be anything but rotten.

# CHAPTER ELEVEN

MIA SAT IN her darkening living room. Monique would be shocked at how sparkly and orderly her place looked. She had worked fiercely to clean every trace of Daniel Mac-Carey from her house.

Conversation fragments kept coming to her mind from the call he had made to her from his car, like *I am so sorry* and *for the best* and *if there is anything I can do*.

Now that she could think clearly, yes, there was something he could do. He could return her building to her. He could love her.

But what she had wished they could have had been a fantasy and the less she thought about him, the better.

Her phone rang. Monique. The perfect distraction.

"Hey, Monique, how's it going?"

"He's packing." Her friend could hardly speak for the tears in her voice. "He's…he's…"

"Who is packing, sweetie? Lenny?"

"*Grand-père.* I stopped over there after work and he's going to Florida." Monique only called grandfather by the French term when she was profoundly sad, like when her mother died and left the two of them alone. "It's the beginning of the end."

"Monique, is he going for a visit?"

"He's visiting the Kellys. Says he wants to see how the other half lives."

"I'm coming over."

"It's all right. Lenny's coming over for his dinner break."

Mia could hear her friend trying to compose herself.

"Are you sure you don't want me to come over?"

"I don't want to scare Lenny. We're a pretty intimidating pair. I think he took so long to ask me out because he knew he'd be dating a woman and her fierce protector friend."

"You're afraid I'll beat him up if I come over."

"Something like that. If he's not breaking up with me, he's in for a big test. He gets to see me all weepy-eyed and scared."

"Well, for sure if that scary sight doesn't send him running in the opposite direction, he's in for the long haul."

Monique bubbled a laugh. "I'm so glad I called you."

"Did your granddad say when he's leaving?"

"No. He needs to finish helping on Jim O'Connell's boat, so he doesn't have a definite date."

"I'm so sorry, Monique. Are you sure I can't do anything for you?"

"You already have."

"Call me back if you change your mind and want me to come over. And about your granddad, maybe he's scared, too. To paraphrase a good friend of mine, I cannot see Edwin Beaudin sitting under a palm tree with an umbrella drink in his hand."

"Oh, Mia, I hope you're right."

"Now go blow your nose and put a cold washcloth on your pretty face."

As soon as she hung up, Mia pushed up from the couch and headed for the door. She couldn't fix her own heart. She couldn't help with Lenny, but she knew where Edwin Beaudin hung out this time of day with his cronies. Maybe she could go swat some sense into him, or at least feel things out.

In ten minutes, parked in front of Braven's Tavern, Mia

leaned against her SUV, looking into the darkness across the street. Pirate's Roost would one day attract tourists, provide a few modest jobs and be her anchor. She hoped.

She shook her head.

Well, she couldn't fix the Roost right now. She strode across the quiet street with purpose and opened the old door to Braven's, one of those heavy, solid wood doors that held the mystery close until you pushed on the worn brass handles and let yourself inside. The tavern was almost as old as Liam Bailey's building. Another town treasure serving beer for almost two hundred years.

Inside, there were seven fishermen at the U-shaped bar, three at the bottom of the U and two on each leg. Each with an empty seat or two between himself and the men on either side. "In case a good-looking woman comes along. I don't want to be sittin' next to an old bag of wind when I can be sittin' next to her," Edwin Beaudin had explained to a twelve-year-old Mia, only he and most old-time Mainers pronounced "her" as a version of "h-ah." He had gotten a swat from his daughter for such an explanation, but that didn't make it any less the truth.

The arrangement worked out well tonight. She took the seat on the bottom of the U between Edwin Beaudin and Whister Carmody, ex-brother-in-law of the widowed cat lady who pestered Monique with her fake Persian rug and cat poop.

Both men turned to see who had come to invade the space between them. As one they grinned at her. Whister quickly turned back to his beer, red-faced. Edwin grabbed her in a big hug that made her wonder if her ribs would survive.

"What brings you down here, a beauty among all these hairy beasts?"

"I came to see you, Edwin Beaudin."

Edwin took a big gulp of his beer. "Well, I'd like to be all kinds of flattered, but what'd I do?"

"What can I get for you?" the bartender asked, clearly happy to be serving someone that didn't have bushy whiskers and rumpled clothing.

"Whatever white wine you have open, Michael."

"My kind of lady. Not makin' any trouble."

She didn't take offence at that. Michael Erickson had been giving her a hard time since they were in the second grade.

"How's Francine?" she asked.

"The sweetest woman on the face of the earth," he said and went to get her wine.

Mia sipped her wine and listened as the fishermen talked about what they had brought in that day or hadn't. Edwin told her his granddaughter could be expecting another lobster soon. Jim O'Donnell was paying him in the catch of the day.

"I could sell 'em, but I get the best kick outta seein' that grand-daught-ah o' mine smile when I give 'em to her."

"I hear you're going down to Florida," Mia said and carefully watched the look on Edwin's face.

He twitched a little and rocked on his stool. "I gotta check out my options, eh. Wint-ahs are hard on a' old guy like me."

The conflicted look on has face told Mia he wasn't set on anything. That should be encouraging to Monique.

She leaned forward and back to see all seven of the men at the U-shaped bar. "Have any of you ever left Maine?"

"Ah-yuh." Charlie Finn around the corner from Edwin wrinkled up his face in distaste. "My wife made me go to Chicago for our honeymoon—in January. Colder than a— Oh, well, no palm trees growin' there, I can tell you."

The other guys laughed.

"I had to go to some tiny lake ne-ah Bemidji, Minnesota, with mine." Barrel-chested Harley Davies sat near the end of one of the legs of the U, the closed end that abutted the wall, and he spoke without moving his darkly whiskered face from its position of hanging over his beer. "I still don't know exactly whe-ah that town is. Stayed with a bunch of her cousins at a lake cabin. Good thing I didn't mind sand in my bed sheets. Bless h-ah, she loved me for goin' and that was enough for me."

Heads nodded and beer got sipped.

"Almost left once." Short, round, white-whisker-faced Bill Schroeder said, piping up from two stools past Whister. "One of my daught-ahs thought we should all go to New Aw-leans for her weddin'. Convinced her we could put on a much prettier show if we didn't have to pay for all those hotel rooms. Gas wasn't nothin' then."

"Wasn't that something? Imagine how good life would be if we paid a quarter a gallon again."

That raised a row of cheers.

"What about you?" Harley leaned forward from his far-flung stool and asked her.

"Ah-yuh, I left Maine for almost six years. In Boston, the university, a job, you know." She couldn't help but think she'd be down there still if she hadn't been downsized out of two jobs and hadn't failed at romance.

"How'd that go?" he asked.

"I'm back, aren't I?"

That got a round of chuckles and more sipping.

Mia drank more of her wine because she was getting woefully behind. "Fellas, I had a lot of time to think about what's important about where I live and I gotta say, it's Maine things, the families raising children with good stout values, the young people who stay here because it's home, and it's you guys and all the older generation."

There was almost an embarrassed silence. She knew

these guys loved compliments as much as anyone, but they had the hardest time taking them.

"Older generation?" This was the bartender. "What about us youngun's?"

"And who's you callin' old?" Whister Carmody did have a voice.

"Sorry about the old crack," she said as she put a hand on the bar near him. "You have all lived here long enough to be the polished gems of the town."

"Ah-yuh, that's us. Gems," said Stan from the stool around the corner to the right.

"Hey, Edwin, you an opal or a topaz?" Harley called.

"He's an opal. He's soft in the head," white-whiskered Bill piped in. "Me, I'm a nice shiny piece of quartz."

"Naw, you're a big old chunk of watermelon tourma-line," said Charlie around the left corner.

"If I'm a watermelon, you must be—"

"All right. All right." Mia stood on the rung of her bar stool and raised both hands.

"Careful, Miss," Michael said as he leaned over the bar in front of her. "If you incite a riot here, I'm gonna have to charge you for a round just to quiet 'em down."

They all cheered.

She sat back down. "You're gonna get me into trouble here, Michael."

"So, how's that coming over they-ah?" Edwin tossed a thumb over his shoulder toward Pirate's Roost as he spoke, and Mia felt a pang that she was in no position to hire him and may never be.

"Well, we are trying to figure out who that was in the wall." Mia stretched and looked exaggeratedly around at them all. "I don't suppose any of you were around when that guy got himself walled up."

"Bill was," Whister said without missing a beat, and

Mia knew he was kidding. Apparently when you got him into the conversation it got easier for him.

"Watch out, Whiss, or I'll collect on that bet I won off you in 1898," Bill shot back.

Laughter ensued and the guys ordered another round. When the bartender brought her wine he said, "You should come more often. A good-looking woman is very good for business."

"So you people are pretty hush-hush over there." A new voice was heard from. Earl Smith, the only man who could be considered skinny in this group, spoke from the opposite end of the U from Harley. "Tell us wha's going on 'cause if we have to wait for our wives to find out from those two at the yarn shop, we get way behind. We did hear about that man who keeps coming around from the university."

"Yes, that's Dr. Daniel MacCarey. He's a forensic anthropologist."

"Like that TV show where they study bones," Whiss said.

"He's the one who's going to tell us exactly how old the bones are."

"Is he a Maine boy?" Bill asked.

"I didn't ask him."

"He's not bad-looking. You might want to snap him up if he is," Edwin said from her elbow.

"I guess I'll have to check and see if he's a Maine boy. But hey, you guys, I'm looking for information about what would make life around here better for people."

"We were kind of looking forward to that place of yours getting finished, eh," Harley said as he looked up from his beer.

"Wouldn't have to drive so far from town to take our wives to a nice dinner," Stan added with enthusiasm that was seconded by some of the others.

That surprised Mia. She had no idea these men even thought of such things.

"Or maybe a date, eh, Whiss?" Bill teased the other man.

Mia expected Whister to dive into his beer mug, but he grinned. She wondered who the lucky lady was, but she didn't want to push his burst of extroversion past its limits by asking.

"A hand of cards in a nice warm place in the wintertime, maybe after a warm breakfast and a good cup of coffee." Harley looked as if he were daydreaming as he spoke. "That might be good."

She thought of the big windows she would like to have put in the front of the restaurant and the smaller ones in the back. They'd let in a lot of light. She'd planned on supplementing central heat with a large stone fireplace. It should be cozy.

She could even see these guys at a couple tables in the corner in the back laughing, harassing the waitstaff for more coffee. But what if this was the kind of thing that kept them here. Kept the heritage in Maine.

If she ever got it built.

"So what do you think?" Whiss leaned toward her. "Are you gonna make that place over there work for us?"

She hadn't thought about breakfast, or card games.

"So wha' if it's that pirate you've got over there in that wall?" Skinny Earl spoke before she could answer. He had moved down to sit at the corner of the bar next to Charlie Finn.

She laughed. "Then I named the Pirate's Roost well." If she could deflect him, that might be very helpful for the peace in the town.

She turned away. "You haven't said much, Mr. Beaudin, what would you like to see the Roost offer?"

"I don't much care," Monique's granddad said and it was almost a mumble.

"Hey, Stan, maybe you could'a had the baptism celebration there for that surprise grandchild of yours," Earl said louder than he needed to be heard by everyone in the bar.

"Stan, I heard he's the cutest grandbaby ever born," Mia said because she knew Earl had just shot a dig at Stan.

"You must have been talking to my wife," Stan said, maintaining his jovial tone. "Strappin' boy if I ever heard one."

"Gave his opinion several times in church that day. Make any granddad proud," Edwin added.

"So can we come across the street and have a look?" Earl seemed to be feeling his beer and she wasn't sure that was a good thing.

Mia wanted to talk to Edwin more, but decided the best way to get away from Earl's questions was to remove herself. She swallowed her last sip of wine and slid off her bar stool.

"I had a great time, fellas. Do you mind if I come back, say Saturday?"

"Anytime, Ms. Park-ah," and several variations thereof came from the patrons at the bar.

"See ya, Mia," the bartender added as she heaved open the heavy wooden door.

She hurried out into the cool air. A good night for a walk. She patted her neon green car on the hood and hiked on up the street toward home. One of the great things about a small town. There were a lot of places one can walk to and from.

The closer she got to home, the more the night cleared her head.

Edwin Beaudin seemed to have been prepared for her subtle inquiries, or maybe she hadn't been as clever as she had wanted to be. She had wanted to be able to report to Monique about which way the wind was blowing with her granddad.

She thought of the darkened windows in the Pirate's Roost and wondered if she would ever make them bright with life, if folks would ever play a hand of cards or celebrate a baptism there. If they could, would people like Edwin stay?

She smiled when she thought of Stan's sweet cherub grandbaby. He was the cutest thing ever. Even Father Murray didn't judge a child for being conceived before marriage.

Her thoughts traveled to another time. Two hundred years ago Archibald Fletcher's daughter might have married under similar circumstances. If the woman had been in love with Liam Bailey and then married so quickly after Bailey disappeared, maybe there had been a baby involved.

If there had been a baby and if that baby was born, say, six months after the wedding, Liam Bailey could indeed have an heir. Holy cow. Tomorrow she'd have to check the records at the church.

She hurried the rest of the way up the hill to her house. When she got there she sat on the porch swing and looked out over the town and the people she loved. Dappled moonlight shined through the pine boughs and stars twinkled overhead.

Eventually the cold slipped inside her coat and she went indoors for a long warm shower. That and the wine should make her sleepy.

When she finally lay in her bed, she couldn't keep her eyes closed.

Could she really keep people here if she got Pirate's Roost open? Could the Roost give the residents of Bailey's Cove a place to hang out, a place to gather?

Did Liam Bailey have a child?

Could she find out in the church records? Luckily, the

priest had kept them in the rectory in the 1950s because the church was so small. That kept them safe from the fire that nearly destroyed the old church. She needed the wedding date…birth date…

Sleep. She needed sleep.

An hour went by and all she could do was think and plan. Try as she might, she could not reckon how she could talk Markham Construction into opening up a new spot for her or if the bank would restructure for her so she could lower her payments.

*Sleep!*

*No. Use.*

A good run would help her sort out her jumbled thoughts. She could pick up her car so tomorrow when she was too tired to drag her pitiful self around town, she'd have wheels.

She donned her running gear and jogged down Blueberry Avenue's hill in the twin beams of her headlamp cap. There were no streetlights on the side streets, but she'd soon be down on the main street and there would be less chance of twisting her ankle or tripping over a night creature. She and a raccoon had almost collided on one such restless night. She wouldn't soon forget the challenge in those piercing eyes.

As she turned on Church Street, the crisp night air in her face made for a wonderful run. To the old church and back home was her six-mile route. Tonight it would be easy.

The old brown dog that roamed the streets of Bailey's Cove and that everyone fed met up with her at the corner and loped without effort at her side. He had gotten left behind by someone passing through town, maybe on purpose. He never seemed to pine for whoever left him, he just adapted. Maybe he wasn't left, maybe he chose to stay.

"Hey, Brownie. You can't sleep, either?"

The dog trotted on silently, his tongue hanging out of the side of his mouth.

"Well, I'm glad for the company."

She passed the post office. Bailey's Cove was one of the lucky towns. They still had their own tidy little redbrick post office. After the post office came the hardware store and the small building with paper covering the windows that used to have a deli on the ground floor. She wondered if the people who had owned the deli had left town yet. Rumor was they were going to find jobs that didn't suck the life out of them.

She wished them well.

As she and Brownie trotted closer to her car, she noticed there was light coming from the windows of Pirate's Roost, bright light. It was then she realized the car parked on the street across from hers belonged to Daniel.

Her heart thudded hard as she stopped close to the dirty windowpane and Brownie ran on. "See you later, boy."

Daniel stepped into the half-demolished doorway of the back room holding two of the pieces of granite in his gray-gloved hands. He didn't look up at her and was trying to see if the pieces fit together. He was reassembling the crypt.

The backlight put him in silhouette, chiseling his features and his fine body into art.

Mia remained perfectly still, so as not to attract his attention, watching as he put one of the pieces on a tarp he had spread out and picked up another. She wondered if he wanted any help.

Suddenly and with only subconscious permission, her hand leaped out and rapped hard on the window.

Silly hand. She stuck it in the pocket of her warm-up suit as the other waved at Daniel, who was squinting to see what mad person was outside disturbing his work at two in the morning.

She let herself in and Daniel met her halfway across the front section, granite pieces in his hands.

"Good morning?" She smiled at him.

"And you're up in the middle of the night because?"

"Couldn't sleep. I jogged over to get my car and saw the lights on here." *I wanted to see you, to kiss you and have you hold me in your arms and see where our feelings take us.* "And you?"

"Working the 3-D puzzle."

"Because you always work at two in the morning?"

He put the pieces of granite into one hand and reached the other out to her. When he lightly touched her cheek with the back of one gloved finger, it felt like warm silk touching her and she closed her eyes for longer than a blink.

She had the feeling his hands gave his deepest desires away, too. He wanted her as much as she wanted him. That did not help quench the desire inside her.

"Couldn't find a way to get to sleep, either. Do you want to help me?" He gestured toward the other room and she followed him in.

"An insomniac's dream." She pulled a pair of gloves from the box on the corner tarp. He had set up two lamps and spread out the tarp for serious work.

She hunkered down near where he had separated out the most promising shards.

"Have you found anything?"

He picked up several pieces and crouched beside her. "I started collecting pieces with discoloration on them, but they're harder to sort out because I think there is discoloration from more than one cause. See the different shades of brown."

"Where do I start?" Her breath trembled in and out as she tried to function, to think when his body heat seeped into her, his warm scent filled her. *Where do I start?* To find the strength to resist her feelings for an unavailable man.

"Chances are, when the stones were knocked loose, they flew as a group. So if you pick up stones from the same general area, that might help find matches."

His eyes moved over her, caressing her, stoking the already blazing fire. *Where do I start?* To begin to dig him out of her heart, because that is where he was firmly lodged.

"Are you trying to put together the whole thing or just the area with markings?"

"I think the markings will tell us all we need to know for now."

They sat, hunkered down or wandered, picking up pieces of the tomb and patiently fitting them together.

"Mia, is there a possibility you could move Pirate's Roost to a different location?" he asked after they had worked in silence for a while.

"It seems like such a simple solution, but I passed the point of no return on this place a long time ago."

DANIEL SAT ON the plastic tarp and listened to what Mia had to say. If he was going to destroy her plans, he needed to know how much damage he was doing and if he could help.

"I put a lot of effort into planning Pirate's Roost. I made and revised a business plan about ten times. I chose the site by looking at traffic flow in the area, the visual appeal and the view, of course." He remembered that view of the harbor, of the sea birds soaring and the bustle. Great view for a restaurant. "I have given everything I have to Pirate's Roost, and have too few resources left to move anywhere else."

She did not seem embarrassed by what she was saying, but sadness was something he knew well, and she radiated hopeless loss at this moment.

"You did everything right."

"Everything except check the walls for skeletons."

He studied her face and it wasn't hard to see there was more. "Tell me the rest of it."

She looked down at the two pieces of granite in her hands and after another moment, nodded.

"I got a building big enough to do the job. Made sure there was ample parking. Lined up money from the historical society, local citizens, two banks via the small business association, even my granddad has chipped in a little of his savings."

She dipped her chin.

"What were you hoping for? Not the business, but what did you really want to do with this place?"

She shook her head and turned away.

He pushed up from the floor and pulled her into his arms. She came willingly. He knew she would, and how much of a cad did that make him?

He kissed her silky hair. "Tell me."

"I want them to stay. I want the families who breathe life into Bailey's Cove to stay. I want the young people with their imagination and drive. I want the retirees, the people who are the living history of the town to stay and to hand their wisdom and legends down to the next generation."

He held her against his chest and let her talk.

"I didn't even know how much until I sat down and started listening to them. I knew I wanted to be here because Bailey's Cove is a paradise of the normal and… and…I don't know. I love life here."

She took a slow breath and continued. "If the folks of Bailey's Cove don't reinvent this town, there are only two choices. The town continues to fade away or the outside world moves in and has it their way."

She leaned back and looked up at him.

He picked up the tail of the long red scarf she always

seemed to be wearing. Lady in Red, he thought and the song begin to play inside his head. When he started to sway, she looked up at him.

A smile curved her lips and lit her face, made her more beautiful than he had ever seen her.

"What are we dancing to?"

He brushed her nose with the tail of her scarf and told her.

She put her arms around his neck and her cheek against his and they danced to the creaking of the old building. Daniel had never heard more beautiful music.

"Thank you." Her whisper brushed his ear and he wondered if he could let himself love her, and if he did, could he keep her from loving him?

And he wondered how many ways he could let himself break her heart before he had to walk away from her and stay away.

"I think the music stopped," he said as he stepped back.

"Does that mean *get to work, slacker?*"

"I don't think I'd have used the term slacker, but it fits."

After a few minutes of studying the pieces with markings she looked thoughtfully over at him. "What do you think we'll find if we get all the pieces together?"

"That's one of the things I like best about this science. Sometimes we aren't looking for a specific answer. Sometimes we're just searching for whatever might be there. One thing's for sure, whoever wielded that hammer after the bones were removed did more damage than necessary to break the tomb apart."

"Stupid hammer has caused me all sorts of trouble. Maybe the person using it was mad because there was no treasure here."

"Tomb robbers have all sorts of motives. Sometimes it's just to destroy things."

She held up a hand, came closer and whispered, "Did you hear that?"

He listened. "Sounds like old building noises."

"I know this old building. There's no wind and it's not cold enough to make her wood creak like that. It sounds like someone is walking around upstairs."

He leaned over and whispered in her ear. "We're not alone."

She giggled and huddled closer. "Oh, Danny, you've got to save me."

Sudden pain shot through him. He stepped quickly away and clenched his fists.

It was all happening again. Sammy's face as they put the tiny boy into another scary, noisy piece of high-tech medical equipment. Mandy pleading, "Danny, you've got to help me find some way to save him. There must be something we can do. He's only a baby, Danny."

Then Mandy trying her best not to lay blame exactly where it belonged.

On him.

# CHAPTER TWELVE

MIA WATCHED DANIEL stiffen. His face ashen as if he were in the middle of some horrible nightmare.

"Daniel, are you all right?"

She put her arms around his stiff body and hugged him. Slowly, he dropped his chin until it rested lightly on top of her head.

They stood like this until he relaxed in her arms, and then she leaned back to look into his face. "You don't get hugged much, do you?"

His expression remained grim. "Not many huggers in my life."

"What about your family?"

By the look on his face, that was one huge step backward. Something terrible had happened to his family, something so dark he couldn't bring himself to talk about it.

"Come on." She took his hand and led him toward the door. "You need some sleep."

"I need to check upstairs."

"Upstairs it is."

They were careful to avoid several sets of large sneaker prints on the stairs and in the hallway leading to a back room. Funny, she couldn't feel anything but annoyance tonight about the sneaker prints. Tomorrow would be soon enough to worry, if then.

The window gaped open and outside a ladder leaned

up against the building. Whoever had been inside left in a hurry.

They closed and locked the window, put the ladder inside and locked up the building. The police could look at things tomorrow, or today after the sun came up.

They stood outside the building in the chilly air. Mia knew they needed sleep, desperately.

"Come to my house."

"That's not a good idea."

"If you're worried about gossip, rest assured they've been talking about the two of us since about three minutes after you first arrived at Pirate's Roost."

"I can't let you…"

She put her hand on his cheek and made him look at her. "It's a small town. We've got a movie theater that gets movies after they've been at the budget theaters in Bangor and Portland."

When he didn't look convinced, she said, "We've no symphony, not even mini-golf. Our shopping mall has eight little stores and our yarn and craft store specializes in gossip. What's a person to do?"

Brownie came over to see what was up. Sniffed each of them and then moved on.

"Brownie thinks it's okay."

He gave a quick nod.

A few minutes later, she let them in her front door and turned on the lamp in the small foyer. The dim light spread into her living room of neutral colors with splashes of red, filled with the odds and ends of life.

He looked around and smiled. "Thanks, Mia. I like your house. It's welcoming, like you."

"You're welcome here anytime, Daniel."

She hung her red scarf and coat on a hook behind the door and took his vest and hung it beside them. "I'm going to brew some tea. Make yourself at home."

She flipped on the light above the sink and started the teakettle heating.

"What kind of—" She turned and stopped quickly. "Oh, sorry. I didn't mean to yell in your face. I didn't hear you come in."

"I didn't want you to wait on me."

"Then the cups are there—" she pointed to a cupboard beside her sink "—and the tray's over there. How about Rishi's Serene Dream? It's got, let's see, valerian root, lemon verbena, lemon balm, chamomile, lavender and spearmint."

"I have no idea what most of those ingredients are."

"Serene Dream it is." She scooped loose tea into her teapot. "Oh, you can light the fire if you would, please."

He nodded and backed away.

Left alone in her kitchen, the tight knot that was supposed to be her heart relaxed a little. This was totally new ground here and she had no idea what she was doing. She and Daniel had spent so much time together in the past three days it felt like a month, at least her poor struggling heart thought so.

She rubbed her chest. Real, unselfish feelings for a member of the opposite sex were things you didn't know until you knew. She now realized there had never been a love of her life. She already felt more for Daniel MacCarey than she felt for any man in her past, men she thought she'd marry and spend the rest of her life with.

Ironic. She wasn't going to spend the rest of her life with this one, either.

When the teakettle started to steam, she poured the hot water into the teapot and carried the tray into the living room. Daniel stood in front of the crackling fire, the light doing that gorgeous stuff to his hair again.

"It'll steep for five minutes and then we can drink it," she said as she put the tray on the table.

"I'm sorry, I guess I should have asked you if you wanted to be left alone to get some sleep. I'm still so awake and there isn't a crack in my ceiling I haven't mapped tonight."

"Sleep's not my forte these days." He retrieved both of the pillows and put them on the floor in front of the fire.

"I'm trying not to feel awkward about this," she said as she brought the quilts over near the fire and sat down. "New territory for me."

She stretched out with her toes toward the fire and stared into the flickering flames.

"As long as you don't get hurt." He sat on the floor close to her.

"By this, whatever it is."

"Yes."

After a few minutes, the microwave timer in the kitchen chimed and Daniel placed the tray with the teapot and cups beside them. When she reached for the pot he said, "I'll get it."

He poured the steaming Serene Dream into their cups.

"Smells nice." She picked up her cup and leaned her face over the column of rising moisture.

"Don't fall in."

His friendly teasing reminded her of the things, the little bonuses she would get if she had this man for her own.

This was dangerous thinking.

Still she didn't care.

She intended to take pleasure in every enjoyable thing Daniel MacCarey offered.

"A mini facial," she said as she lifted her face from the steam. "I take one every time I have bedtime tea."

"They must work."

"Oh, a compliment. I'll take that."

"Don't you have a string of guys out there waiting to spend time with you?"

She snorted and almost spilled her tea. "There was somebody, but he wisely ran away."

"I'm sorry."

"I'm not. Been there done that. Right now, I'm in the 'I'm perfectly fine with me' phase. I'm actually quite happy to have run the gauntlet without marrying any of the toads I kissed."

This time when she leaned forward over her tea, he tucked the strand of hair behind her ear.

"They were lucky toads. Well…you know what I mean."

They talked about his work and the university. They talked about Rory and her previous boyfriend and this was the first time she had ever been truly able to laugh about those relationships.

She quite enjoyed talking with Daniel. She couldn't ever remember having a man for a friend before. That may be where her problems were with the others. She couldn't imagine sitting around chatting with Rory.

"So what do you think of our little town? Wait. Sorry." She held up a hand. "If you'd like me to shut up and just let you rest, I'm good with that."

A soft smile spread across his face. "It's fine, as long as you don't mind my less-than-sparkling conversation."

"You sparkle just fine."

"What do I think about your little town? An old coastal fishing village and the prospect of finding an early Maine settler would have been great news to share with my aunt Margaret."

"You mentioned her before. She must have been important to you."

"She was a wonderful person. She was ninety-two when she died."

"I'm so sorry she's gone."

"So am I. You would have liked her. She'd have liked you."

Something about his professor appearance made him look more uptight.

"Thank you." She reached over and ruffled his hair. "I like it better that way."

He scowled but she knew he didn't mean it.

"Margaret MacCarey knew a lot about the world," he said.

"The world before the internet. Before space travel."

"Born about the same time as the cake mix. She had a 1956 black Cadillac convertible when she died. Bought it new. It's still in her garage."

"So you have something to remember her by."

He seemed to study the fire while Mia poured more tea for both of them.

"She left me something else." He spoke very quietly as if thinking about each word.

She put her teacup down and focused on him.

"She left me a ring."

He reached into his pocket and pulled out a small, cloth bag. If the flames told it true, a light lavender pouch with frayed ribbons, and he handed it to her. "I haven't taken it out since the night she died."

Mia held up the bag. The fabric was thin with some of the velvet worn away.

She looked up at him and when he nodded, she tugged at the ribbons to loosen them and opened the delicate purse.

Into her palm she poured a heavy gold ring with a large pale blue stone encircled by what were probably diamonds.

"It looks old—even I can tell that, and very beautiful."

"I never saw her wear it. The hospice nurse gave it to me after Aunt Margaret died, and it came with this." He pulled an envelope from his shirt pocket and handed it to her.

Mia took the envelope, scooted closer to the light and read the note she found inside.

When she was finished, she looked up. "She was a lovely woman, wasn't she?"

"She was the best. The nurse also gave me a last message, said it would be up to me whether or not I shared or kept the secret."

A family secret. Mia wasn't going there, definitely not going there, so she tucked the note back inside the envelope and held the ring up to the firelight.

"Is this your family's coat of arms on the inside?"

Daniel sat forward. He cupped one hand under hers and gently took the ring. She couldn't help it. When he touched her he stoked the fire.

Fires she could control...

She hoped.

She poured more tea into her cup.

He examined the ring for a long time. Then he got up and turned on the lamp on the end table and looked at it more closely.

"There's a magnifying glass in that drawer under that lamp."

She wanted to bite her tongue off as soon as she said it. That drawer was currently chock full of condoms.

He opened the drawer, and without a moment's hesitation, pulled out one of the little devils and then pretended to use it as a magnifying glass.

"You are one sick puppy."

He raised one eyebrow at her.

"Very sick."

"I think that's a compliment these days."

"It fits."

He smiled a relaxed smile and exchanged the condoms for the magnifying glass.

She drank the rest of her cooled tea, but what she really wanted to do was use a fistful of the packages.

"There is a wafer of gold that seems to have been added

after the ring was made. On it is a coat of arms and it's not the MacCarey coat of arms."

"Oh, secrets galore."

"They're holding the package at the post office. I guess I should pick it up, but I keep trying not to do things that will remind me she's gone." He looked up from the ring. "I would have been here sooner if it weren't for her funeral on Saturday."

"Kind of makes me feel bad for thinking all those evil things about that unknown person who was supposed to be coming from the university. Sorry."

He turned off the lamp and returned to sit beside her in front of the fire. The warmth reached out and wrapped around them. He put his hand on hers, but didn't say anything.

She squeezed his hand in return. "I won't ask, but if you ever feel like telling me, you can."

He smiled a small smile, one that seemed to say something had lightened inside him. That his life just got a little easier. She hoped so.

Time and tea had taken hold. She reveled in the feeling of sleepiness as she leaned back in to the pillow and relaxed. Daniel did the same, then he put an arm around her and drew her close. She turned over so her body fit into his and he breathed a sound-asleep sigh.

THURSDAY AT SEVEN-THIRTY in the morning Mia awoke to the sound of her shower. She sat up and folded the quilts. That was so much better than a note.

As she pulled the pillows back to their corners, she wondered if Monique had heard yet that Daniel had spent another night on Blueberry Avenue.

More, she wondered how Monique and Lenny were doing. Since all was quiet from the neat little house on White Pine Court, things must be going very well.

With the quilts folded and placed on the arm of the couch, she went out to the kitchen.

Light streamed in her kitchen window as if starting up a new day meant something different this morning. She touched the hanging crystal and watched the rainbows dance.

As the coffeepot started to gurgle, she got out the pan for oatmeal.

When Daniel entered the kitchen looking damp and sexy, she grinned a nice friendly grin. "Good morning."

He came over and kissed her on the cheek. "Good morning and thanks for such a good night's sleep."

The touch of his lips made her blush and if she wasn't careful, that blush was going to turn into a raging fire.

"Do you know how to make oatmeal?" she asked.

"That one I can handle."

"Good, I'm going to shower." She took off, abandoning the burbling coffee and the water about to boil. Whatever he needed... Her kitchen wasn't big, and she need a shower, a cold one.

By the time she returned, Daniel had added walnuts and cinnamon to the oatmeal along with dried Maine blueberries and butter.

"Tasty," she said as they sat at her kitchen table in the white light of the bright day. "What are you going to be doing today?" she asked, hoping he would let her get back to work in the building.

"I need to get to the university this morning. What about you?"

"I'll go talk to the police about the trespassing and then I need to check records at the church. If I get bored and if it's all right I'll work on piecing the crypt back together, you weren't taking the pieces with you, were you?"

"I can leave them here. You don't mind if I leave you with all that?"

"I need things to do." Besides wrestle with bill collectors and her crazy libido.

Twenty minutes later, Mia stood on her porch and watched Daniel climb into his car and leave.

Friends, she loved being friends with Daniel MacCarey, but—it was not enough, and as his car rolled down the hill and then disappeared around the corner of Blueberry Avenue and Church Street she felt her good spirits crumple.

Squaring her shoulders, she headed back into the house. She was a tough Maine woman. She could love and not be loved, though, now that she knew what that truly meant, and wanted to stomp off and challenge whoever was in charge of romance in the world.

Maybe she'd just go to work.

On the way back to the university, Daniel called a friend of his, Eleanor Wahl, an avid member of the Jane Austen Society and owner of an antique jewelry business. He set up an appointment to meet her at two this afternoon. If the ring from Aunt Margaret originated in Europe, and it easily could have, and if it was as old as he suspected, this woman might know something of its history. Many *if*s but worth checking out.

Then he called the student in charge of studying the remains and left a message to meet him in the lab at one o'clock to discuss the progress.

When he got into town, he changed at his condo and went to the lab even though he was early.

"Dr. MacCarey." The lead student was so excited he could hardly speak. It was clear to see the trio had found something.

"You gotta see this," another of the trio said as she almost danced around a specimen laid out for his examination. A pair of ribs.

"Come and look," the third said, and although Daniel

knew the young woman was just as eager, she was too reserved to show it.

As Daniel held one of the ribs under a magnifying glass,
a roughness on the surface caught his eye. It looked lin-
ear, like nothing that would have occurred from a skeleton
slouching in a crypt. He picked up the sequential rib and
compared the scoring. The ribs each had similar markings,
one more dorsal and one more lateral. The chances of the
scorings being incidental damage, was remote.

"What do you think?" Daniel looked at the three of
them one at a time. He wanted each of them to know their
answer was important to him.

"It's a stab wound," student one blurted out.

"He was stabbed in the back," the young woman said
with enough relish that she dimpled and blushed.

"The location and angle say it was a mortal wound,"
the quieter of the group said.

"What else do you know about a stabbing like this?"
Daniel turned back to the bones.

"Stabbing a man in the back isn't as easy as it looks on
television. The knife needed to go through clothing…be-
tween the ribs, and get through several muscle layers to
kill. So it had to be done by someone strong, experienced
or just lucky." The information was pieced together as a
group paragraph.

"Good. What else can you tell me?"

"There was no war in this small coastal town during
the window in which this man could have been put in the
wall."

"And how do you know the time period?"

"It's an extrapolation, sir."

Daniel nodded. "So the wound was not a war wound."

"And self-defense wounds are rarely in the back."

Daniel looked at the trio again. He knew by their faces

they were dying to tell him their favorite answer. "What does that leave?"

"Murder," the three of them chorused.

Daniel knew he'd have to examine the evidence closely, but this man, whoever he was, had most likely gotten in someone's way or pissed them off.

"Ms. Vock, Ms. Diaz, Mr. Miller, it looks as though I chose well. Now that the exciting stuff is over, what about the clothing?"

"The cloth was manufactured in Europe in the early 1800s because of the type of fiber. The cut of the clothing takes a more colonial direction than European. There are no fasteners and no metal accessories, so we can't be exact. Although it does appear as if the buttons have been cut off."

"There is DNA in his teeth, Dr. MacCarey, and some of the bone, should we run it?"

"What will we compare the DNA against?" Daniel asked. Heather Loch's name sprang to mind, but he wasn't jumping there just yet.

"Oh, yeah. There is that."

"But preserve it all. There may be a day when it will be useful. See what you can do with reassembling the clothing. Get started on the computer facial reconstruction model."

He left the students with the remains and instructions and headed back to his car with plenty of time to make the trip to Mrs. Wahl's home.

None of what the students had found proved the man had been an important historical figure. It did not disprove it, either.

He found himself smiling at the enthusiasm of the trio. He remembered being twenty-four. He had been invincible, and he knew everything that was important to know about archeology and anthropology. He was two years away from meeting the woman who would become his wife and mother of his child. He was years away from being knocked to the ground by something he had no control over.

He had wondered if he'd ever get up, until Mia Parker made him feel as if he were finally able to gain some footing. She did something to him, brought out his sense of humor. One of those things he thought might be gone forever.

He left the university behind for a place that always amazed him. If there was a home that said gentile more than Eleanor's he'd not seen it. He met Eleanor through his ex-wife, Mandy, and their mutual interest in Jane Austen.

When he stopped his car and got out in front of the meticulously kept home of Eleanor Wahl, he could only feel awe. Built by her late husband's great-grandfather, the home had a brick sidewalk, sweeping front porch and an ornate three-story chimney. The chimney running up the front of the house had the name Wahl spelled out in brick at the base.

"Daniel dear, come in. Come in." A tall, ample woman, dressed in a flowing flowered top over equally flowing brown pants. She met him at the door and led him into the parlor, a room with the kind of leggy, firmly upholstered furniture that was meant for sitting, never lounging. In front of a fireplace was a brass peacock with tail feathers spread that looked as if it didn't dare tarnish. On a table in front of the bow windows stood a palm tree, its branches lending warmth to the decor.

"Do you want anything to drink, Daniel? Are you hungry?" Eleanor asked him.

"No, thank you." He smiled. Eleanor's generosity had not flagged over time.

"Let's see it."

Now he laughed. "I knew I should bring it to you. Who else would be so enthusiastic?"

She grinned knowingly at him and leaned forward eagerly as he removed the old velvet purse from his pocket. He opened the pouch himself because Mia had opened the pouch last and she seemed closer to him right now because she had.

When he poured the ring out into her waiting hand, she gasped. "My, oh, my."

"You recognize it?"

"I recognize it as one very similar to one I know." She looked up at him, her gray eyes sparkling. "One that disappeared in 1808 and was thought to be at the bottom of the Atlantic Ocean."

"My aunt never mentioned its history."

"The blue stone is most likely a topaz, a lovely large one. Of course, those are diamonds." She pointed with the tip of the neatly polished nail of her little finger. "If, as I suspect, it's real."

"I was hoping you could tell me about it."

"I can tell it's gold and gemstones, but I mean, is it a reproduction? Reproductions are often very precise these days. What's its provenance?"

He explained how he got the ring. "My aunt would not have kept it close if it was a reproduction, unless Hathaway, her fiancé, gave it to her, but she wore his engagement ring until she died and there was nothing secret about her relationship with him."

"Let me show something to you."

She led him to an office off the kitchen. "Used to be the maid's quarters, but I don't get up and down the stairs as often as I used to and it's easier to keep my office down here."

She pulled up a website with famous jewelry of Regency

England. She typed in Princess Charlotte and a page of sketches popped up. She pointed to an item on the screen.

"Aunt Margaret's ring belonged to Princess Charlotte?"

"Read about it."

She got up out of the chair and let him sit.

"'Commissioned for Princess Charlotte by her father George IV, then Prince Regent. She never received the ring because it was stolen in a daring robbery of its transport coach and ended up on a ship bound for the colonies. Subsequently, the ship was beset by pirates. Because none of the treasure that was supposedly on that ship has ever been recovered, it was believed the ship sank before the treasure could be confiscated.'"

"Until now." The woman looked at Daniel. "Juicy, I'd say. Your aunt's secret is a very big one. Are you sure you don't know what it is?"

"I'm afraid I've been neglectful. Her attorney sent me a package and I haven't yet collected it."

"I'll be waiting to hear what you find out when you get it."

He smiled at her eagerness. "Do you recognize the insignia on the inside?"

"Let's see." She used a jeweler's loop. "The mark of the jeweler is over here on the side, but the coat of arms has been imprinted on this gold wafer and inserted after the fact. I take it it's not your family's coat of arms."

"Not even close."

"If this is indeed Charlotte's ring, I'd say the insert was put in there by someone who got the ring after it came off the pirate ship."

By a pirate, Daniel thought. What did that mean? His aunt. A pirate.

# CHAPTER THIRTEEN

MIA WAS HALFWAY through a box of files when it occurred to her that if the information at the museum was correct she should have come across the debate about changing the name of the town from South Harbor to Bailey's Cove. So far nothing more than vague references had been made in the log. Maybe the town's name wasn't important to this logger. Chief Montcalm had said there were many varieties of the truth.

She rubbed her eyes, wondering how Daniel was, what he was doing, how the bones were coming, if he'd found out anything.

She'd hug him. She'd hug him every day of his life if given the chance. They had found each other, truly found each other, but something stood between them, and it was more than the granite tomb of a pirate.

Instead of her heart, a hard knot sat in her chest, a frozen thing, afraid to beat.

She dropped her head into her hands. She didn't even know what she was competing against.

Things had gotten so messed up, and she had no idea how to fix them.

She read another file. When she found nothing in that one, she put it back and plucked out another. This folder, stuffed with creased and yellowed papers, was dated February 18th, 1869. She opened it and on the front page was something very familiar and she had to smile. There was nothing for it. A coffee stain almost a hundred and fifty years old; okay, maybe it was tea, but she recognized such a stain. Ones like this adorned many of the pages of her plans for Pirate's Roost.

The notes on February 18th started like all the others of late. Weather reports seemed to be in fashion.

*The sun favored us this cold day. The offshore wind jostles the boats in their moorings and nearly caused Mrs. MacDonald's bonnet to go for a swim. That might not have been a bad thing, as I hate this bonnet she insists on wearing each time we go out.*

*Colleen McClure has raised the topic again of changing the name of the town.* Mia sat up. Colleen Fletcher McClure? The daughter of the man who owned half of South Harbor, and then nearly all of it when Liam Bailey was out of the picture, had married a man named McClure, but there had been no mention of her in the notes for decades.

*She is most adamant that she wants to rename South Harbor after the original founder, the privateer Liam Bailey. Her claim is that South Harbor is too ordinary and if the town had a more exciting name, we might be able to draw more worthy citizens. She proposes the name Bailey's Cove.*

*Sounds too romantic if you ask me,* Sheriff Sean Winchester MacDonald said. *I doubt she'll get her way anyway because her father is apoplectic. Nearly gave him a seizure at the town meeting last night. Between you and me, the town would not be at a loss if that old codger died.*

On August 15th, Sheriff MacDonald entered that two things happened in two days' time. *Archibald Fletcher died yesterday. Today his daughter, with her eldest son, Rónán, that dark-haired boy of hers, at her side, got the town council votes to change the name of the town from South Harbor to Bailey's Cove.*

Mia held a stack of files in her lap, tapping her thumb against the jacket. Colleen McClure had lobbied for the name change with her eldest son in tow. Archibald Fletcher had fought the name change until the day he died.

So Colleen changed the name of the town to Bailey's Cove. She lives in Bailey's home, she brings her first born to the fight about the town's name. If Liam Bailey's hair was dark...Rónán could have been his son.

Conjecture? Yes, but wasn't that how discoveries were often made?

The church records took on a sudden glow of excitement. Mr. Sawyer, the secretary, had told her she could come at two o'clock today. At the time he had put her off she'd thought, why not? Why shouldn't the holy records keep her waiting? She was so good at putting her life on hold these days.

Daniel would be the perfect person with whom to share her theory about Mrs. McClure and Liam Bailey.

Her friend Daniel...

She wondered how he was, what that pain was she saw written all over his face.

She pulled her knees up to her chin and wrapped her arms around her legs. She had seen agony in his eyes, the helpless suffering. She wished she could ease his burden, whatever it was.

She winced. A failing business enterprise, even if it took her to the bottom of the financial barrel, would be nothing compared with devastating personal loss.

What if Colleen McClure had lost Rónán? First her lover and then her child. Mia couldn't even get her head around losing a child.

She rocked back and then forward, back and then forward, staring at the cross patterns at the corner where four tiles met.

If losing a child and maybe even a wife *and* child was what Daniel faced, he deserved all kinds of leeway. The fact that he was upright at all and not confined to a quiet room somewhere said a lot about his strength.

She lifted her chin. Suddenly, all her problems seemed surmountable and she knew she would fight on until she prevailed or they buried her—and she didn't even feel all that brave doing so.

Mia dived back into the files. She was almost at the end of the next box before she realized she needed to reread the passage she had just read. The entry date July 25th, 1924. *The local treasure hunters have stirred things up again. I had wondered when that family would pop up again. I believe they were all born under some kind of curse. Some of them die when they are kids and the rest grow up to be devil witches or ne'er-do-wells, take your pick. They are obsessed with being descended from a man who had no children and they apparently start looking for treasure as soon as they are able to hold a shovel. The most recent offender against our peaceful town is the Loch, Bryon, who made himself heard today by posting the announcement that he has the legal and moral right to any treasure recovered in the village of Bailey's Cove and the surrounding area.*

So at least Heather Loch didn't make it all up. She was just standing on the family platform.

Mia put the file carefully away and slid the box back into line. *Damn you, Daniel. I've no one to talk to about these records except the chief.*

Her stomach growled. Lunchtime.

She put her scarf and coat on and hurried up and out into the sunshine.

"So you're not buried in the hole forever today," Monique said instead of hello when Mia called.

"Nope, and I'm hungry."

"That's unusual. What's the occasion?"

"I'm going to pick up a taco, do you want one?"

"I want two and so do you. Who eats one taco?" Monique spouted the dogma she always did when one taco was enough for Mia.

"Two it is."

"Hey, I heard that Daniel—"

Mia interrupted. "I know what you heard. We can talk about it over tacos."

"How many times—" Monique asked and snickered.

"Over tacos. I'll be at the dry cleaners in fifteen minutes or less with tacos."

"Wait. Barbara's here. She can cover for me during lunch. I'll only be two doors down, after all. I'll meet you at Loco Tacos in five minutes."

With trays of food and drink Mia and Monique sat in the corner as far away from the moms and preschoolers as they could get.

"A few weeks and we'll be able to eat outside," Mia said as she squeezed hot sauce from the package on her tostada, her compromise. When it came to ordering two tacos, she just couldn't do it, but two bean tostadas and she was in heaven.

"Okay. Okay. Out with it, Monique. You look like you're ready to burst."

"Lenny surprised me last night."

"Lenny? Our Lenny? I'm such a bad friend. I forgot he was coming over. What did he do?"

"He brought me flowers. Other than you, no one has brought me flowers, ever."

"So did he ask for another date? If not, let me know. I got a big hammer that seems to be causing trouble. I could do some pretty heavy damage to his kneecaps with it."

"He traded workdays. He wants to take me to a new movie in Bangor. Imagine seeing a first-run movie. Says he already has tickets, just in case I said yes."

"Wow, who'd'a thought? Are you sure you like him, because I'm starting to think I do."

"Can I borrow your hammer?"

Mia laughed. "I saw your granddad last night. I went to Braven's and drank with him and his cronies."

"Okay." Monique gave her furrowed-brow look.

"I knew where he'd be and I went to see if I could feel him out."

"I'm thinking if you had any luck, you'd have already told me."

"I could hardly get a word out of him. But I can tell you he seemed conflicted, like he wasn't sure about anything yet."

"I hope so," Monique said around a bite of taco, a dollop of sour cream on her upper lip.

"Switching topics," Mia said, reaching out with her napkin to get the white splotch.

"About time. Let's have it."

"I have some new swatches of a nice plaid vinyl for the booth covers."

Monique made a face. "You know what I want to hear."

"I can tell you that I'm checking the marriage and birth records at the church this afternoon and then I might have something very interesting I can tell you."

"I want to hear about you and Daniel."

Mia thought for a moment before she answered. "You're going to be disappointed."

"Well, apparently there aren't enough disappointments in my life, 'cause I'm dying to know, anyway," Monique said as she opened her second taco.

"Daniel and I are—um—friends."

"Oh, no. How did that happen? From six to zero a in day."

Mia tried not to spit tostada all over the table. "Hey, I'm eating here."

"Come on, you gotta admit. You two made quite an about-face. It's weird."

"It was—um—eye-opening."

Monique leaned forward on her elbows and put her chin in her hands. "Go on."

"He's in some sort of personal crisis. Something horrible happened to him."

"Awww. Had his heart broken? Haven't we all."

"It's worse than that, much worse. I don't know what it is or how to explain how I know, but whatever it is it makes him feel like he's unable to get into a relationship."

"So what does he think will happen to him if he does?"

"I don't think he's worried about himself at all. I think he's afraid of breaking someone's heart, my heart in this case, but, ha-ha, what else is new?" She put her hands to her head. "For once, I don't think it's me."

"What does that mean?"

"I learned something about myself, something pretty profound and I didn't like it."

"Do tell." Monique slurped her drink to the noisy bottom.

"Daniel and I spent time together, meaningful time, happy, sad, talking about his aunt, about how he no longer has anyone to hug him. It struck me, I'd never made friends with my lovers. I guess I thought as long as we had good sex we had a good relationship. How shallow am I?"

"You don't know, do you?"

"How shallow I am?"

"No. Now, I don't like speaking ill of the living, but have you never sat with your parents. Listened to their conversations?"

"I know they aren't the best of friends, but they love each other."

"Yes, they do the best they can. They might even still lust after each other."

"Are you trying to shock me here?"

"No, I'm just trying to tell you I don't think you had the greatest role models for what a wonderful, romantic relationship looks like. You did what they did, and thank goodness, you didn't get what they got. I'm sorry, honey—" Monique paused and put a hand on Mia's arm "—but Rory would have needed to evolve to make it up to weasel."

"I've started trying to be kind when I remember him, but I can't say you're wrong."

Monique sighed and took a bite of her churros. "I always had such hopes for us, knights on white horses, happily ever after and all that stuff."

"That's what I always thought I was after. Now that I've had a taste of what having a man as a friend and lover might be like, I have to tell you, I could get used to it. I just don't get to get used to it with this particular man."

"Are you sure? The two of you made one heck of a connection and you made it quickly. Can't you find out what his hang-up is and work on it with him? You know, be his friend?"

"You didn't see him whenever we got close to the subject. It nearly laid him out and I don't mean in a good way. I told him if ever wanted to tell me, I'd listen."

"Nice and friendly."

"I guess when I decide to grow up, I do it all at once. I would have thought I had experienced enough of the world to have figured things out before now."

"I suspect we don't ever stop figuring things out." Monique wrapped up the remains of her taco. "So you didn't just stop having, you know, those kinds of feelings for him?"

"No, oh, no. I want him. I want him when he's here and I want him, well… I want him right now."

"How are you all right with all that going on?" Monique squinted into the sunshine now streaming in the window.

"I've decided not to be a mess."

"And you can keep that up?"

Mia huffed out a breath before she spoke. "I will hold it completely together until Daniel MacCarey is gone, and then I intend to get on with my life—somehow."

"Do you think he's the one?"

"Heaven help me, Monique, if he is."

"What are you going to do?"

"What I need to do. I'm going to get Pirate's Roost open if I have to get the hammer and nails myself."

Monique put her hand over Mia's. "I'm so sorry, honey. I wish things were better for you. Is he here in town? Do you have to spend your days avoiding your—ah—friend?"

"He's gone back to the university."

"And while he's gone you don't get to work on the Roost, do you?"

Mia shook her head. "And they're starting to desert the sinking ship. This morning at Mandrel's, I heard that Stella has taken a job at the gas station store out at the interstate. Rufus and Charlie aren't that interested in traveling out of town, so they hadn't found anything yet, but even they have to eat. Jobs might be tight, but almost all employers can pay more than I can afford."

"I have faith in you, honey."

"The thing that troubled me most is Markham Construction called and bumped me for sure this time, and I can't talk them out of it. The best I could get out of them is a *maybe* for the following week."

"Wow. That does so suck," Monique said as she checked her phone for the time. "What do you need to be ready for them?"

"I just need to get the demo finished."

"On that note, I'm sorry, but your friend has to bail on you, and you'll let her because Barbara will have a nervous breakdown if I don't get back soon and I'll have to work all day, every day. So go to the church and check the records and report the gossip."

As Monique walked away, Mia realized she didn't feel any better. Talking to Monique had always lifted her flagging spirits. Not today.

She picked up her tray. Time to start holding it together. *Oh, Daniel, I wish I could make things better for you,* she thought. *Be safe. Take care of yourself.*

When she dumped her trash into the can, her chest felt as if she'd dumped her heart in, too.

THE VISIT AT Eleanor's took longer than Daniel anticipated when it turned out she had invited three of her friends to share their tea.

The women, all dressed similarly to Eleanor, were duly impressed with the ring and even more so with the mystery of how it might have gotten from a coach in transit in England to the pocket of a colonial the likes of Daniel MacCarey in the twenty-first century.

The women she had invited were all tenured experts in various aspects of Victorian and Regency England, the New England states, or the colonial and the post–Revolutionary War United States. They eagerly agreed to research and see what they could find out about Liam Bailey and to consult with the students. In the process Eleanor Wahl had scored a coup among her friends.

His students were gone by the time he reached the lab and he decided that was just as well.

In his office at last, Daniel wrapped up the paperwork he needed to keep the Bailey's Cove project moving, more like chugging, along the slow university track. Then he sat back with his feet propped up on the desk.

Thoughts of Mia flowed into the void. They always did. He found if he wasn't actively working on something, she slipped in and made him want her all over again.

He wanted to touch her, to have her kiss him and caress him, to sit and hold her in his arms. Sometimes when he got like this he started to doubt himself, started to think it was all right to let her in, to tell her. They could figure out a way for the two of them to be together.

But he couldn't do that to her. Just knowing could change her.

He removed his feet from the desk. He wasn't enthusiastic about leaving, but he was even less so about staying. He wasn't sure where he was going, but his car seemed like some sort of refuge these days. It always managed to take him away from places he didn't want to or shouldn't be.

He had just grabbed his vest and put it on when a shadow darkened his doorway.

"Glad I caught you, Dr. MacCarey."

His boss and the department chair, Dr. Gary Donovan stepped into the office. When his boss used "Dr. MacCarey" there was always a want involved.

"What can I do for you, Dr. Donovan?"

"Just looking for an update on our pirate."

"Not much to tell, sir. The man was most likely from the early part of the nineteenth century."

"That's good, isn't it?"

"He was murdered. Knife in the back."

"These people will love the intrigue."

Daniel could see Dr. Donovan loved the idea, not of murder but of the excitement. "The students have started working on clothing reconstruction."

"Good. I'm having a cocktail party tomorrow night and I need you to attend because the pirate people will be there."

Daniel regretted he hadn't left sooner. He hadn't been asked to attend one of the fund-raising cocktail parties in years. Not since his son's birth.

"Where? What time?" Daniel asked.

"We'll be at the botanical gardens, 7:00 p.m. sharp. Black-tie."

Daniel nodded. Dr. Donovan might be brusque and pushy, but the man had given Mandy and him anything they'd needed without question when Mandy was pregnant and sick and when Sammy was struggling through his short life. Because of that, Dr. Donovan could ask Daniel to crawl on his belly across hot coals and he'd do it.

"And, Daniel, you should consider bringing a date, it will help the matrons keep their minds on donations and not other things."

"Dr. Donovan, I'd like to release the site in Bailey's Cove to Ms. Parker. The builder's project is in jeopardy and the sooner the site is free, the better."

"Not yet. We need to see what this donor expects, how much they want to be involved. We may need the raw site as leverage. If it's demolished and plastered over, even if we hang a plaque on it, it won't be distinguishable from any other site where you have to take people's word that something significant happened there."

"I'll invite the builder to come tomorrow night."

"Go ahead. Just make sure he dusts his coveralls off first."

"I'll do that," Daniel said, picturing Mia the first time he'd met her.

"I have to go. There is a nice bland chicken breast and dry salad dinner with my name on it." He patted his spreading waistline and, his business done, scooted out the door.

Daniel drove to his condo, willingly for the first time in a long time. When he got there he kicked off his shoes, poured two fingers of neat scotch and made a phone call to Mia.

## CHAPTER FOURTEEN

MIA TUGGED THE QUILT up under her chin and turned on her side with her phone under her ear. The fire crackled behind the glass doors while she breathed and tried to think of what she was supposed to say.

"Mia?"

"Give me a moment, Daniel."

She took another breath. Excitement clenched in her chest and caution signs flashed wildly inside her head. All she had to do was be polite and friendly.

Maybe he was...

And make no preconceived ideas about this call. *Breathe.*

"How are things at the university?" she asked when she had some semblance of calm.

"The students are working on dating the clothing and will have a reconstruction of the face soon."

"Great." She wanted badly to ask him how he was, but she didn't want to give him cause to lie.

"I'm not calling about that. I have a favor to ask you and I'm sorry this is such short notice, but would you be able to come to a cocktail party tomorrow evening? It's a fund-raiser. My department head will be there, as well as some people interested in funding the work I'm doing with the find from Pirate's Roost."

Mia studied the fire's low flame and wondered if she needed to go out and get more wood. Would this funding get them in and out of her building sooner? Would he ask her if he thought her coming to this party would harm her chances of getting them out of her building?

"Mia? Sweetheart?"

Adrenaline rushed through her, speeding up her heart and making her body tense as if ready for something. *Sweetheart*. She took a breath.

"Daniel, I don't know what to say."

"I asked to get the site released to you today and the department head turned me down."

"And if I come to the cocktail party, I can put a face on the situation here in Bailey's Cove. Make turning me down harder." She needed to get Markham Construction to come to her place next week, not in September.

"Are you interested? Wait, before you answer, it's black-tie."

Daniel in a tuxedo. If she weren't already on the floor, she would have fallen there. "Are you trying to kill me?"

"I'm sorry?"

"You are such a guy. Have you never looked at yourself in a tux? I just got a mental picture of you in a black tux and I have to tell you, if I come up there and spend a couple of hours, I cannot, cannot be responsible for what happens after."

"So will you come?"

She had given up all reservations and she knew it.

"What time? Where? Hold on, I'll need a place to change when I get there."

"Come to my place. The party starts at seven."

"Is 3:00 p.m. all right?" *Come to my place* should be glorious words, but they were somehow frightening.

"What are your plans for tomorrow?"

"Oh, the usual, read records, pray for miracles." Let him figure out for himself what those miracles might be.

"Come for lunch. Pack a bag."

She flopped out spread-eagle, flinging the quilt aside. "I am dead. You realize that."

"Can you use some makeup to disguise that?"

She laughed. Ah-yah, she was in for whatever the man in the city had to offer her. "I'll come, but only if you're sure."

"I am. Are you?"

He hadn't hesitated even for a moment. He was sure, sure of what, she didn't know what that was, and she wasn't going to speculate. But a tux. Really?

"Yes, I am."

"I'll email my address. Is noon too early?"

*Is 5:00 a.m.? How about right now instead of tomorrow?* "Noon would be perfect." How hard was it going to be to buy a black-tie cocktail dress and arrive at Daniel's condo by noon? It would be tight, but she'd die trying.

"I could easily come and pick you up," he offered and she was tempted.

"Oh, I think I'd rather have my own transportation."

"In case you need to flee?"

"In case I need to flee. I'll be there by noon." She said goodbye and then clutched her phone to her chest.

"Are you freakin' nuts?" Monique stood in the living room doorway with their after-dinner tea.

Mia sighed and shook her head slowly, wondering if her friend was right. "I might be. How much did you hear and what have you already made up about it?"

Monique brought the tray with the teapot and cups over and put it on the quilt between the two of them.

"I'll distill it. Tux. Your mother's little black dress. Daniel MacCarey won't know what hit him." Monique stood and snatched the tray up from the floor. "In fact we need to go now if we're to get your mother's dress."

"She and Dad will be watching their show. If they are

in the middle of one of their shows, we'll have to sit quietly in a corner."

"Don't be their kid. The shows are recorded. They can press Pause for their daughter."

"You know she'll be speechless when I ask to borrow a dress."

"She'll just think you've finally decided to grow up and give you that noncommittal *how nice*."

"Speechless, I'll bet you a buck on it."

They smacked palms to seal the bet.

At her parents' house, Mia's mother smiled tentatively when she saw who was on her doorstep. Marianne looked as if she needed an appointment at the hairdressers. Her overly large blond hair didn't have its usual puffy shine.

She held the door open and let them into the house. The first thing Mia noticed was the TV wasn't playing, and then that there were no lights on except in the kitchen. When Marianne Parker led them into the gleaming well-lit room there was, oddly, a crossword puzzle half-worked on the kitchen table.

"To what do I owe this pleasure?"

"Mom, are you all right?"

"Of course, I'm fine." She pushed at her hair. "You must have come for a reason, dear."

"Mom, I need a dress."

She nearly dropped the package of cookies she was about to pour onto a plate to serve to them, with milk, of course. "I'm trying to guess whatever for. You meet your bankers dressed in khaki slacks, you come to church dressed in the same manner, you…"

"Mom, I need your black cocktail dress."

Her mother's expression changed to confused as she pulled three glasses from the cupboard. "It will fit you, yes, very nicely, but whatever for?"

"I'm going to a cocktail party, a fund-raiser."

Her mother's face softened. "I can't remember when you last asked me for anything, Mia. You're so independent."

"I learned from the best, Mom."

Her mother shook her head and lined up the three glasses on the table. Marianne Parker was going to eat milk and cookies. Mia had never witnessed such an event.

"I'm afraid you did learn from me, dear, and sometimes I'm sorry about that. Of course you can borrow the dress."

"I'll be careful with it."

"Of course you will."

"We'll take really good care of it, too," Monique added because Marianne Parker trusted the dry cleaners where Monique worked to take care of her exquisite vintage clothing.

"It's important to me, you know," Marianne said as she looked from one girl to the other. There was a frightening sadness in her mother's voice.

"Yes, Mrs. Parker."

"I'll go get the dress." Her mother hurried away and Mia followed.

"Mom, it's Thursday. Why are you sitting at the table working a crossword puzzle?" she asked when they were in the spare bedroom. Her mother had opened the closet and seemed to be trying to mentally bury herself in the contents. "Where's dad?"

"Your father huffed off somewhere. He does that more and more often."

"Why?" Mia knew the single word was an accusation and she could see by the set of her mother's jaw, she did, too.

"Your father's and my business is not yours."

"Hey, you're my parents and I love you."

Marianne let a breath out slowly as she rubbed her hands down the front of her knit slacks. "Your father wanted to do something different tonight and I don't see that there is anything wrong with what we always do."

Then her mother reached into the closet and pulled out the dress encased in a plastic bag, but did not hand it to Mia.

"Mom." Her mother seemed not to hear her and she took hold of the sleeve on her mother's sweater to get her attention. "Mom, I learned something and I'm going to pass it along. You can use it or not. Try treating him like a friend."

"I don't know what you mean, dear. He's my husband." She lifted the plastic and ran her hands over the light-weight chiffon with black crystal beads sewn along the V-neck bodice.

"That's just it, Mom. What if Maxine said she didn't want to go to Mandrel's for breakfast on a Sunday morning?"

"Why would she? Where would we go?"

"Maybe she decided to learn to cook and she invited you to her house."

"I guess, if she had it all planned, I'd go, of course. She's my friend."

"So when Dad does something like that, try pretending it's Maxine asking and react accordingly. Be his friend, Mom. It might be reciprocated."

Her mother handed the dress to her and then reached into the hanging zipper bag and pulled out shoes and a purse. "You'll need these."

Mia put a kiss on her mother's cheek. She'd have hugged her if her hands weren't full.

Her mother shooed her back out to the kitchen and Mia knew that meant shut up, subject closed.

Monique looked up from where she sat at the table filling out the crossword.

"It was good to see the two of you." Her mother picked

up the three clean glasses and put them back in the cupboard. The cookies followed.

Mia and Monique filed out like schoolchildren during a fire drill. When they got into Mia's car Monique snapped her seat belt on and turned toward Mia, who was securing the dress, shoes and handbag safely in the backseat. "What the heck was that?"

After they were rolling down the road, Mia replied, "They're in trouble."

"'Cause they're not watching their shows?"

"Did you see that? She was going to have milk and cookies with us."

"Ah-yuh, that's bad. So what's going on?"

Mia drove on silently, thinking about the rituals her parents lived by, like watching recorded game shows. If those fell apart, they may have nothing else. What if they had one of those shell marriages because neither of them believed in divorce?

"She said dad wanted to do something different tonight and she refused. And I think I learned something really important from my friendship with Daniel. Be a friend."

Be a friend. A real friend like Monique was there for life, glitz and warts notwithstanding. Cocktail dresses and tuxes. TV shows and breakfasts.

"And you told her… Come on, I'm pulling teeth here."

"And I asked her, what would she do if Maxine wanted to change their routine?"

"What did she say?"

Mia did a quick shrug. "She threw us out."

"Hey, no matter who else does what, you've got me."

"You're the M to my M. I love you, Monique. Don't ever forget that."

"I wish I could fix your world, Mia."

"The Parkers. Experts in creating messy lives."

"Listen, you can't take on your parents' troubles."

Mia knew her friend was right. She had so much on her plate and now she had taken on a cocktail party.

"I know, but I'm still concerned."

"Of course you are."

Mia laughed. "You want me to drop you at home, or do you want to help me try on the dress?"

"The dress, of course, and we can also try to do something with all of this." Monique picked up a lock of Mia's hair.

"Do you suppose weddings and baptisms, and movies with cocktail parties, have been enough to prepare me for facing university-patron types?"

"You will break hearts and open even the most secure wallet."

MIA SAT IN her car in a parking spot outside Daniel's condo, fifteen minutes early. The little black dress on its hanger in the bag draped over the backseat. On the floor behind her seat sat a bag with everything else, including a few condoms. Heaven help her, just in case.

She had spent the entire two-hour drive wondering how she was going to look Daniel in the eyes, those gloriously rich, dark diamond eyes, and kiss him on the cheek and then…

But that was her problem. Daniel wanted to be friends.

She could do that. Soon. She could do it soon. She got out of the car and hurried up the sidewalk and then up the stairs to the second floor.

Calm and relaxed, yeah, right, she rang Daniel's doorbell.

*Breathe, just breathe. Everything is under control.* If he looked too tempting, she'd remember she was his friend. She'd come to get her construction project underway and chat with a friend.

He opened the door. What he was dressed in hardly

mattered. All jeans and sweaters looked the same on him. Devastating.

Oh, wow, if she had to be a good friend to this she was dead.

She shoved the dress bag at him and then her small suitcase.

He took everything and smiled. Dead. She was so dead. No one would ever want to be her friend again.

"Daniel."

He dropped everything and reached for her. His mouth descended over hers, stopping any breath, any thought except to have him.

She broke away and kicked the door closed. "I'm a bad friend."

"I love having a bad friend." With his hands at her waist, he rained kisses on her face, her neck, her mouth, and when he lifted her sweater and tossed it aside, rained more kisses on her chest, over her new bra. "Lace."

She pushed him backward out of the foyer.

He wrapped his arms around her, turned her back to front, kissing her neck, her ear and her hair. Nearly overcome with pleasure, she dropped her head back against his shoulder and panted for air. Then he swept her off her feet and carried her, through the living room and down a hallway, kissing the hollow at the base of her neck, then her lips again.

In his bedroom, long desperate seconds passed as they stripped off their clothing. "Wait," she said as he was about to toss her jeans aside. "Pocket."

He opened the package and she snatched the condom and looked up into his face as she rolled the soft latex down onto him. Then she pulled him on top of her and into her where she needed him to be.

She luxuriated in his kisses, unwilling to give them

up until she let herself go, let the waves of pleasure crash over her and over her...

Wrung, sated and gloriously happy she stroked his brow and laughed. "Hello."

"Welcome to my home," he said as he ran his fingers through her hair.

"I am so happy to be here." *And I love you, Daniel MacCarey, my dear friend. Someday I hope you want to know it.*

After their breathing returned to normal, he shifted onto his side and flipped the bedspread over both of them.

"Well, I practiced for hours and hours, so that I could be in your presence and not jump you," she said, smiling.

"How'd it go?"

"Not well, but I'd be willing to go back out and try it again." But she didn't move, other than to sigh and touch his face to assure herself she wasn't still sitting in her car having a daydream. "And if that doesn't work, I'll go back out..."

"You make me crazy. I can't look at you and not want you." He hugged her as though he cherished her.

Yet, she knew there was desperation in those words. She felt the same when she thought of how much she wanted him and how much he needed to maintain his distance.

She lay beside him measuring each breath, wondering which one of them would flinch first. It was as if they stood nose to nose on a tightrope, each needing to get to the other side but neither willing nor able to pass the other. She breathed in the warm musky scent of him, felt his steady heartbeat under her hand.

Eventually, pride and responsibility won out. She patted his chest. "I need to go hang up the dress."

He kissed her and she slid out from under the spread, taking his robe from the chair and wrapping it around herself.

When she came back into the bedroom with the dress and her bag, he was coming out of the bathroom with boxers on.

They hid nothing. He couldn't make the wanting go away any more than she could make wanting him go away.

He took the dress and hung it in his closet beside another garment bag, his tux she'd wager. Daniel in a tux.

"You can put the rest of your things in there," he said, indicating the bathroom.

When she came back out empty-handed she said, "You may think I eat all the time…"

He flicked his eyebrows.

"Well, I'm hungry. Did you have a place picked out for lunch or should I go forage?"

"We can eat here if you don't mind."

"If you at least have peanut butter and bread, I'm good with here."

He invaded her space, leaned down and dropped a kiss on her lips, and when she was ready for more, he stepped back and said, "I think we can do better than peanut butter."

Her stomach growled loudly.

He unfastened the belt of his robe from around her waist, bent over and put his lips to her stomach. "Right away. Right away," he said to her belly and planted a sloppy kiss.

She laughed and pulled his face into her. He nipped softly and sidestepped her hold.

"We need to feed you."

She retied the robe as he led her out of the bedroom.

"Sex and food. Can I come and visit you often? This feels like a vacation."

His smile held a touch of longing.

"My balcony gets full sun and it's very warm on a day

like this." He led the way to his dark blue tile and white kitchen with wood trim and accessories.

"Wait." She put out her hands to stop him. He did stop and she continued. "You did *not* pick out this kitchen scheme."

"I did not. It was available when I needed something."

In a hurry she bet. More of his secret, more of where his pain came from.

She smiled at him when she wanted to hug him. "Lunch outside would be wonderful. Do you mind if I wear your robe on the balcony, or will it stir up your neighbors?"

"The neighbors will be pleased for the lovely distraction."

"Hey, I've got some scoop to tell you about while we dine."

"As luck would have it, I have some for you."

"Can we eat now?"

"Grab those." He pointed to a stack of table linens and dishes.

"I love dinner plates. Yum, they have so much fiber."

He laughed and pulled out a tray of delectables from the refrigerator.

When she returned from putting the place settings on the balcony table, he had slipped on a T-shirt and plaid flannel lounging pants. Barefoot and tousle-haired he looked sexy and relaxed. She liked to think she had something to do with that.

She grabbed the glasses from the counter and the carafe of chilled water and headed back through the living room with dark gray and blue furniture with wooden trim. She was starting to see the theme in this place.

ON DANIEL'S WARM and sunny balcony, they set up a feast of gourmet food he had ordered from the deli down the street and large glasses of orange juice. Mia was right, it did feel like a vacation.

"Tell me your scoop and I'll tell you mine," she said, bliss written all over her face as she made it halfway through a turkey sandwich on a petit bun, with the domed part of the bun hollowed out and filled with lettuce and some kind of herbed mustard-mayonnaise.

"My great-aunt Margaret's secret involves the ring. Apparently, it was destined to belong to Princess Charlotte of Wales, who died in 1817." He told her about tea at Eleanor Wahl's home. "Charlotte was the daughter and only child of the man who became George the IV."

"How did your great-aunt Margaret get the ring?"

"Mrs. Wahl and several of her friends, experts in the era, are trying to find out, but there's more."

Mia rubbed her hands together in anticipation and he put his fingers on her cheek and let them wander lower.

She gasped when his fingertip brushed the side of her breast. Clearing her throat, she said, "I love a good mystery."

He gently caressed the warm, giving flesh of her breast and wondered if the neighbors would call the cops or just keep watching.

She pressed his hand and then sat back and closed her eyes. "Hey, you'd better keep talking or we'll get arrested and it'll be worth it. Sex in the sunshine. Glorious."

When he pulled his hand away, she grabbed hold and brought his knuckles to her lips before she gave the hand back to him.

He shook his head and grinned at her. "And the coat of arms stamped on the inside does not belong to Charlotte's family nor her husband's. Mrs. Wahl and her friends are working on finding out whose it is, feverishly, I'd wager."

"There's something, I'd wager." She gave him a suspi-

cious look. "You didn't go to the post office and pick up
that package from your aunt's attorney, did you?"

"You're wrong. It's sitting on the desk in my office
here."

"Unopened. And yet you seem so manly and brave.
Open the package already."

"I thought you might like to help me, since you were
nice enough to come and be arm bling for a fund-raiser."

"That's what I am?"

"It's what my boss believes. He also believes you are
two people. I told him I was inviting the builder. Your
other persona has a dirty pair of coveralls and probably a
comb-over." He put his fingers in her hair and brushed it
all over the top of her head.

She burst out laughing and looked so lovely with the sun
glinting off the golden highlights in her hair. He wanted
her now and always. He wasn't even going to ask himself
what he thought he was doing. He was just going to sit
there and take it.

Mia smiled and put her hand over his. Her expression
seemed wistful. They sat like that for a while, feeling the
sun, letting the passion fade to manageable.

"Mia," he said when he thought some of his sanity had
returned. "How prepared are you for this to be the remains
of a town founder?"

"Worse, I think I'm finally prepared for this to be the
remains of Liam Bailey, the long-lost pirate with a relative living in Bailey's Cove."

He wasn't sure why, but those words caused a kind of
relief in him. "What do you know?"

"Do you want to go 'hmmm' or roll your eyes first?"

"Hmmm."

"All right. I've found out the man who owned the half
of South Harbor that Liam Bailey did not own, Archibald
Fletcher, had a daughter who fought to have the name of

the town changed to Bailey's Cove. Fought hard against her father's apparently apoplectic objections, and the day after her father died she convinced the town council to make the change."

She put her hand over his lips. "That's not the hmmm part. When she went before the council, her son Rónán McClure was with her. This Rónán was referred to as the 'dark-haired one,' which leads me to believe the other children were not."

"Hmmm."

"So, first of all, and this is just an aside, I don't think I told you Bailey named his hotel the Sea Rose Inn. He also built that large white home on the hill overlooking town. After he disappeared, Colleen insisted her father acquire it and she lived there with her husband and children."

She took a big breath and plunged on.

"So add all that to this. I went to the church yesterday and looked up marriage and birth records. Shortly after the pirate was supposed to have disappeared, Colleen *Rose* Fletcher became Colleen Rose McClure. That was in May of 1818. In September of 1818 the McClures had their first child baptized, Rónán Uilliam McClure. Liam is a shorter version of Uilliam. Since a baby that young has only a small chance to survive in today's world, this was no premature baby."

She gave him a quick look, and he wondered if she had seen the distress he suddenly felt because she hurried on. "So much for 'hmmm.' Are you ready for eye rolls?"

"Ready."

He struggled to stay with her instead of getting lost in the past, but he did a practice eye roll. "Ah-yuh."

She giggled and he'd bet his life she didn't do that very often.

"Turns out Heather Loch comes by her fascination genetically. In 1924 the chief of police mentioned— Let me think of how he said it."

She looked out over the lawn and the small lake surrounded with side-by-side condominiums and then spoke again. "He said they were obsessed with being descended from a man who had no children and they start looking for treasure as soon as they could hold a shovel. He thought they were cursed because most of them grew up to be, well, less than stellar citizens, and some of them died when they were kids."

"*Died* when they were kids" punched him right smack in the gut. He refused to double over, and he had to force his breathing to be normal.

"He said the most recent offender against their peaceful town was Bryon Loch. Daniel?"

He pulled it together and looked at her. "Loch."

She scooted her chair over next to his, put her arm around his shoulders and didn't say a word more. She was a good friend. The best.

So why was he doing this to her?

## CHAPTER FIFTEEN

MIA GOT UP and kissed him on the forehead. He could see in her face she knew his demons had raised their heads.

"Sit here," she said gently. "I'll clean up. You stay. Take in the sunshine."

He leaned back, turned his face up to the warmth and closed his eyes, but after a minute pushed up from the chair and followed her into the condo.

She put the last glass in the dishwasher and turned to smile at him. Her delicately featured face held the effects of everything going on in her life and he knew he was one of her problems.

He took hold of her hands and pulled her toe-to-toe with him. "Mia, we can't keep doing this to you."

She bowed her head. "I know. I thought I could deal with it. I thought I could be close to you, have you, and keep my emotions in check."

"It's not your fault."

"My part is my own fault. I thought it didn't have to matter if we made love, had fun sex and then walked away." She put her cheek on his chest and broke his heart the rest of the way.

He held her close and pressed his lips to delicately fragrant hair. "I knew better and I let us get involved."

She pushed away and looked at him, at first confused and suspicious. "I'll get my things together and be gone in a few minutes."

"Please don't do that." He held her hand when she started to walk away.

"What do you want me to do?"

"I want you to be able to meet these people this evening. I want you to have the chance to let them meet you, see the human consequences of delaying your project."

Emotions played across her face and she came to a decision. "I'd like that. Bailey's Cove deserves that."

"Do you think it's possible we've defused the situation between us enough that we can manage to get through the next few hours?" He watched her face for any signs of doubt or fear, signs he should back off. "Especially since we have something to do to distract us."

"The package on the desk in your office? I'd better help you or it'll sit there forever, won't it?"

"It might."

She looked up at him and smiled, a smile bright enough that it might have held forgiveness.

Relief he didn't know he'd been waiting for surprised him. If he had broken her unflagging spirit, destroyed another woman, he might as well bury himself in the vast Maine forests away from civilization, from her.

"I'll get the package," he said as he slowly released her hand.

She nodded.

He picked up the package from his desk and hefted it on the palm of his hand. It had turned out to be a postal box with a standard printed label, black and white, bar codes, the works.

When he returned to the living room, Mia was dressed in her jeans and sweater and sitting on the edge of the sofa. One of his kitchen knives sat on the coffee table.

"I didn't know if you had a box opener or a utility knife, so…" She picked up the knife.

"So that's for the package?" He trusted her. He trusted her with his life and he knew it.

Mia looked up toward the ceiling and clasped her hands. "We love you, Great-Aunt Margaret, and I'll help this sorry nephew of yours through this package of stuff if I have to tie him to the chair and prop his eyes open."

She unclasped and then reclasped her hands. "And thank you for taking such good care of your nephew all those years."

"She did, too." He took the knife, slit open the package and pulled out the contents.

"The MacCareys." Mia put a hand on his arm as she read the cover.

He had seen the fat binder before. "Aunt Margaret worked on this all the time I knew her. She never tried to coerce me to help with or even look at it. It's the family genealogy. At first, as a kid, I wasn't interested, and then I was too busy." And then, well, he couldn't.

He couldn't because there were bound to be other children, other MacCareys who had died young, from the same genetic flaw his young son had gotten from him.

He opened the binder to the most recent entry and glanced at the page before he opened the book wider so Mia could see inside. Margaret had mercifully left out any information about himself except to note him below his deceased parents. The chapters had many photos and much text augmented by clippings, letters, handwritten and typed notes, apparently from the present to long ago. The older pages had been encased in plastic page covers to preserve them.

"It's wonderful how the handwriting seemed to go from typed to ball point to fountain pen to quill," she said, pressing a fingertip to one of the covered pages with quill writing.

When he reached the oldest pages, the beginning of the

MacCarey line in the United States, he knew by her gasp Mia recognized the coat of arms at the same time he did.

"Daniel."

The page held an image of a carefully drawn and colored coat of arms. A similar image had been stamped on the inside of the ring from Aunt Margaret. The faded greens and yellows must have once been vibrant. On the triple-peaked shield divided into quadrants of alternating color, the blade of a sword crossed with a tree, and a ship floating on the ocean sat in the background. The stamp on the ring had only the sword and the tree. The ship and the waves would have been too much detail for such a small stamp.

Inside the pocket of the back cover of the binder sat a letter-size envelope with "My Beloved Daniel" handwritten on the front.

"She must not have wanted to scare you off by putting the letter in the front pocket," Mia said in a soft voice. "Smart woman."

He ran the tip of his finger over the writing and opened the letter so both of them could see it.

*To Daniel MacCarey, or if he never looked in this book that troubles him so much, to anyone who will give a thought and perhaps a prayer to the MacCarey family.*

Mia pressed her body against his, put a warm hand on his leg and squeezed, a gesture of comfort. He opened the letter.

*Daniel, I wanted to give you the underpinnings of your family line in case you ever read this.*

*Alas, the origin of the coat of arms is lost to me. This drawing and the ring have been passed down for a century and a half. The ring belonged to Colleen McClure, given to her by her lover. Her oldest child was not fathered by her husband and we, Daniel,*

*the MacCareys, are descended from the child con-*
*ceived out of wedlock. This may not be a shocking*
*horror in your day and age, but it was then and Col-*
*leen wanted to make sure the secret was never for-*
*gotten. The secret passes with the ring and the coat*
*of arms. I think she might have been afraid the fam-*
*ily would reject her first son's heirs as illegitimate if*
*the truth was known about the father, so she refused*
*to name him outright or to say anything at all about*
*the mystery man.*

*Unfortunately, and it distresses me to say this, one*
*branch of Fletcher/McClure descendants, twice re-*
*moved from the child born of love, was obliterated by*
*someone keeping the records and there is no informa-*
*tion about who might have been added and then taken*
*away. I will leave you to make your own conjectures.*

*Other than that, we are an ordinary collection*
*of geniuses and outstandingly good-looking human*
*beings.*

*Have a wonderful life, Daniel. I knew you would*
*read this—eventually.*
*Your great-aunt Margaret Irene MacCarey*

"Did I tell you Great-Aunt Margaret was a terrific
woman with a delightful sense of humor?"

"Well, she certainly wasn't wrong about the good-
looking part."

"Yes, she was a beautiful woman."

She gave him a light elbow in the ribs.

"I'm starting to put a name to the mystery man. Since
I'm not a scientist or an anthropologist, I can make up anything I want." She scooted to the edge of the couch and
turned to face him.

"The pirate Liam Bailey is you grandfather about eight
or ten times removed." When he reached for her, she leaped

up and danced away. "Arrgh, matie, shiver me timbers. Yo ho ho and a bottle o' rum, I believe it's time for me to get in the shower and get ready."

"Towels are in the cupboard." He started to follow her.

"It's a bathroom. I think I'll find everything I need."

Daniel sat back on the couch and pulled the book into his lap. Was Mia right? Was it possible for coincidence to be so facetious as to make him related to the man in Mia's wall?

Then he closed the book. How could it possibly make a difference to anyone except a historian, or perhaps an anthropologist?

He gathered up the book and tapped on the bathroom door. "Mia. I need to leave for a half hour or so."

"I'll be here when you get back."

Mia hung her clothes on the hook on the door and stepped into the shower. As soon as the water poured down over her head, tears poured from her eyes.

She had been so smug. Had known everything there was to know about a broken heart. In fate's retribution, here she was, left to spend several more hours with a man who couldn't reject her, but couldn't love her, either.

When mere tears didn't seem to be enough, she leaned against the wall and sobbed until she was sitting on the floor in the flow of the water trying to wish the pain from her heart.

She loved him.

She loved him and could not find an opponent to fight to win him over.

Yet she needed to do battle this afternoon anyway. She needed to convince these people whom she did not know that she mattered, that the folks of Bailey's Cove mattered.

And she would. That's what she did. That's who she was.

She stood and shook herself to try to clear all the negative thoughts from her head. Then she lathered soap all over herself. Once again she cleansed the touch of Daniel MacCarey from her body and, if she was the unluckiest woman ever, soon it would be from her life.

That she had been too cavalier about getting her heart broken was yet another of those life lessons she had not known she needed to learn.

Now she had learned and relearned.

She would open Pirate's Roost or she would become a sorry old cliché and die trying. She needed to throw herself into the work. It didn't matter who that was from her wall. Pirate. Arrgh, she'd deal with the lookers. Treasure hunters? Bring 'em on. A woman with a broken heart had a lot to compensate for, and one thing she knew about herself, she could fight hard.

The past six months of hands-on work at Pirate's Roost had taught her a lot. She wasn't kidding when she told Monique she'd wield a hammer herself if need be, and the nails, screws, saw.

She got out of the shower and wrapped a fluffy towel around her head. She dried off her body briskly with another. No matter how deeply she dug in her bag of supplies, however, she could not find her toothpaste. She could brush without it, but that always seemed like wasted effort.

This time she put on her own robe and opened the bathroom door to let out the steam the vent was not handling and flipped on the mirror lights. She needed to assess how much damage she had done to her face and eyes by crying.

Not too bad. She splashed cold water on her face over and over.

Once again, she looked for the elusive toothpaste. No luck.

Everybody had toothpaste, so must Daniel.

She opened the medicine cabinet, found the tube and squirted some on her brush. As she put the tube back, she realized on the shelf above there was one of those small, wallet-size photos standing, slightly curled on the shelf behind the shaving cream.

Daniel kept close the photo of a woman and child, where he could see it every day. Not displayed out in the open where visitors could see it. Hidden where only Daniel could see—unless a visitor ran out of toothpaste.

Mia scooted the can aside and picked up the picture. The woman was beautiful and the little dark-haired child so cute, but a little sad even though he smiled.

When Mia looked more closely at the child, she saw a distorted version of Daniel looking back at her.

She winced and started as Daniel strode into the bathroom and took the picture from her.

The steel of determination shuttered any reaction he might have had to finding her holding his secret.

"It's them." The words came out on a breathy gasp.

He put the picture in the pocket of his shirt. "How did you know?"

"Put your hackles back down." She rubbed his chest to reassure them both that this was not a breach. "I don't know much and what I thought I might know you just confirmed."

He looked suspiciously at her and the dark pain began to slowly dance in his eyes. He forgave her the transgression or he would not have let her see his emotions at all.

"You are a very strong person, Daniel. I've never doubted that, so when I called you Danny, just the sound of the name brought up something so terrible it took you out as if I had hit you with that hammer. That had to be the name you were called in your family unit. Whatever happened to you was so dark and so profound it had to involve a child. That's all I thought I knew."

When he turned away from her she knew she did not

know it all yet. She wanted to go to him and demand he tell her, but a promise was a promise.

"Hey. I'm sorry."

"That's just it." He turned back. "You don't have anything to be sorry about."

She nodded acceptance. "I'd like to air-dry my hair some on the balcony if you would like to use the shower."

Now he nodded.

"I just need my brush." She grabbed her things from the bathroom, including the toothbrush, which she stuffed into the plastic bag it had been stored in. The toothpaste smeared and mushed all over the inside of the bag and she hoped that was not a prediction of the next few hours.

She glanced up to see his reflection in the mirror. He looked...alone.

When she left the bathroom with her bag over her shoulder and her arms full of stuff, he stopped her and placed a kiss on the top of her head.

Forgiveness, complete and full of sorrow.

She turned and hurried away.

Dropping everything on the couch except one towel, her hairbrush and the robe she wore, she let herself out into the warm afternoon sun.

Every brush stroke seemed to sooth her. Every minute she sat in the nurturing sunshine healed her a little more. Maybe by the time she got ready to meet these people, she would be strong enough to get through the night. Smile. Chat. Smile. Chat. And drive herself home.

*I think I can...*

By the time her hair was dry and smooth, Daniel had come out onto the balcony dressed in a robe with a towel draped around his neck. He looked refreshed and that bolstered her strength.

"You can have the bathroom back."

She hung the dress on the back of the bathroom door

and in the relatively dim light of the bathroom she scooped her hair up and realized the upswept comb-over she and Monique had planned didn't seem right anymore. She just twisted her hair at the back of her head, pinned it and inserted the black crystal-studded hair fork.

She applied more makeup than her usual modest amount because construction work didn't require much in the makeup category.

With the side zipper of the black dress tugged up into position, the dress molded tightly around her waist. She felt a little uncomfortable with no bra, but the dress did not. The whole intent of the design was to glorify a woman's natural curves in swaying black chiffon and shining crystal beads that ran in a two-inch scattered row on either side of the modest V of neckline and joined to make a four-inch swathe to the waist. The back of the dress dropped open to her waist.

Monique had talked her into a deep red matte lipstick that, Mia had to admit, looked smashing on her full lips. "It'll stay on," Monique had said. "And it says, oh baby, oh baby, there is absolutely nothing ordinary about this woman."

Mia had been skeptical and she still was.

"Now make a moue," Monique had said, and when Mia pushed out her lips, "Oh, yes, now it says, oh, honey, you're not good enough for me. Go away until you're better-looking, richer and fantastic in bed."

Hey, Mia thought as she repinned a loose lock of hair and gave it a good spray, maybe there was a good-looking donor just waiting to back a pirate restaurant.

She put on her earrings and necklace and modeled for herself in the mirror. Her emerald-and-gold necklace and earrings from her grandmother weren't the best fit, but they were pretty and they would have to do. Her phone told her it was six-twenty. She hoped Daniel had everything he needed from the bathroom before she closeted herself in.

With one hand on the sink for balance, she slid on one of the four-inch black patent-leather heels and then the other. Tipping her foot to the side, she admired the cap-heel and open-sided pumps. *D'Orsay style* according to Monique and to which Mia had responded, "If you say so." The toes of the shoes had three bands of leather crossed over each other. The band crossing over the top of all of the others had black crystal beads similar to the dress.

Thank goodness for Monique. She had insisted, before the mani-pedi, Mia walk around the house in the shoes. Once she had found her balance last night, things had gotten easier. Now she moved around the bathroom and had her balance after only a few strides.

She was ready.

She loaded the matching purse with essentials and gathered up all her things. She stopped and put down everything but the purse. Daniel might not be her lover anymore, but he was a guy and she wanted to get the full effect when he saw something he had never seen before. Mia Parker in full fancy-dress mode.

She stepped out of the bathroom ready for a taa-daa moment, but Daniel's bedroom was empty. He wasn't in the living room or the kitchen. He must be in the office. She perched on one of the blue bar stools that lined the counter dividing the kitchen from the dining area to wait.

A moment later she heard his footsteps approaching. Since the dress would have more impact if she stood, she slid off the stool and put one hand on the counter, standing up "I rule" straight.

He walked out of the office concentrating on the box in his hands. The lines of his tux showed off the killer form of his body without looking overly done. His dark hair was brushed back and slightly wet-looking.

Bruce Wayne sexy and James Bond aloof…and when he was only a few feet from her and looked up, he took one step back and grinned at her, Indiana Jones charming.

He made all the effort worthwhile.

"You look beautiful. Astonishing."

"And you look good enough to be with me."

She approached him, touched his chin with the tip of one finger and then sashayed away, presenting the back of the dress.

He coughed and sputtered. "Um, wow."

She turned back around. "Does that mean you like it?"

"I knew you had a lovely back, but I had no idea how good it would look framed in black."

"So what do you think?"

"You make that dress the most beautiful thing I've ever seen, and—" he touched the corner of her mouth "—I think that lipstick was designed to make men grovel at your feet."

"I won't ask you to go that far."

He held out his hand and led her over to the mirrors behind the dining room table. "I'm not saying your lovely necklace isn't charming and beautiful, but I wondered if you were interested in borrowing these."

She took the black velvet jewelry box from him and lifted the lid. Inside were a diamond necklace, a bracelet and a pair of earrings. All matching. All glittering and gorgeous. "Great-Aunt Margaret?"

"Yes, and they don't get much use from me."

The three pieces were simple strings of set diamonds. Round, marquis and emerald cut diamonds set in white gold or platinum. Each piece a single strand. The earrings dropped three inches and would almost touch her shoulders.

Mia took her jewelry off and put it on the table. Daniel draped the necklace around her neck and it fell to just above the rise of her breasts as if designed for her. She made herself ignore the effect of his warm fingers on her neck. He fastened the bracelet around her wrist and then glanced up to look into her eyes. She put the earrings in without looking away.

"One last chance. Do you want to face these people?"

"These people who will think Dr. Daniel MacCarey has finally come back out of his shell?"

"They might at that."

"Come on. We'll shut them up. Kiss me on the cheek once in a while. Act protective and they won't be able to talk about poor old Daniel MacCarey any more."

"I won't be pretending to be protective. There are always a few in attendance who must have missed out on manners class."

"So let's go pluck some dollars for the university out of some bank accounts."

When they arrived dutifully a few minutes early, the foliage of the botanical gardens was lit with twinkle lights, and the waitstaff was ready to serve. Daniel introduced Mia to Dr. Donovan, making sure his department head knew this was the woman whose project was being put on hold for the pirate dog and pony show.

Daniel's boss looked the pair of them up and down. "Well, you two certainly have all the bases covered."

As they strolled away Mia thought she heard a low wolf whistle and leaned into Daniel. "It's the dress. I'm still just a girl with a hammer and a fistful of nails."

He leaned down and said intimately in her ear, "You've never been just a girl with a hammer and fistful of nails."

She smiled up at him for his charm and they ventured out into the gathering crowd.

## CHAPTER SIXTEEN

The nose of Mia's pea-green SUV ate up the road as she sped toward home. When the party broke, she had returned Great-Aunt Margaret's jewelry to Daniel and drove away from him as he stood in the parking lot looking as bereft as she felt.

Turns out the Owens, the pirate dog and pony show people, loved the hammer and nails description, especially from a woman dressed so "divinely." It didn't hurt to have Dr. Daniel MacCarey by her side to get such a response from the people who did not know her at all. The last thing they said they wanted was to get in the way of her "divine" project. She didn't hold much hope they would push to get the site opened to her, but at least they probably would not block it, either.

The evening had been a smashing success, according to Dr. Donovan, who had found many reasons to spend time with Daniel and her. He gave, however, no more than vague responses to the question of releasing the site. For her part, Mia brought out all her impressive people-handling skills. While giving no offence, she made sure Dr. Donovan knew her plans for the property and the importance of the building project to the town.

"He's most likely waiting for the results from the lab. He can't afford to give up a piece of history," Daniel had told her. "But the Owens pledged another sizable chunk to sponsor more than one project for the anthropology department."

"And, as much as I hate to say this aloud, I don't want him to give up any history. It would be a piece of Maine history, after all," she had said in response and then looked up at Daniel. "I hate both the rock and the hard place."

As she sped onward, lights from the oncoming cars passed in the darkness of late evening. If the university's wheels just moved fast enough for her to get the site back by Monday, she might be able to complete the prep work by the following Sunday and pray Mr. Markham forgave her for not being ready for them by "next week" and would tuck her into the schedule for the week after.

Halfway home her phone rang, and she chucked the handbag with the phone in it over her shoulder in case she did something crazy, like answer any calls. A minute later the voice-mail signal played from the backseat. It was too early for Monique to call, too late for her mother, probably too late for anyone to be calling about the Roost, so that left Daniel making sure she was all right—as if. She knew she could not hear the sound of his voice right now.

She hissed out a breath between her teeth. Did she never get a break?

The phone rang again and she was glad it was in the backseat. It saved her from having to chuck it out the window.

By the time she reached Bailey's Cove the clock on the bank across the road from the museum read ten o'clock and, of course, the last thing she wanted was sleep.

She changed into her mint-green tank top and blue plaid flannel shirt and jeans and headed for Pirate's Roost.

Tonight she took her aviation-style headphones, good for keeping the music in and the world out. No creaking building. No passing cars. No thinking. Just music.

"Hi, Marcella," she said when she called the evening dispatcher at police headquarters. "This is Mia Parker. I just wanted to let you all know I'm at Pirate's Roost for a while. I didn't want them to worry about the lights being on."

Marcella said she'd let the squads know and wished her a good night.

Mia clicked on the lights Daniel had brought for the task, and with her headphones offering Jimmy's lessons learned from Margaritaville, she sat down on the tarp and started piecing together granite chunks.

She did just what the man in the song had done, learned from life's experience.

Exactly and in great detail, she had truly learned this time just what a broken heart felt like, and not just an inconvenienced heart as with the likes of Rory. She also learned how nonsensical it was to walk willingly, in sloppy armor, into the fray.

Okay, so the no-thinking part was failing already.

She sighed and worked on.

Eventually, frustrated with the puzzle of granite not fitting together, she got up and collected more of the pieces she thought looked promising and added them to the ones on the tarp.

Monique had tried to tell her it would matter if she got her heart broken, but noooo. She had to listen to her own faulty wisdom. She wondered how Monique knew in the first place. What had she missed when she was away from Bailey's Cove and Monique was still here? What emails had she made light of or glanced over and relegated to her overstuffed read-later file.

Mia was about to put all the pieces of the crypt aside and get more when she looked down at the markings on the collection in front of her. They made an odd sense. She had been trying her best to make a shield, a coat of arms out of the pieces, a pirate flag or symbol. No matter how she put them together, took them apart and put them together, the pieces did not seem to go together. If they did go together, they did not form a recognizable picture.

What was it Daniel had said? Sometimes anthropologists look for what's there, not for what they expect.

She examined the pattern again with the pieces laid out in the way the stone seemed to fit together, and then she pushed the pieces together in the circle of her hands.

The puzzle made sense.

"Oh, Daniel. It's a rose," she said aloud and checked again to make sure she wasn't making a mistake, making things up in her head as she was so good at it as of late. She was sure she saw what was there. A rose, about eight inches in diameter. It even had leaves and a stem. Colleen Rose Fletcher McClure. Liam Bailey. Rónán Uilliam McClure. How much circumstantial information would tip this thing over the top?

She sat with the shards on the tarp in front of her, holding as many of the pieces together as she could. From what she could tell, they were the lighter side of the stones, from the outside of the column, not the inside. Liam Bailey's crypt had an image of a rose on the outside.

Now she had enough information to convince the university—to take over the sight forever. They'd pay her some token amount so she could eat in her tent for a few weeks before she shambled off with rags for shoes and a cardboard box for a hat—alone, adrift.

She laughed at her pitiful self to the tune of James Taylor's "Fire and Rain." She always thought she'd see him, see Daniel, again.

A toe nudged her.

She slipped off her headphones and looked up to see Monique and Lenny standing next to her.

"So you're sitting in the middle of the night, in a deserted building, telling jokes to yourself, are you?"

Mia picked up the cardboard box she had brought in

case she wanted to take some pieces home with her and put the box on her head. "What do you think?"

Lenny looked quizzically at Monique. Her friend put her hand on the arm he had linked with hers. "Not to worry, honey. She is obviously in the middle of one of her woe-is-me scenarios. It will pass, it always does."

Then she turned to Mia as if Mia would not have heard what she said to Lenny. "It looks lovely, dear. I do think you could use a silk flower or two on it."

Mia shrugged and took off her "hat." Her friend could almost always hit her moods on the nose. "How was the movie and dinner?"

"They were the best time I've ever had." She looked up at Lenny who didn't even need to puff out his heavily muscled chest, but his grin spread across his entire face.

Mia motioned for Lenny to come cross the tarp to where she sat. He hunkered down beside her without hesitation. "Lenny, you made an outstanding choice, picking Monique, and I love you for it." She pulled him down until she could kiss him on the cheek.

"Are you all right?" he asked as he stayed hunkered down beside her.

"I am." *I think I am.* "I am. Now take my dear friend away and be very good to her."

"Go home, Mia." He made the words sound like a gentle request rather the command from a police officer.

Lenny stood and Monique took his arm again.

"I think I will go home," Mia agreed as she pushed up from the floor and nearly toppled.

They both grabbed for her and she put her hands out. "High heels. My feet are still very annoyed with me for walking around in spikes for three hours. I'm good. I'm good."

By the time they left, she was sure neither of them believed she was "good." To their credit, they understood she was best left to herself.

Mia gathered the crucial pieces of the puzzle into the box. Maybe she wasn't supposed to remove them from the site, but they weren't going to punish her for keeping the rose safe.

When she saw the taillights of Lenny's car pull away from the curb, she raised a fist of cheer. "Monique and Lenny together forever."

She was so happy for her friend she could cry, but she knew if she cried it would be tears for herself.

When she got home and finally put her head on the pillow, she sat right back up again.

She had it.

One more of the puzzle pieces fell into place. Liam Bailey built the column as a hiding place, as a treasure vault. Who would think to look for treasure in a closed-up wall in the middle of a hotel?

The hiding place was very clever. The wall was extra wide with a closet at either end. If no one ever measured the depth of the closets, no one would realize the wall was a few feet longer than the combined length of the closets. The closets themselves were most likely used for table linens, extra chairs and such, making the width of the dividing wall look like a feature and not a cover-up to conceal the vault.

The only mark he put on the vault was the rose in honor of his Colleen "Rose" Fletcher. Charlie's hammer had shattered the rose before anyone had paid attention to it.

Liam Bailey had unknowingly built his own crypt. Whoever stabbed him must have hefted him up and into the vault. All they had to do then was to seal off the opening, finish the wall and make sure no one had use of the building for a couple years—because they made sure they got the property from the courts—Archibald Fletcher.

*Shame on you,* she thought.

Some of Bailey's treasure must have made it possible for the pirate to become a land baron, and he didn't plan on needing the rest of the loot for a long time. He planned to put his and his Rose's security in the wall, a sort of 1818 safe-deposit box.

She fluffed her pillow and laid her head back down.

The next time she sat up, it was seven on the dot. Mia got up, dressed and ran her six-mile run. When she returned she put water on for oatmeal and showered. After a righteous bowl of the hot cereal, she thought of calling Dr. Donovan for an opinion, but Saturday morning was never a good time to call university offices. She'd call on Monday morning at about ten o'clock. Plenty of time for even the slowest Monday morning PhD to be up and on the job—to be able to make the decision whether or not he would be relinquishing control of her site anytime soon.

She thought of trying to piece the column together, but she decided she'd done enough damage to her cause. She wasn't going to help them hang a neon sign above her door announcing Pirate Within.

She settled on accruing ammunition for the fight. She took a tablet and started writing down her proposal list, the things she would request permission to do if they didn't let her back to do full renovations right away. Maybe tear the rest of the wall down. Surely she could clean the upstairs and basement. Have the finishing completed in the bathrooms and kitchen, have the back deck installed and the new windows. She walked around for an hour, thinking of every item she could. More to barter with if it came to that.

By the time she was ready to go drinking with her new pals, she had cleaned the windows in both Pirate's Roost and her house, finished laundry and pinned Monique down about how things had gone with Lenny after they had left her the night before—stupendous—and showered again.

The bar had around thirty-five patrons when she arrived on foot. All the tables in the place had been taken up with people having a good time and only two bar stools stood unoccupied. Of course, Saturday night would be much more crowded. She shouldn't have expected less.

The open bar stools were on the left side of the bottom of the U. She and Edwin Beaudin had sat in those two seats when she had come in the last time. She was disappointed to see Monique's grandfather missing, but she had said she was coming and here she was.

"Miss Parker," Harley Davies called to her from his usual seat at the end where the bar attached to the wall.

She came around to the end and smiled. "Hi, Mr. Davies."

"Hi, yerself," he said when she stopped near his perch. "Ed said he'd be here by seven-thirty, but that oth-ah seat is saved for you." Davies pointed across the bar to the two open seats.

"This is a nice crowd," she said, gesturing around the room.

"Unusual. That's what it is. I guess each one of us told somebody and here they all are. My wife's over there with Cindy Carmody and Helen Schroeder, oh, and Charlie Finn's wife, Mattie."

"And they all came because...?"

"Well, because you said you'd be here."

"That's great," she said, having absolutely no idea what she was calling great. "I'm looking forward to talking to everybody."

"You can start with the girls, I mean..." He dipped his big black beard toward his barrel chest. "The ladies."

"It's okay, Harley. I get so confused by what's politically correct. I can't even do Halloween right any more."

He grinned shyly at her. "Good to see you again, Miss Parker."

"See you later." She waved and moseyed over to the table of women Harley had mentioned.

They smiled up at her as a group and borrowed an empty chair from another table. Mia sat down and asked them how they were doing.

Cindy Carmody started off the conversation. "We're so glad you decided to come and talk with us."

"The mayor is out of town for another month and the town council never asked us before what we wanted for Bailey's Cove. It seems ever since the paper folded we don't get much in the way of news unless we go down to the bank and read the bulletin board," Millie Davies said as she smiled with her bright coral lipstick on her sixty-year-old lips. She looked great, ready to have a good time.

Motion caught her eye and Mia glanced up just in time to see a tall dark-haired man come in the door and turn away. Her heart nearly caught in her throat until she realized the man wasn't Daniel. Ah-yah, she was so not clear and free of thinking about him.

Helen Schroeder was speaking and belatedly Mia gave her her attention. "...getting too old to have all the kids and grandkids come and stay with us. Said just the other day, wouldn't it be nice if we had a nice motel? You know, one of those chains with an indoor pool and all."

"Do you think you can get something like that started, Ms. Parker?" Cindy Carmody asked. "I don't even have kids, but maybe us girls could have a girl's night, like they do in the movies."

"We could treat ourselves to dinner at a nice restaurant and go for a swim," Millie Davies put in.

"I guess we have all been dreaming about what kind of things our town could use." Mattie Finn spoke shyly but smiled brightly when every other woman nodded her head.

"I can't tell you ladies how thrilled I am to hear all your

enthusiasm about Bailey's Cove," Mia said, wishing people in the town had spoken up sooner.

When Pirate's Roost opened, she was more sure than she had ever been that the town would support her business.

Other tables called her over and indicated she should drag her chair. Her phone rang and she stopped the sound without looking at the screen.

By the time she had made the rounds to the small tables, an entire enterprise of businesses had been suggested for the town. A few, like a couple big-box stores, were out of the question, but a bed-and-breakfast, the motel with an indoor pool, a shop featuring Maine crafts and many others made sense for the necessary growth of the town. Someone even mentioned the starting of a town blog by Shamus she thought.

Mia was having a wonderfully distracting time. The only table she hadn't visited was the long one against the far wall, where eleven of Bailey's Cove's most experienced townsfolk sat. She got the feeling they had been talking about something private when she approached with her chair.

They welcomed her and regaled her with stories of Bailey's Cove. How their grandparents had stood, sat and laid on their bellies watching for submarines during World War II. The times their grandparents shared their catch with each other and bartered with the farmers when the depression took away so many of the jobs. Their parents had told them about such things as the first use of electricity followed by the first radio, washing machine and vacuum cleaner. And they talked about how they raced to launch their boats to safety during the biggest storms, and how each brought in the biggest catch ever. Or, as Sarah O'Brien had put in, had eight kids and lived to tell the tale.

"And we might have been the last spot in the country

to get internet, but even more unbelievable that Shamus here was the first to get in on it," the longtime boat captain Camden Flynn put in.

The table of people chuckled and jostled the elderly man.

"Maybe we should tell her about—" Shamus Willis started but Mr. Flynn stopped him.

"Oh, Shamus, she'd not be interested in our shuffleboard club," Mrs. O'Brien interjected as she gave what sounded like a forced chuckle.

Shamus looked chastised but also a bit rebellious. She wondered what he had truly meant to say.

When she next scanned the bar she noticed Edwin Beaudin had come in, and there was somebody on the stool next to him.

Monique turned when Mia tapped her on the shoulder.

"Hey," Monique said, "Miss Popular, about time you came and gave us some attention over here."

"I'm flabbergasted. I had no idea there were so many people so interested in the town's long-term future."

"We're quite progressive," Monique said, and her granddad chuckled and took a swig of his beer.

"Lenny must be working tonight."

"And you were nowhere to be found, so here I am." Monique smiled and offered Mia half her bar stool.

"When are you meeting him at Mandrel's?"

Monique checked the time and grinned. "In thirty-four minutes, with the usual caveat that urgent police calls take priority."

Edwin grinned when Monique spoke of Lenny.

"I see you approve." Mia put her arm around Mr. Beaudin's shoulder.

"Officer Gardner is a fine man, in spite of all the teasing the two of you did when you were growing up."

"Edwin, how are things going on O'Connell's boat?"

"It's good to be handling a boat again every day." He took a sip of his beer. "There's a problem, though."

Monique turned to him. "You didn't tell me about a problem."

"'Cause you're part of it."

"What did I do?" Monique put a hand to her throat and gave a sham look of dismay.

"Now you got three people, and the lobsta I got for you only has two claws."

Mia caught the joke and played along. "I suppose your granddaughter could watch Lenny and I eat the lobster. You must have some little old bottom-feeder you can bring for her."

Monique laughed. "I might eat the whole thing myself. Let those without fight over the bottom-feeder."

They spent time talking and Mr. Beaudin laughed more times than Mia guessed he'd laughed in a long time. It was almost as if his daughter were still alive and the four of them were together for a summer meal during one of Maine's long evenings when the sun didn't set until after 8:00 p.m.

When it was time for Monique to leave, Mia said good-bye to the groups of townsfolk, told them she'd like to meet with them again—to which they readily agreed and walked with Monique to her car.

"He's too happy," Monique said as they stepped out onto the sidewalk.

Mia couldn't help but glance up at Pirate's Roost. If the lights were on… Her heart sank low and miserable when there was only darkness.

"What's wrong with your granddad being happy?" she asked when she was sure she could speak without begging for a hug.

"It's like he's no longer struggling, like he has his mind made up and he's leaving."

"I'm here if he does, and we'll find a way for you to live with him being gone for a little while."

"What if he leaves forever? I can just see what he's thinking. If I have Lenny, he's off the hook. He can leave me behind."

"I don't have the answer. I wish I did." Mia tugged the curls back off her face. She had no answers for anything these days.

Monique hugged Mia and got in her car to seek refuge in Lenny's arms.

By the time Mia started back toward Blueberry Avenue, she was convinced Monique was worrying for nothing. Edwin Beaudin might go to visit his friend, but he'd return satisfied Bailey's Cove was the best place to live.

Besides, the recurring notion she got from talking to these people was that they were all watching her and Pirate's Roost, rooting for her, waiting for her success. Then they would not only support her, they would begin to support each other's dreams and wishes for the town's survival and growth.

As she started up Blueberry Avenue her phone chimed, telling her she had a new text message. She pulled it instinctively from her pocket.

The text was from the woman who would be her chef when Pirate's Roost was ready. "Please check your voice mail."

Mia did as asked.

"Mia, I am so sorry. I wanted to speak directly with you, but you didn't pick up my calls. I have taken another job."

Mia stopped cold. Her heart jerked with a painful thud. Her chef had quit. The chef she had searched for until she found the right fit for Pirate's Roost and the perfect woman to do the job.

Mia replayed the message because she had stopped listening after *taken another job*. "I'm moving to Cleveland next week. I just wanted to thank you for having faith in me and I'm sorry things didn't work out. I love Maine, but I'm going home."

Home. Pirates. Terrible secrets. Why were the enemies in her life so complicated?

The opening date of Pirate's Roost had been put off three times, and if she had to tell the contractor she wasn't ready, the fourth would be the death knell. She suddenly saw all the dreams and wishes of the people of Bailey's Cove crashing and burning.

She turned and hiked back down Blueberry Avenue.

Now, she did not care.

## CHAPTER SEVENTEEN

DAYLIGHT WOULD SOON break. Daniel left the lab and went for a run instead of calling Mia as he wanted to, as he always wanted to, even though when he did call he got voice mail. She had said it didn't matter if her heart got broken, but he had seen from the beginning the hurt in her lovely blue eyes. He had been kicking himself for three days since she had gotten in her SUV in that devastating black dress and had driven away from him because he had told her she must, that there was nothing for her with him.

She believed him this time, and all he had to do now was convince himself to follow what he knew to be the truth. No, that wasn't all. He planned to be there when Dr. Donovan arrived in his office this morning. If there was any reason to be found in this whole skeleton in the wall scenario, he'd make Dr. Donovan see it and let Mia get her crew back to work. She did not need to keep hearing the same excuses over and over.

He jogged down the steps and around the building to the path through the campus and to the forest beyond. If he ran hard enough, maybe he could forget for a while.

The early-morning breeze cooled him and the birds sang to him, but every step he took made him think of Mia Parker. The touch of her hand, the feel of utter completeness when he held her in his arms, listened to her sigh. The hope he felt was like nothing he had ever felt.

He pounded harder and faster on the running trail as he tried to think of his past, of the reasons he should not want

Mia to love him. Each time they came up, they faded and she took their place, her smile, her rare giggle.

He stopped on the bridge over the river that ran through campus. When he peered down at the water he saw life moving on as it should, but the river remained the same. He could move past the horrors, but they would never change. The reason they happened would not go away. Ever.

He started running again until he was so tired he wasn't sure he could go on, and then he turned around and ran back the way he had come, back to the lab where he could shower and meet with his students before he saw Dr. Donovan.

Daniel entered the lab, hair slicked back with water, dressed in jeans with no major worn parts, a button-down collared shirt and a newer version of his gray old beater sweater.

The three students were each sitting at a computer terminal calling out changes for something on the screen. "He's here," one of them said and the computer screen Daniel could see from the doorway went dark.

"Dr. MacCarey," Ms. Vock called.

"Good morning, everyone. Did you find anything more about the skeleton?"

"There's more damage to the bones, but just a broken wrist from childhood. He had already lost two of his teeth when he died," offered first Ms. Vock and then Mr. Miller.

He could see in the eagerness in their faces they were dying to show him the computer images.

"All right, what do you have?"

Mr. Miller sat down at a computer. "First we took into consideration his height and, based on the size of the crypt, the maximum girth, and based the possible fat deposits in his face on that."

"He's trying to say we think he was probably a bit on

the skinny side." Ms. Diaz brought up an image and turned the computer to face Daniel.

The stilted computer-generated image of the face looked homogenized enough to resemble a tenth of the male population on the planet, but the image most likely would have been recognizable to the people who knew him. The students had given the man modest whiskers and dark curling hair.

"And here he is dressed." The next image showed a standing figure dressed in early American fashion, waistcoat and all.

"Of course, for completeness we added, per the suggestion of Dr. Mitchell, the walking stick, a three-cornered hat and shoes with large buckles." Dr. Mitchell was one of the early-America experts Daniel had met at Mrs. Wahl's house for tea that day. "And a cravat. And the buttons on his clothing."

"We think he had twenty-six to twenty-eight buttons, none of which we found on the clothing. Nor, as Ms. Vock implied, did he have a cravat, which was the norm for the day and the manner of dress."

"He was wearing his socks, however."

"Did men really wear shirts that hung down to their knees that they tucked into their pants?" Mr. Miller squirmed as if trying to imagine tucking a knee-length shirt into his jeans.

"Did Dr. Mitchell tell you they did?" Daniel asked.

"Yes, sir."

"Then it's true. Know your sources and use them for as much authenticity as possible."

"Dr. Mitchell assures us the clothing was upper-class and was made in the early nineteenth century, probably before 1815."

"Where can you go now with the investigation?" Daniel asked, and got furrowed brows from two, but Ms. Vock stepped forward. "We can search for images from the era and the area and see if we can find out who the man is? Maybe his descendents would like to know what happened to him."

"You've all done well."

"Wait. Wait. We are so not finished, Dr. MacCarey," Ms. Diaz said as she made a few keystrokes.

Onto the screen popped the image of a pirate, a dressed-down Captain Jack Sparrow, sans beard beads and eye shadow.

He had to laugh.

"I need three copies of each of the images." What would Mia think? His gut twisted.

"We don't have any photo paper."

"Regular paper will be good enough for now. Make sure the pirate does not get on the internet and don't show it to anyone until I tell you it's all right."

That finished, he went to Dr. Donovan's office, turning the last corner as his department head arrived, coffee and keys in hand.

"Come in, Daniel."

Dr. Donovan hung his coat on the old wooden coat tree and took a seat behind his equally old desk with his coffee in hand.

"I have good news, Daniel. I'm taking the Owens to Bailey's Cove tomorrow. They are eager to see the site, sit in the ambience I believe is the way Mrs. Owen put it."

"As I've said before, there isn't much to see. The crypt is in pieces and the remains are here."

"You're sure there is nothing more to find at this site?"

"Not without knocking down walls or getting out a backhoe." There was a little more excitement in his boss's voice than Daniel liked. "It's all in my notes."

"I see you brought something." He reached a hand across the desk toward Daniel with his palm open.

"The students are searching for an identity," Daniel said as he handed over the first two photos, keeping the pirate to himself.

He did not add that his great-aunt Margaret had claimed a relationship to the pirate, because the identity of the man in the wall could only be hinted at with circumstantial evidence.

"Always good to have a face for these kinds of things."

"The students have dated the remains found in Bailey's Cove from very early in the town's history."

"Those three are an eager group. Will they be at the site tomorrow?"

"I'll see that they are there if at all possible. Sir, I'd like to suggest we allow Ms. Parker to do some demolition away from the sensitive areas at the site. Allowing the site to remain undeveloped is doing a disservice to the small community and the owner."

"I need to do what's best for the department and the university. Daniel, if you're too close to this, I can send you out on a dig. Elliot Smith can take over in Bailey's Cove. He'll never impress the donors like you can, but he's relentless."

"Ruthless." As Daniel said the one-word rebuttal he looked his boss in the eyes so there would be no mistaking what he meant.

Dr. Donovan rearranged the papers on his desk. "He does have that quality, but he makes a good stout club when such a thing is necessary."

A threat. Daniel knew this day would come. Having his boss take the gloves off was all right with him. Everybody had to move on and, above and in spite of all other things, Mia had done him a great service by agreeing to accompany him to the fund-raiser, helping his colleagues realize he was ready to face the rigors of academia.

And he would remember those scarlet lips.

"If your students could name this man, and the evidence is piling up in the direction of the town founder, the pirate, we could give the Owens some guidelines they can follow in making their proposal for the site."

Apparently the Owens had bought privileges, so to speak, with the size of their donation, and just as apparently Mia didn't have any. "I think you should reconsider letting Ms. Parker begin work on areas the Owens won't need to see."

"Absolutely not until after the Owens have had their visit. It's very important for Mrs. Owen to experience what she calls the raw site and she will put her nose into everything. You have left instructions that no one is to be tramping all over inside the building."

"That is currently being taken care of." Daniel thought of the prints from the athletic shoes on the stairs.

"What about work on the outside of the building?"

"It's only one more day. It can't really make that much difference." Daniel knew if it were a large developer, the attorneys would already be around the table. He was also sure Mia didn't have the funds for that kind of backup.

"Any delay makes a difference to her. She's on a tight schedule."

"The matter will be decided tomorrow." His boss started to stand, but thought better of it. "I need photos of the site."

"You'll have them as soon as I get back to my computer."

"Do you have something else for me?" Dr. Donovan pointed to the remaining papers in his hand.

Daniel only wondered for a moment what his boss's face would look like if he gave him the picture of the pirate.

Ecstasy at Mia's expense.

He rolled the images into a tube. "Copies, sir."

"I'd appreciate if you would help Ms. Parker remove anything from the site that might detract from the Owens' experience, and have her open the site tomorrow morning by nine. If she can be there, we'd all love to see her again."

"If that's all, sir."

Dr. Donovan pursed his lips. "It's not, Dr. MacCarey. There are two new finds, one in Guatemala and one here in Maine. This department will have a hand in the development of both of these. The one in Guatemala will go a long way in helping bring forensic truth to this more modern site. The one in Maine, much less prestigious but still important, is an early-civilization site. I will be assigning you to one of these and Mr. Elliott to the other." He moved his paperweight onto the stack of papers. "That's all. I'll see you tomorrow morning at 9:00 a.m. at the site in Bailey's Cove."

Daniel was down the hall on his way to his office before he let himself think about what Donovan had just done.

In essence he had used Elliott to make him toe the mark. If the site in Bailey's Cove was not handled to his liking, Daniel would get second pick of the assignments after a doctoral candidate.

The site in Guatemala would most likely be a mass grave site, and Dr. Donovan knew Daniel's career mission statement, *to find out where humans came from so we can aim at a better future,* dovetailed with this kind of site. What Dr. Donovan didn't know is that Daniel would pick through garbage in Bangor rather than harm Mia any more than he already had.

He owed Dr. Donovan a lot, but the man was using up chits rapidly, and most of them at Mia's expense.

When he got back to the lab, he found the students setting up another meeting with Eleanor Wahl to try to put a name to the face. He gave the three information on how to get to the site and suggested they all show up by 9:00 a.m. and learn a bit about the other side of academia, the politics of money.

In his car on the way to who-the-hell-knows he called Mia…again. He couldn't stop the horde from descending, but he could warn her. She hadn't answered since she drove away on Friday.

One unanswered ring followed the next. One more ring and he'd get her voice mail…again. This time he'd just drive down—

"Hello, Daniel."

He inhaled a sharp breath. "Mia, thanks for answering."

An apology sprang to mind, but saying he was sorry would mean he somehow thought anything could change.

"Please, tell me what you want."

"I'm calling to warn you Dr. Donovan is sponsoring a site visit. At nine o'clock the Owens are coming, as well as the three students I have working on the remains. Apparently Mrs. Owen likes to sit with the site."

"Are you coming?" she asked.

He couldn't tell by her tone what she wanted.

"I thought I would come down early tomorrow morning."

"To make sure I haven't built a restaurant in place of a pirate's tomb?"

He smiled. She could have said the words with spite, and would have been justified, but her words teased.

"Something like that. I'll see you at eight."

MIA OPENED THE DOOR to Pirate's Roost before eight o'clock the next morning and returned the pieces of the rose, carefully arranged so they looked like nothing until she pushed them together in the circle of her hands.

Today she had dressed up. In honor of the rose, she wore her pink button-front pullover shirt with a pink cardigan, and jeans, of course.

She loved the rose and what the beloved flower meant

in this case. There was some peace in knowing how much Liam Bailey loved Colleen Fletcher.

When a car door slammed, she stood to see Daniel coming to the door. By his clothing, she knew Professor Daniel was here, and he carried a brown paper bag and a tray with two coffees.

He smiled when he saw her and kissed her cheek when he stopped at her side. "Hello, Mia. You look lovely."

"Hello, Daniel." She wasn't sure what to say to him. Her mind just went blank where seeing him used to fire her imagination.

"I thought I'd come with breakfast."

"I've already… Wait, no, I haven't eaten. That would be nice."

He held up the bag. "Mandrel's oatmeal pancakes with maple syrup."

"My favorite." She took a coffee when he held the tray out to her.

"I had help. Priscilla at Mandrel's said you order these almost every time you come in for breakfast or lunch or dinner."

She let a smile spread across her lips. She couldn't hate him no matter how many times her heart broke over him. He was so convinced that he was doing the right thing that she would be the last person to fault him for integrity.

They sat on the floor in the sunshine and ate pancakes in a friendly silence. Because she didn't hate him didn't mean she knew what to say for conversation. Random things like "kiss me you fool," "take me I'm yours" and "you're such a jerk" all occurred to her, but none of them seemed quite right.

When they finished, and there was still time before the rest arrived, she took his hand. "Come on. I have something to show you."

She led him to the other side of the dividing wall.

There shouldn't even be an *other* side. Yesterday afternoon Markham said he could hold the building supplies for another week, but still left the impression that fitting her in next week or even the one after that was futile.

Rufus and Charlie had started new jobs yesterday. She had no idea how she'd get the building prepped and ready, as was her part of the contract, without her workers.

The crushing feeling of failure pressed in on her from all sides, and if she lost her battle so did the residents of Bailey's Cove.

Daniel tugged on her hand until she faced him. "Are you sure you're all right?"

She gave one of those little, not-quite laughs. "I'm not sure I know what *all right* feels like anymore."

Then she quickly held up a hand. "No, please, I was just thinking logistics again. That always gives me sort of a blank expression."

When she dropped to sit on the tarp, he sat beside her and watched as she gathered the pieces of stone together in her hands.

"A rose," he said with the same wonder she had felt when she first figured it out.

"This might be the closest we get to the missing link."

"Let me hear it. Let me hear your theory."

She took a few seconds to put her thoughts in order. "The pirate Liam Rónán Bailey falls in love with his Rose, Colleen Rose Fletcher. He has a beautiful blue topaz ring, part of his pirate treasure, retrofitted with his coat of arms and gives it to his Rose—which she, of course, keeps in a velvet purse, they called little pouches purses in those days, and out of Daddy's sight. He also plans on staying in South Harbor, now Bailey's Cove, forever, and builds a granite vault for his treasure, in the wall of the Sea Rose Inn—soon to be Pirate's Roost. He marks the vault with a rose, a sign of his everlasting love for Colleen Rose. He also builds a mansion on Sea Crest Hill for them to live in. Colleen's father disapproved of the relationship and put Bailey in the wall—convenient, since Bailey already had it built. A pregnant Colleen marries Mr. McClure. She insists her father install her and her new husband in the home she planned to live in with Bailey. The child of the red-haired man and blond-haired woman has very dark hair and is born six months after the marriage. Two hundred years later, Charlie Pinion comes along with the big hammer and shatters the rose before anyone gets a good look at it—until now. Daniel MacCarey, that was your ancestor in my wall. You are related to a pirate."

She let go and the rose fell into disarray.

At first he didn't say anything, just looked as though he was considering the matter. Then he smiled at her, an easy smile. The kind she just wanted to taste. *No. Think of something else.*

"The brown color, what do you suppose that is?" she asked.

"We'll analyze it, the rose is probably an ink or dye that changed color over time."

The front door opened and they got up from the tarp. Daniel went out to the front room and Mia put the rose shards back in the box and followed. The three that walked in gawking around and looking a bit wide-eyed had to be the students.

"Dr. MacCarey, this is an awesome old building."

Before Daniel could make any introductions, four middle-aged women all dressed in flowing, flowered clothing stepped through the open door.

"Who—"

Daniel leaned down and said close to her ear, "They're with me."

The warm whisper of his breath made her want to turn and kiss him. *No and no.*

"Welcome, everyone." Clearly these people had arrived just in time to save her and she smiled brightly at them. "Hello, I'm Mia Parker. I'd like to welcome all of you to the future home of my restaurant, Pirate's Roost."

She stepped up to the tallest, most stately looking of the women of the quartet. "You must be Eleanor Wahl," she said and reached out a hand to the woman.

The woman grasped her hand and shook firmly. "Our Daniel has told me so very little about you. The least he could have said is how pretty you are."

Mia smiled in Daniel's direction and then back at Mrs. Wahl. "He speaks very highly of you, Mrs. Wahl."

By the time everyone had been introduced, the Owens entered, and it was such an entry; big smiles, gracious greetings, friendly introductions.

"Mrs. Owen, you look ready to begin." Mrs. Owen had told Mia she was an amateur archeologist and was looking forward to getting a look at the site where the bones had been found. Mia held a hand out and let the women precede her to the back room. The woman was even dressed for the role in her many-pocketed olive-green pants and a delicate tool belt. "I thought you might want to get in here before the crowd invades."

"You are so right. Thank you, Mia. My husband gets bored sometimes, so I like to move quickly. If you could keep them at bay for a bit I'd appreciate it. I want to sit with the site for a moment or two in peace."

"Gladly, and as you can see, the site is pretty self explanatory," Mia said, and left Mrs. Owen to "sit" with the rubble.

When Mia returned to the other room, Dr. Donovan had still not joined the group. Those who had arrived smiled at her as a group. She clasped her hands together smiling back hard and wishing they would all go away. "I hear

Dr. MacCarey has you women to thank for your historical expertise."

"We are sorry we haven't found any men resembling the computer image of the man," Mrs. Wahl offered.

Mia paused, one finger in the air. "Could you hold that thought for just a moment."

Then she turned to Daniel with her finger still up. "Computer image, Dr. MacCarey, of the man from my wall?"

"I am remiss, Ms. Parker," he said to Mia and then turned to the young man. "Mr. Miller, if you would retrieve the envelope from the front seat of my car, I would appreciate it."

Miller was gone and back in a flash. He handed the envelope to Daniel who handed it to Mia. She started opening it and stopped.

"You have all seen these?" she asked as she looked around. When they each gave an affirmative, including Mr. Owen, she continued. "If you'll all excuse me, I'm going to go outside and have a moment with these. If you all could stay in this room until Dr. Donovan gets here…"

They all nodded and Mr. Miller stopped his edging toward the other room.

She took the envelope and departed.

Outside in the cool morning air, she sat on the bench to the right of the door and held the unopened envelope as she gazed down toward the sunny waterfront. Once she took the photos out, she'd look into the face of the man who died because he loved too much. She would also see the face of the man who had given her trouble.

Had her life changed so completely in two weeks? Had Pirate's Roost gone from a possibility to an extreme challenge in the blink of an eye or the sweep of a hammer? Had she fallen in love, impossible love, in such a short time?

"Would you like some company?"

She moved over and Daniel sat down beside her. He took the envelope she held up to him and slid out the photos.

She hesitated but then took the top two photos he offered to her and held one in each hand.

He had dark hair in the reconstruction, dark eyes and a narrow face. "Look at him, all dressed up. He looks like a stranger. I guess I expected to recognize him or something."

"Maybe you will recognize this one."

He handed her a picture of Liam Bailey as a pirate.

"Ha. No wonder he chose such a nefarious occupation."

"Why is that?"

"He's so much better-looking as a pirate."

She put the photo down on her lap and turned to study Daniel's face. Then she held the picture up to his face. "Nope, I don't see the resemblance, but maybe if you got yourself up in pirate gear…"

"Check with me next Halloween."

He held up one more photo.

"The coat of arms from Great-Aunt Margaret's genealogy book," she said as she took the photo to examine it more closely.

"I thought you might want a copy. You can tack it up on the wall next to the sign Pirate's Bones Found Here."

"Nope. I'm going to build a huge shrine with all sorts of seashell and crystal roses and charge admission."

"I'd pay."

"You might, but on second thought, I don't think I'd like to take all that space away from my diners." If she ever had diners. She put the copies in the envelope and held it out to him.

"Those copies are yours. I haven't shown the pirate to Dr. Donovan as there is no hard proof of the man's identity."

"Okay. Thanks for keeping me company while I looked at them. I wasn't sure what I'd feel."

"And what do you feel?"

"Sad for Colleen and Liam. Mad at Archibald Fletcher. And I want so damned badly to be angry with you."

He nudged her shoulder with his. "I've spent too much of my recent past being angry. I thought I had it all under control, but when Aunt Margaret died I got angry all over again. Anger feels like a drug. No matter how much it seems to feel right at the time, it sucks the life out of me. I think I have you to thank for all that starting to go away."

"Me?" She was not going to ask what she had done. She remembered all of what she had done with him. She remembered the touch, the feel, the sound and smell of him, the feelings of rapture, the sweep of his hand on her cheek when he knew she was troubled.

"Look at you, Mia. You're not mad at me and you could be."

"It might still happen."

Dr. Donovan pulled up right then and climbed out of his overly large SUV.

Mia looked at Daniel and he shrugged.

"Fine day it is, you two. Shall we go in?" He held his arms wide and let them precede him.

"Mr. Owen, I'm glad you could make it, I take it Mrs. Owen is in the other room." Mr. Owen nodded.

"Mrs. Wahl, how nice to see you and your lovely friends," Dr. Donovan continued and then moved on to the students and greeted them as a group.

The front door burst open, drawing all eyes.

"You people need to show more respect. It's enough you have desecrated the grave of my ancestor."

Heather Loch stepped inside, her white hair flying and her purples clashing.

# CHAPTER EIGHTEEN

EVERYONE STOOD STUNNED, except Mrs. Owen, who came from the back room with her camera in her hand. She just looked puzzled and then snapped a photo.

"Do you have to turn his resting place into a circus before he's even put to rest again?" Heather Loch asked, the fierceness of her feelings etched across her face.

"Madam, I'm sure I don't know what you are talking about." Dr. Donovan started toward Heather as he spoke and she stopped and glanced around her. "But I'm certain you're trespassing."

The closer Dr. Donovan got to her, the more she seemed to cringe, but she held her ground.

Daniel stepped in and reached out a hand to her. "Ms. Loch, it's good to see you again."

She almost flew backward to avoid shaking hands. The small faded blue velvet pouch with a tattered ribbon she had been clutching in her hand fell to the floor.

As it lay there looking oh-so-similar to a faded lavender pouch, Mia snapped her gaze to Daniel whose face held a smile of understanding.

Before anyone could retrieve the small bag for her, she snatched it up and brandished it at them all.

"These are proof."

"Ms. Loch," Daniel tried again and she stepped away.

"Heather, come outside with me for a minute." Then he leaned toward her and spoke so only she could hear.

She nodded and went back out the door with Daniel fol-

lowing. Everyone seemed to gape as Daniel and Heather
Loch sat down on the bench to the left of the door.

"Well, now that's over, we can all get back to business."
Dr. Donovan addressed the room. "Mr. and Mrs. Owen,
tell me what you need."

Mia watched Daniel and Heather Loch speaking ani-
matedly out on the bench.

"I'd like to tour the rest of the building," Mrs. Owns
replied.

"Would one of you students go with Mr. and Mrs. Owen
and help them with anything they need."

Heather got up and started to walk away. Daniel called
to her and she turned. Mia couldn't hear what they were
saying, but then Daniel held his faded lavender pouch out
toward her.

"The other two of you can take a look at the site and tell
me if there is anything else you think needs to be done."

He turned to the four women. "Ladies, what can I do to
make your visit to our site more enjoyable?"

Mia listened as Dr. Donovan took over her world and
watched as Daniel traded his pouch for the bag Ms. Loch
had dropped on the floor. Then each examined the other's bag.

That was enough for Mia and she was headed out the
door. Undoubtedly more fun was going on out in the street
and she didn't much like the dog and pony show inside.

When Heather looked up and saw Mia approaching, she
shoved Daniel's bag at him, holding out her hand for hers.

He handed her bag back, but did not reclaim his own.
"She's all right, Heather."

Heather clutched her bag to her chest.

"Hi, Ms. Loch," Mia said. "I can't tell you how good
it is to see you."

Heather looked at Daniel.

"What's going on in there?" Daniel asked with a nod toward the building.

"Mayhem and some sort of dictatorship."

Heather grinned.

"See? Just like I told you, Heather," Daniel said.

"Have the two of you been talking about me?"

"But she has a really big ego. Thinks people are talking about her all the time."

They started slowly down the block to the vacant store that used to sell confections. Mia missed that store, and they sat on the bench in front, Daniel between the two women.

"You really ought to look inside my bag, Heather. If what you say is true, then what's in this bag will knock your socks off."

"Knock my socks off, huh?"

"At least down around your ankles."

She laughed a slow chuckle, but handed her bag back to Daniel, then watched while Daniel checked out the contents.

He poured a bunch of buttons out onto the palm of his hand. The buttons were tarnished brass with the thread and clumps of the cloth still clinging to them, as if they had been crudely cut from the clothing. Daniel counted buttons and Mia almost tore the envelope trying to get at the picture of the nineteenth-century man.

"Twenty-six," Daniel said with awe in his voice.

Heather nodded. "The Lochs have had those buttons for many, many generations. They were from his clothing. Ma McClure passed them down through the females of the line and that's how they came to me."

"There looks to be twenty-six buttons on this man's coat and waistcoat," Mia said as she studied the photos.

"Be that he?" Heather put a hand over her heart. With her other hand, she took the stack of pictures Mia offered.

She scrutinized each one. "Yes. Yes. I can see it."

Mia wondered what she saw.

When Heather came to the picture of the flag she leaped up and waved the picture of the coat of arms.

"Where did you get this? You have no right to this."

She shoved Daniel's pouch back at him and grabbed the bag with the buttons and took off down the street with the photos clutched in her hand.

"Okay, that was odd."

"Heather, wait," Daniel called after her but she marched on.

"Why do you suppose she got so angry over the photo of the coat of arms?" Mia asked.

"I would guess she has one like it. For so long people have been ignoring or denying the claims of the Lochs." He turned toward Mia with an eager smile.

"What? You have that fanatical anthropologist look."

He held up his fist, turned his hand over and opened his fingers. A button sat perched on the palm of his hand.

"You stole one of her buttons?"

"I borrowed it, so I'm sure she'll at least open the door when I follow her to the museum."

"Do you want me to go with you?" she asked.

"If you would police the crowd in your building. I think I can get Heather to let me borrow the button."

"She likes you Daniel." She touched his cheek. "We all like you."

Back inside the building they were all gone, or it seemed that way until she heard footsteps and voices upstairs, and after a minute, downstairs.

The four women came down from upstairs laughing.

"This is such a great adventure, Ms. Parker," one of the women said. "We've each picked out our rooms, so we hope you get the bed-and-breakfast up and running quickly."

Dr. Donovan returned just then with the Owens and the students in tow.

He pulled Mia aside. "Dr. MacCarey seems to be right about there being nothing more here to explore, but it would be a shame to have the remodeling process destroy anything more. I'm sure you understand that there needs to be a further investigation of the whole building."

"There is no treasure here, Dr. Donovan."

He didn't do a fake shocked look very well. "The history of Maine's early days may be at stake here."

"My livelihood is already at stake. I need to get work restarted now."

"Soon. I think we can get things restarted here soon."

"Soon was last week, Dr. Donovan, and a week more is disastrous for this project."

"Ms. Parker. I have the authority of the state to take this building away from you if I see fit."

"Excuse me, Dr. Donovan." Mrs. Owen put a hand on Dr. Donovan's arm. "My husband and I need to leave, but we'd like to speak with you first."

"I'll be right with you. Ms. Parker, it was nice to see you again," Dr. Donovan said.

With that, he turned and followed the Owens outside. Shortly after, the rest of the crowd filed out. The students jumped into the short dark-haired student's beater of a car and chuffed off down the street.

Alone once again, Mia took a seat outside on the bench with a view of the harbor. Birds flew overhead, sunlight sparkled off the water, children laughed in the park just up the street and cars passed by her. No matter what happened to her, where she ended up, she would never forget the view of life from this old bench.

Last night she had gone over every possible source of money available to her. Even if she drained her retirement account to the bottom and charged every credit card to the max, she couldn't hold off the bill collectors for long.

The only thing left to do was to get the prep work done by Monday morning so Markham could get his people there.

If the university wanted to take her to court, the worst that could happen was they would force her into bankruptcy sooner. A nice quiet jail cell was starting to sound good to her right now.

She pulled her phone from her pocket and Mr. Markham himself answered. "Mia Parker here. You can start work on Pirate's Roost on Monday."

When she pocketed her phone, she gulped down a couple of sharp breaths. She knew she was truly skating close to the edge now and when she saw Daniel coming back up the street, she stood to meet him.

He could not be a part of this. He'd lose everything he'd worked so hard to hold on to the past several years.

"How'd it go?" she asked.

Daniel pulled the small plastic bag with the buttons from his pocket. "I was going to give this to the students, but I see they're gone."

"What did you say to Heather to get her to go outside with you?"

"I told her I believed her and that I might be able to prove it."

"Daniel, that was so nice of you. I doubt anyone has ever given her that kind of validation."

"She's, as you said, an interesting lady, and she follows a strict set of her own rules."

A thought occurred to Mia. "You let her keep the ring as collateral."

"She was only going to go so far with trusting me."

"She still would not have entrusted those with just anyone. She believes you, too. Does she know you could be her cousin?"

"We'd had enough sharing for one day."

"Could you prove that with DNA analysis? Or does that come under the 'would I, could I, should I' conundrum?"

He stared into her eyes. She was sure the question had come and gone without consideration.

She knew she should at least step away, but she could not. She wanted to stand there forever, bask in his warmth, his scent, crave his touch. "You have to leave Bailey's Cove, now."

"I do?" He felt it, too. "I thought I'd read more of the records."

"I finished them. And I found a couple of fascinating things. Archibald Fletcher bought the doors for the church, and they were installed just before the baptism of his first grandson. My guess, a bribe to the priest. The chief said to thank you for your help."

He gave her a speculative look. "I also planned to have the students collect the granite pieces, if you're finished with them."

"I am."

"I'll send them back and I'll get more pictures for you. Heather insisted on keeping the ones I brought for you."

"And I'll keep you posted on how things are going if you like."

"I'd like that," he agreed easily.

He leaned in and kissed her on the mouth, a sweet lingering kiss, a reluctant goodbye kiss, an "I'm going away forever" kiss.

She forced her hands to stay at her sides. If she put her arms around his neck, it would be all over for her heart.

He turned and walked toward his car.

"Goodbye," she whispered into the salty breeze. She would most likely see him again, Dr. Donovan would most likely be arranging that, but she expected to feel less and less for him as time passed. Distance in this case would let the heart settle into a solid routine of beating without breaking.

She thought she heard the little angel on her shoulder sputter out, "Yeah, right."

DANIEL FOUND THE STUDENTS back in the lab, each on a computer writing a collaborative report on the site visit while it was still fresh in their minds.

"Today or tomorrow, you need to go back to Bailey's Cove and collect the granite shards." He reminded them that these were not pieces of rock but delicate gems and should be treated as such. "And take another set of the four photos."

They all stood. "Yes, sir."

Then he took the buttons from his pocket. "See what you can do with these."

They crowded around.

"Are those the buttons missing from the clothing?"

"You tell me."

He placed the bag of buttons on the counter and left the three of them giddy with the prospect of solving more mysteries.

He wanted to be that eager about something again, he thought as he bypassed his office and headed straight to his condo.

When he had the information about the buttons, he would tell Mia that Heather Loch had shown him a flag with the same image. A flag she said Liam Bailey flew on his ship.

He didn't realize why he had gone to his condo until he found himself sitting on the balcony in the sun, drinking orange juice and thinking of Mia Parker.

MIA CHIPPED AWAY at more of the plaster. To work again felt so good. As soon as Daniel had left, she went home, dressed in her old clothes and came back to restart the demo. The contractor would arrive with his crew on Monday and expected to build out and finish the Roost. It had all seemed so easy when she had three people to help her.

Who was she kidding? It had never been easy.

The day of the crypt discovery, the demo had been about twenty-five percent completed. The wall would be another twenty percent.

The sun had slid down, indicating it was past noon when she looked around behind her. She had been working for several hours. The ladder abandoned outside the building by the intruders had come in handy as Charlie and Rufus had taken theirs back to use on their new jobs.

The Dumpster that had sat out back collecting nothing now had a modest layer of old wallpaper with plaster and some of the lath still stuck to it. Modern insulation mixed with a variety of degraded materials. Mia did not care to think about the abandoned mouse nest on the bottom.

Two fishermen from the bar, Whiss Carmody and Bill Schroeder, moseyed in after work. Before sending them away, she had contemplated asking them for help, but being here meant she was technically breaking the law. She couldn't let anyone help and thereby break the law for her sake.

As she went out to dump more debris, she realized the sun had set. She supposed she should be hungry, but she had eaten an apple and a yogurt for lunch. That should be good enough for a while longer.

When her phone rang again, she ignored it, three times. She thought she should be tired, but the methodical prying and chipping, pulling of nails and pulling down insulation had almost gotten easy, until as some point she sat down on her bucket and she could not get up.

She rested for a while, stripped her gloves off and pulled her phone from her pocket.

She sighed. 1:30 a.m. Wednesday. Five more days to get this done. She could do it. She had to do it.

## *CHAPTER NINETEEN*

THE SOUND OF her alarm at six o'clock was fully distressing since rolling over and reaching the bedside table seemed out of the realm of possibility.

"Shut up. Shut up." Clocks did not listen, at least not the one she had. She swung her feet over the edge of the bed and reached for the off button.

Two toaster tarts today, and a yogurt. She'd need her energy. She made a peanut butter sandwich and took it with her.

As she went flying out her door she ran smack into Monique.

"Don't you even think about it. You don't answer my phone calls, but you'll have to knock me to the ground to get around me."

Mia smiled at her friend. "What's on your mind so early?"

"Lenny."

There was a topic Mia didn't think she should push aside. "Come on in."

Monique sat at the counter while Mia made a cup of tea for each of them. When they were sitting side by side and her friend had said nothing, just sat there and looked sad, Mia asked, "Are you going to tell me what's up, or do I have to guess? Oh, wait. I'll guess. You and Lenny had sex and he disappointed you terribly. Or you found out that if you got married his mother was moving in. Or... Well, I give up."

"He said he loved me."

Joy and utter heartbreak swamped Mia at the same time. "And that's not wonderful?"

"I thought when a guy told me he loved me, fireworks should go off and the world should suddenly seem brighter."

"Does that mean you don't love him?"

"I do. That's the hard part. I do. But when he told me it felt like good old memories and my favorite dessert. No fireworks."

"Okay." Mia sipped her tea.

"Don't you see? He's better than my favorite dessert."

"But he's also old memories. You have so many memories of Lenny. Well, tell me what happened."

"It was after work last night. He said he'd loved me forever, he just didn't want to push me."

"Points in Lenny's favor, you have to admit. Wait. All those times we thought he was giving us both the eye, it was only you?"

"Sorry, pal, you're not as attractive as you think."

Mia laughed. "So was it romantic at least?"

"Oh, as romantic as I could ever want it to be. We watched the moon come up over the ocean. He brought flowers and this."

Monique put out her arm. Today her wrist was adorned with a sapphire tennis bracelet, Monique's birthstone.

"The dog. How could he?"

"Don't tease me. I know. I know."

"Are you afraid?"

"Of Lenny? No, never."

"He won't leave you."

"It's not... Maybe it is. Oh, Mia. What should I do?"

Mia put her arm around her friend. "Give it some time. If in say, fifteen, twenty years he's still hanging in there, maybe you should demand fireworks."

"He's waiting to take me to breakfast. Do you want to go with us?"

"I'm going to work."

"What are you doing?"

"I'm doing demo at Pirate's Roost."

"That's great. They gave you an all-clear?"

"Not exactly. I'm just doing it because it has to be done."

"Does Daniel know?"

"No way. I couldn't get him into trouble. It's just me."

"By yourself?" Monique gave her an exaggerated bug-eyed look.

"I don't feel right about asking folks to help me. I'm not destroying anything of substance unless a mouse nest counts."

"Won't *you* get into trouble?"

"If I find anything that has any value, I'll stop or work around it. So far all I've found is old building materials and crud."

"You can't do all that by yourself. You have both the dining room areas, the kitchen, the hallway between the bathrooms and the kitchen."

"I have one of the walls in the dining room almost completely finished. The one behind where the counter will be."

"What about a chef? Any luck on hiring a new one?"

"Pfffff."

"Translated?"

"I don't even like to go there. I have a couple leads from the chef who quit. Otherwise I have feelers out at culinary schools."

"Do you still believe?"

"I still believe Pirate's Roost will be the best."

"Sweetie, do you still believe in love?"

"I liked talking chefs better."

"Rumor has it he was here yesterday with a whole group and you got a good long goodbye kiss."

"That's exactly what it was."

"The M&Ms are being trampled by love. I believe. I believe." Monique slugged down the rest of her tea, hugged Mia. "Don't kill yourself working." She dashed out the door.

Did she still believe? Of course she did. She believed for Monique and Lenny.

By the time she arrived at Pirate's Roost, it was an hour later than she had planned. *Nothing for it, just get to work.*

Before she could climb the ladder Chief Montcalm came to the door. She let him in. The teens Thompson and O'Connell followed him looking wholly contrite.

The chief stood with his hands together behind his back and looked at the two young men. Mia had an idea of what must be coming and she had to press her lips together to keep from smiling.

They stepped up to her and looked her reluctantly in the eyes. She shifted her gaze between them. "Yes, gentlemen?"

"I'm sorry for sneaking into your place without permission." First one said it and then the other. Chief Montcalm had coached them well. "I'd like to know if I can come after school and help you," they chorused and she was impressed.

"I would appreciate your help. I'll see the two of you as soon as you can get here." Maybe she could find something for them to do that wouldn't seem like breaking the law. They could be her luggers.

"Get to school now," Chief Montcalm said firmly.

They walked politely from the building and then ran for all they were worth.

"Thank you, Chief."

"I'm sorry to tell you, I do not believe those boys destroyed the crypt."

"That's interesting."

"We have a lead we are working on."

"Thank you and all the police department for putting a modicum of fear and respect in that pair."

He tipped his hat to her. "Have a good day, Mia."

*Mia.* She smiled. "You too, Chief."

Alone, Mia put on her gloves and picked up her tools. Halfway up the ladder and she realized this was going to be a long day.

The students from the university came and collected every scrap and tiny chunk of the granite. They left her a batch of shiny photos, including copies of Colleen McClure and Princess Charlotte.

Mia's muscles had finally loosened up by the time the teens arrived after school. They came with a bag of corn chips and three candy bars. The three of them sat, semi-hiding in case the chief happened by, on the floor in the back room and enjoyed the bribe.

"You know I'm keeping your dad's ladder—" She pointed back and forth between the two of them until Mickey raised a sheepish hand. "Until I'm completely finished with it."

After all the munching Mia hopped up. "Sorry, guys, I still gotta put you to work. You can start by gathering up those piles of plaster and lath and getting it all in the Dumpster, and watch out for the top step. It's weird, deeper than a step should be."

They did a good job and after two hours of hard work she let them go home to do their homework. Who knew? It could happen.

At least she had gotten food out of the deal, and the front wall of the room had been stripped and carted to the Dumpster.

The sun had been down for a while and she had the lights on when Monique showed up dressed in jeans and a sweatshirt.

"Where can I help you?"

"Thanks for coming. Do you want your shoulders to ache or your calves?"

"Such great choices." Monique put her finger to her chin. "I'll take calves."

Mia pointed up the ladder. "There doesn't seem to be a reliable method that works for eighty-year-old building materials. The pry bar seems to make it shatter most of the time, but when it works, it works great."

Monique took the tools and climbed. She teetered once and Mia dropped two buckets of debris to catch her, but it wasn't necessary.

"And I got it, be careful."

Mia reloaded the buckets. "And be careful."

They worked for a half hour before Monique decided she could no longer safely climb the ladder. "I'll carry stuff for a while."

"Are you sure? You worked all day, too," Mia said, feeling guilty that her friend was taking on her burden.

"I'm good. I don't meet Lenny until he gets off work tonight."

Mia picked a bit of stuff out of Monique's hair. "You'll want to leave time for a shower."

"That still gives me an hour."

She gamely grabbed a couple of the heavy buckets and headed out to the Dumpster. Belatedly Mia realized Monique didn't know about the old wooden steps.

"Monique," she called just in time to see her friend's head disappear from sight.

"Monique." She ran across the room and out the door. Monique was on the ground and she was not moving. "Oh, my God, please be all right, Monique."

Mia pulled out her phone and dropped to the cold ground beside Monique and dialed 911. When the dispatcher answered she told the woman who she was, what happened and where. "And please send Officer Gardner. It's Monique."

"They're on the way, honey. Now you stay on the line and tell me how she's doing."

She put her phone down and took her shirt off to cover her friend against the chilly wind. "Monique, sweetie, please wake up."

She should have never let her friend help. She shouldn't expect anyone to bail her out. These were her choices.

"You still there, Mia?" the dispatcher called over the speaker of Mia's phone.

"I'm here. She's still unconscious."

"Try to keep her warm."

She put her mouth close to Monique's ear and her arm around her chest. "I'm here, sweetie. I won't leave you. I'm here."

The paramedics showed up first and it took a couple of long minutes for them to come to the back of the building. "Back here," Mia kept shouting. "Back here."

Two paramedics knelt beside Monique and Mia had to move away to let them work. A third tried to take Mia inside, but she refused.

The woman wrapped a blanket around Mia. "I need to ask you some questions, and it would be better for your friend if your teeth weren't chattering so much and you could tell me what happened."

Mia nodded and went inside with the woman, but she stayed near the window so she could see. They had put a collar around Monique's neck and applied a bandage to her head.

"Is she bleeding? I didn't see any blood." When they

rolled her friend to the side, Mia could see a darkened spot on the ground where the back of her head had rested.

Mia didn't have much to tell, so the interview was over before they were ready to convey Monique to the clinic out on the edge of town near the police station.

Mia gave back her blanket and they left her alone and the lights and sirens went screaming down the street. The commotion brought the patrons of the bar out onto the curb. Harley trundled over to her where she stood on the stoop watching.

"Who'd they take away?"

"Is Edwin Beaudin in there tonight?"

"He's gone. Got in his car and left town today."

"That's not possible. His granddaughter didn't tell me and if she didn't tell me then... Oh no, she doesn't know."

"That her in the ambulance? She hurt bad?"

She shook her head. "I mean, yes, it's her, but I don't know if she's hurt bad. What did Edwin say? How long will he be gone?"

"Said he was going to call Monique when he got there. Didn't want her to try to talk him out of going."

"Where's there, Harley? Where did he go?"

"All the way to Florida if you can believe it. Said he had a friend from the army there who's been asking him to come down."

"But what about Jim O'Connell's boat?"

"They're back. It's twins." Harley grinned.

"Oh, heaven help all of them." She patted Harley's arm. "I'll tell Monique you asked after her. I gotta go."

The first person she saw when she arrived at the clinic was Officer Gardner. His girlfriend was hurt on her watch and it was her fault. She didn't even know what she would say to him.

He met her at the door and pulled her outside away

from the waiting room full of people and the Emergency
Department staff.

"I'm sorry, Lenny. I'm so sorry. All my fault." She
started to shiver again and it was hard to talk.

Lenny took his jacket off and put it around her shoulders.

"She's all right. She woke up in the ambulance. By the
time she got here, they said she was fine except she'll need
a few stitches."

She looked up at him.

"Shouldn't you be in there with her?"

"She sent me to look for you. She's worried about you."

"I love her all to pieces. Please, go tell her I'm fine. I'm
just fine." Suddenly, she was bawling, head bowed, shoulders shaking, all out. "I'm sorry." She pushed his coat at
him. "Thank you. Go"

When he didn't leave she pushed on his shoulder. "Go."

He did not budge.

She looked up at him. "She said I was to make sure
you were all right and I wasn't to take your bull, her word
not mine, about being fine when you aren't. Clearly, your
friend knows you well."

He put his jacket back around her shoulders and led her
across the street toward Mandrel's.

"I should get back to work."

"You trying to get me into trouble? What did you eat
for dinner?"

"Corn chips and a candy bar."

"I thought only kids ate that badly."

"Kids made my dinner."

He held the door and they took seats at a booth. "I don't
have my wallet."

"Hey, Kelly, do you know where Mia lives?"

"She forget her wallet again?"

"Really, shouldn't you get back to Monique?"

"I'll go as soon as I see you take the first bite of your food." He looked at Kelly. "She'll have the grilled chicken breast sandwich with lettuce and tomato on a whole wheat bun, carrots and a glass of orange juice. I'll have a coffee to go."

"She fell. I never should have let her help me."

"She loves you."

Mia looked up at a man she'd known since he was a boy. Until Monique had opened her eyes, she hadn't recognized what a good man he really was.

"I would tell you she loves you, but that's not for me to tell."

He smiled at that.

"Are you mad at me?" she asked, looking for a clue in his face.

"Yeah, but not as mad as I was when you and Monique stole my math homework and I had to do it all over again—in detention."

"We only did that because you told Monique she was too skinny to be a movie star. Being movie stars was very important to us in fifth grade."

"She'll be fine," he said as he sipped his coffee. "We just found each other, so that's the only thing I can believe."

She put her hands over his clenched one on the tabletop.

"I'm good. I'll eat. I promise. Go to her."

Just then Kelly set the plate in front of her and she grabbed up the sandwich and took a bite.

"See?" she said with lettuce poking out the corner of her mouth.

She handed him his jacket and he almost bounded away.

Mia smiled to herself. Her friend was going to live happily ever after.

She thought of herself and Daniel so at home with each other, so loving, on the floor in front of the fire at her house, sitting on the balcony in the sunshine at his.

How was that wrong?

She finished her food and hurried over to the Emergency Department at the clinic. By the time Monique was ready to leave, Lenny had found a buddy from the night shift to come in early and cover for him and he became Monique's "someone to check on you every hour during the night."

As soon as Monique left the clinic with Lenny, Mia had gone back to work. The rattled wide-awake feeling lasted until almost three in the morning. By that time, she had the rest of the large sidewall completed.

Lenny had a training class in Portland at ten in the morning, so by seven she was at Monique's doorstep ready to relieve him.

"She still doesn't know about her granddad," he said as he leaned in to give her a kiss on the cheek and sprinted out to his car.

*I got your back, officer,* she thought as she watched him drive away.

"Hey, are you out there flirting with my boyfriend?"

"Sorry, I let him go," Mia said as she entered Monique's living room. "I didn't know I was allowed to flirt."

"You're not."

"Don't you look all queenlike ensconced there. I see your loyal vassal slept in the chair."

"I saw them."

"You saw what?"

"Fireworks. When I hit my head I saw fireworks and then Lenny came to check on me and he was even brave enough to check on you. Did you really eat when he told you to?"

"So does he know you love him?"

"I tried to tell him, but he said he'd waited so long he could wait until we were sure it wasn't the head injury talking." She sat forward. "I could go to work today—"

"You could not."

"But Mr. Wetherbee and Barbara would be there with me. You could leave and go get some sleep, which you so desperately need."

"I'm fine. I'm here until Lenny gets back."

# CHAPTER TWENTY

"WHY ARE YOU doing this, Mia? It's Saturday night and you've been at it for four days."

The streetlight made the rain sparkle off the windows of Braven's across the street. It was so pretty. Mia heard Monique's words, but instead of answering, she climbed back up the ladder one more time. Every time she wanted to quit, she climbed back up one more time.

When she came down the ladder to fill the buckets with debris, Monique shook her by the shoulder. "Please, answer me."

Mia looked at her friend. "Because I'm too scared to stop."

"You don't eat well. You don't sleep well. This is killing you, don't you see?"

"Do I give up? Do I give it all up and walk away? The walking away has to stop, why shouldn't it be me first?"

"Because the sun does not rise and set just because you have arranged it. Because this is a town full of people who, like it or not, are going to make up their minds the way they want to about the future of this town." Monique's voice rose as she spoke. "For the record, though, I hate the thought of you walking away. I missed you when you lived in Boston and Portland and I know I couldn't stand it if you left again."

Mia put a hand on Monique's heaving chest. "I've made you mad, sweetie. You don't get mad. I'm so sorry."

"Does that mean you'll come with me and get some dinner?"

"Later. I just need to get a little more finished."

Monique's shoulders drooped. "If you're still here in two hours when Lenny gets off work, he'll either help you or he'll carry you out of here."

"Don't have Lenny come. I can't have him getting into trouble on my account. Please, promise me."

"But you can get into trouble on account of the town?"

"Maybe you should leave. I need to get back to work. Please don't send Lenny."

"But I'll—"

"Just go away, please."

Monique walked away and Mia immediately regretted her last words. Her friend did not deserve to be treated badly. As soon as this was all over, she'd make it up to her, somehow.

A COUPLE HOURS after Monique left, Mia was about ready to take a break. Eat the sandwich she had made this morning for lunch, a lunch she should have eaten hours ago. Get some water because she was really thirsty. She lowered herself down the ladder. Each muscle in her legs screamed until she got to the floor. Then she moved the heavy ladder to the next spot.

When she checked to see how much she had left, she was not sure she had the strength to do the rest. Maybe she could leave it. No. Mr. Markham had said the first people in on Monday would be the inspectors to see what needed to be fixed before the electricians got there shortly after that. If he was to get the work done on time, she was to have held up her end, the demo.

*Just get these buckets out and emptied,* she thought.

The empty buckets seemed to weigh a ton each. The three steps up into the Roost, Mount McKinley. She needed to go home, rest, eat something before she couldn't even stand.

Back inside with the buckets, she decided on just one more trip up the ladder. She put the buckets down and got the small claw hammer and crowbar. As she stepped up the ladder, she lost her grip and her balance. Her heel flew out from under her and she hit the floor.

A split second later and she knew the ladder was coming down on top of her. The only recourse she had was to duck.

She threw her arms over her head—

And nothing happened.

The ladder seemed to be suspended at an impossible angle and then it actually moved back into place against the wall. In that instance her addled brain figured out she wasn't alone.

Slowly, afraid to look, afraid not to, she tried to focus her gaze. Daniel MacCarey stood next to the ladder.

His dark eyes glittered in the harsh work lights, the work lights he had left behind, and for what seemed like the thousandth time since she met him, she could not breathe.

"Daniel." She had to force his name out with the air left in her lungs.

He extended a hand and she shook her head. "I'd get you dirty." She collected the hammer and pry bar and struggled up from the floor.

"You look very sexy wielding a hammer."

"Oh, you are so cruel." She knew just how she looked. Sweatband around her head, a flannel shirt so old, no one could possibly remember who the original owner was over a faded orange tank top with a juice stain between her breasts. Dust from the top of her head to the tips of her toes.

"Finished?"

"What?"

"Doing an 'I look terrible' inventory because you're wrong."

She took in a short breath to try to banish the tremble her chin seemed to have adopted. He knew her so well. He was such a loss, a great loss.

"Daniel." She breathed again because just saying his name turned the tremble into quaking. She tried to turn away, but her feet wouldn't move. Fatigue made her knees sag and she slumped toward the floor.

Before she knew it, she was being lifted into the air and pulled close to Daniel's chest. He didn't say a word as he carried her to his car and put her into the passenger seat. Five minutes later he carried her up to her bathroom and sat down on the edge of the tub with her on his lap.

She curled up with her head down, too tired to be embarrassed. He tugged the kerchief from her head. Next her boots and socks went, followed by her jeans and flannel shirt.

She vaguely heard him speak to her and then he slid off her tank top and sports bra followed by her panties.

He must have turned the bathroom heater on because she didn't feel the cold at all. When she slid into the water she felt herself falling sleep almost immediately.

The next thing she remembered was waking up with Daniel next to her on the bed, and her kissing him and snuggling against him as she nodded off to sleep again.

When she awoke the next time it was still dark but she was alone. She must have dreamed Daniel had been there. She wondered when those dreams of him would fade away.

She stretched to look at the time but what she saw seemed wrong. It was nine o'clock?

She sat up.

Daniel *was* there. He came to Pirate's Roost and kept the ladder from falling on her head. But that couldn't be. It was almost one o'clock in the morning when he got there.

Things were fuzzy after that. A bath. She had a bath. He was beside her in bed.

She hurled off the covers and stood up until dizziness made her sit down again.

She couldn't have slept all day.

Pulling her arms into her robe, she staggered down the stairs.

He was standing in the moonlight in the kitchen.

"How could you?"

He turned toward her but he didn't say anything.

"How could you? I needed to finish that work before the end of today. I had to get it done. How could you?"

"It's done."

"No, I still have so much to strip and clean up to get done and I have to—"

"It's all done."

"How is that possible?"

"Did you know there was a group of men and women just waiting for you to ask them to help you? Heck, if they hadn't been so afraid you'd chase them away, they would have done it without waiting to be asked."

"What do you mean?"

"Mia, you can't do it all. None of us can do it all."

She tore off upstairs and a couple minutes later she raced back down dressed. In the front hall, she rummaged through the key dish. No car keys.

"I'll drive you."

"I'll drive myself." Where were her keys? She raced to the kitchen. Sometimes she left them there. They weren't.

She grabbed her jacket and headed for the door.

"I'll drive you."

"No. I'll walk."

"Mia, stop it."

She stopped and kept trying to get her arm into the

sleeve of the jacket. Dull anger floated amid the confusion inside her head.

"You do not understand," she said through clenched teeth.

She started for the door again and he grabbed her arm and spun her to face him.

"You can't do it all yourself."

"I need to, it needs to get done. Don't you see? I thought this was just a restaurant, but it's, it's…" She pulled her arm away.

He grabbed her again, but this time he wrapped his arms around her and pulled her to his chest.

"Please, Daniel, please let me go."

"I'll drive you."

She nodded against his sweater and recognized it as her favorite old raggedy one and inhaled a breath of comfort. "Thank you."

A chuckle rumbled deeply in his chest and she looked up into his smile. "Now was that so hard?"

A smile slipped onto her lips. "Immensely."

He smoothed back her hair, probably her wild hair, and dropped a quick kiss on her lips.

She pulled away before she burst into flames. "Let's go."

He made a call on the way to the car. All he said was, "We're leaving." Then he pretended that he had made no phone call at all when she asked what that was about. Who did he call?

When she got into the car there was a bottle of orange juice on the seat and he didn't pull out of her driveway until she drank it all.

"Why do I feel as though I'm being manipulated?"

When they arrived at Pirate's Roost all the lights were on. She jumped out of his car and ran up to the front door.

The place was clean. She ran into the kitchen. Not a

speck of the old wallboard remained. Even the old sink had been scrubbed.

The stairways had been sealed off with tape and plastic to keep as much of the insidious drywall dust from getting upstairs as possible. "They cleaned up there, too, and the basement."

"I can't believe it."

"Can we close this place up and go back to your house?"

She turned and smiled. "What if I want to stay here?"

"I'll just have to make another phone call. They'll all come here. If you just let me take you home, they will have come and done their mischief and gone away like giggling little pixies."

"Did they really giggle?"

"There was one big guy with a dark beard and his wife who could not stop."

"I'm definitely being manipulated, but I guess home it is."

When they got to her house, the lights were on, but then she'd not been careful about shutting them off when she left. Smoke curled from the chimney and once inside the door the definite smell of food filled her house.

On the counter in a bucket of ice was a bottle of white wine.

"So you knew I'd sleep a long time and I'd wake up mad and demand to go to Pirate's Roost. And that I'd be hungry?"

"I think the bottle of wine and fire are just nice extras."

She pulled open the oven. "No way. Millie Davies's fried chicken and Mattie Finn's scalloped potatoes."

"I believe there's a coconut cream pie in the refrigerator and a couple of salads."

"Mandrel's. Don't eat the pie."

"It looks like great pie."

"It is. Hard to stop once you start."

With plates full of food and glasses full of wine they sat on the floor in front of the fireplace and Mia ate the first real meal she'd had in days.

DANIEL WATCHED THE firelight play in Mia's hair. They had dragged the pillows and quilts out and had nestled in front of the fireplace.

"Thank you for refusing to take no for an answer. I don't know how to be rescued. I don't think I've ever known."

"Mia, there is a world of people out there who would love to do things for you, if you'd just give them a chance."

"It's hard."

He watched the firelight play in her hair and the emotions on her face. "Tell me."

She swallowed. "I waited and I waited for my parents to do for me, like other kid's parents did for them. When I was in fourth grade, I got myself up, packed my lunch and got myself to school before the sun came up so I wouldn't miss the field trip to the museum in Portland.

"Other kids got sandwiches and homemade cupcakes and I got whatever I could find to put in my lunch. If I didn't get it done, it didn't happen. Eventually, I decided it must be wrong to expect anyone to help out. And then by the time I figured out that wasn't right, either, I couldn't seem to change. I was afraid to change."

She sat there quietly for a long time, then she turned and studied him.

"Daniel."

"Yes, Mia." He wanted to take her in his arms and reassure her she was enough, she was a whole and wonderful person. He wasn't sure he could trust himself with a hug.

"I know I'm not the reason you need to stay clear of a relationship. I almost wish it was me. Maybe then I could dye my hair or learn to be funnier."

He shifted to face her. "It's just self-preservation."

And he wouldn't touch her for the same reason.

"Monique called you. That's why you're here?"

It wasn't an accusation. It was more like the sound of nearly exhausted hope.

He still wasn't sure he could tell her or should tell her why he would go away again.

"Your friend is a very forceful person. She called me and told me I had to come and stop you because you wouldn't listen to anyone else."

"I love her. I made her mad. She never gets mad. That must be when she called you."

"Then she said I had to tell you why we can't have a relationship. She said she didn't care if I was an ax murderer and a vampire, I had to tell you."

"She said that? You don't have to tell me, you know."

"She said I was killing you."

She breathed quietly almost as if she might break.

"I want to tell you," he continued.

"You'd do that for me? You'd tell me?" Her expression was open and amazed. He broke his promise to himself and he ran a finger down the line of her jaw.

"Are you sure you want to hear it?"

"I can open another bottle of wine if you want more."

"No, thanks."

"I've tried to talk myself out of being—um—attracted to you, but I haven't had any luck so far. For purely selfish reasons I'd like for you to tell me, but now that we're here, I don't know if I can have you look at me while you tell me."

She turned away so she was facing the other direction, and when he reached for her, she moved back against him and he wrapped his arms around her. She waited for him to start, breathing quietly, pressing his arms into her body with her own.

"We knew we were the happiest parents on the planet when we got pregnant." She rubbed the back of his hand.

"I was well on the way to tenure. Mandy had just turned down a huge promotion at her company because it would have meant travel and she knew she wanted to be a stay-at-home mom.

"Everything in our lives was perfect. We had tried for only two months and we were pregnant, but Mandy didn't feel well for most of the pregnancy and then Sammy was born six weeks early, but we were still blissful. We had a son.

"It didn't take long for any of us to grasp there was something seriously wrong with Sammy. He had a hard time taking to her breast. He didn't even do well with the bottle, and then the doctors told us his heart was malformed. He didn't thrive. He just seemed to be fading away in our arms. Then he started to turn blue when he cried hard. The doctors said if we could get him a little stronger they might be able to repair his heart.

"Every day brought fear and pain for all of us. Sammy suffered the worst, test, needles, big cold machinery, unfamiliar beds and faces changing every day.

"When he was just two and a half years old, they took him to surgery. Eighteen hours later, they came to us and told us Sammy had died during the operation. We didn't even get to hold him when he died. He was just gone."

She kept very still and listened.

"One thing they were happy to tell us is we could try to have another baby right away. They could do genetic testing to make sure the fetus wasn't affected. By then I already knew Sammy died that terrible death because of me, because of something I carry within my genetic code.

"If I had paid attention to what had gone on previously in my family, I would have known there was a chance of a genetic flaw. Mandy and I could have made different decisions."

He paused to let his breathing even out.

"Afterwards, Mandy and I tried to hold things together. One day I came home to find her bags were packed. She said she couldn't look at me without thinking of Sammy and she left. No matter how much I told myself our son's death destroyed Mandy, I knew my ignorance and then my reaction was as much to blame. She was a wonderful, loving woman and I had brought her to her knees.

"I was almost happy to see her go. Without me in her life, she would be able to find someone else. She had a chance for a complete life. She could have children with another man, healthy, happy children who would grow up to make refrigerator art and go to prom.

"I can never do that to a child or a woman ever again." He paused to collect his thoughts.

"The hardest part to explain is why I didn't tell you in the first place, why I never wanted to tell you. The mere act of telling you changes you, telling any woman would change her. There is a part of you that will say, 'It's all right, we could do without a child.' I would never ask that of you. Or you might think we can work around the situation. The logistics of that option are difficult from many different angles. I wouldn't ask that of you. The option to go on having a great sexual relationship would only delay the inevitable.

"The point being you should not have to choose those things. You should be able to go out and find someone who can offer you the total union of a man and a woman making a baby. I have been there and I know how utterly amazing that is."

He stopped, hoping she would hear and understand completely so she could free herself. The fire died down behind the glass doors of the fireplace. The house seemed to breathe and Mia did not.

He started to go, but she held on tightly. He kissed her hair. "Let me go. I'll leave, let you get some rest."

"Could you just relax? I'm thinking."

She stayed so quiet, he started to think she had fallen asleep.

"So, you failed to know there was a genetic flaw that might occur in your family." She spoke slowly as if choosing her words carefully. "I get that you feel responsible, but I'm wondering how much punishment is enough. I'm not asking for an answer, but someday please answer that for yourself."

She turned over in his arms and pulled him close.

He tipped back and peered deeply into her eyes. "I'm going to leave now, Mia."

"Yeah, I know that." She stood up and reached down for his hand and helped him up. "Thank you for all you did for me."

"There is a world full of people who are not your parents willing to help you. You might consider letting them."

"Do you think I can do that?"

"It'll take some practice."

She gave him a quick hug and let him go. "Will you try to be a little less hard on yourself? And try to find a hug once in a while. Like Mrs. Wahl. Given half the chance she'd hug you. And, of course, they're always available here on Blueberry Avenue. Heck, buy a couple rounds at Braven's and you might get a whole bunch of whiskery hugs."

He left her smiling, but that didn't make him feel any better.

He pointed his car down Blueberry Avenue and hoped it knew how to get home because all he could think about was Mia Parker. She was everything he could possibly want, if he allowed himself to want. He hoped telling her helped her move on. With Pirate's Roost opening soon, she had a great adventure coming.

He turned onto Church Street and when he was almost

to Pirate's Roost, he realized there was police tape across the door the way it had been the first day he came to town, and there was a notice tacked on the door.

He stopped and got out to look.

The university had gotten an injunction to stop any construction at the site. When the contractor with all his supplies arrived in a few hours, he would be turned way.

Daniel's first instinct was to turn back to Mia's, but there was nothing she could do tonight. Let her have a peaceful night's sleep. He couldn't do anything here to change things.

Her friends would rally around her, while he worked from the university end.

## CHAPTER TWENTY-ONE

MIA WOKE UP excited because the world was tipping back onto its axis even without Daniel MacCarey. Today Pirate's Roost would begin to take real shape. Markham Construction would be swift and competent. They expected to be finished in two to three weeks. She could be ready to serve her first customers in five to six weeks. Woefully behind what she had planned, but the tourists would still be wandering through for several months afterward.

She had planned to be ahead of the construction company, but there were already pickup trucks parked along the street. They were milling around outside the door. Waiting for her. Oh, no. Bad show for her first day.

She parked and hurried up to be met with a group of worried faces. Was she that late? They parted so she could get to the door.

The crossed yellow tape confused her at first. Then she saw the notice.

"It can't be."

She turned to see Henry Markham approaching. His face was grim when he shook her hand.

"Ms. Parker, I'm sorry, we have to leave. The supplies will be returned, but the suppliers will charge restocking fees. Please call the office and reschedule when you can. I hope things go well with you." He tipped his hat and walked away.

The crowd around her dissipated and she stood alone on the steps of her own building.

A squad car pulled up beside her and Chief Montcalm got out. "I'm sorry, Mia. I would have called you last night, but all that would have done was ruin your evening."

"Do you forgive me for breaking the law in your town?"

"From what I understand, it's your town. I would have had a jail full of you trespassers if the university had asked that charges be pressed."

"I can't believe the townsfolk did that for me. Ghosts they were. I didn't see a single face of the perpetrators."

"Mia, you are tough. You'll get through this, too."

She took solace from his words because she suddenly knew this man had been through tough times; he knew them inside and out and here he was.

As THE DAY passed, the storm of her failure raged on. She spoke with the bankers and all loans were withdrawn. They could offer her a low-fee refinance on her home, but that was all they had.

Pirate's Roost was in true limbo. The university had laid claim by the right of eminent domain and the banks could not repossess it until it was released.

Monday turned to Tuesday and then another Monday and another. The building sat empty. No one visited at all as far as she could tell. No hordes from the outside world appeared. The town could probably thank the university for not putting the pirate news on their website.

Negative responses began to come back from the dozens of resumes she had sent out. She knew from experience many of them were just shredder fodder, and she'd never hear from those companies.

Monique had long ago forgiven Lenny and her for not telling her about her granddad the night she fell and hit her head. With Lenny's help she was coping, but Mia did not give up hope that Edwin Beaudin would return one day and for good.

Monique and Lenny helped her get through some of the lonely times, but she refused to be what she called a date killer.

Mia had even watched a few game shows with her parents, and one Thursday evening they played Scrabble and her mother and father seemed to have fun.

Her meetings at Braven's tapered off, took on a different tone, but they all seemed to have fun when she did go. The city council had invited her as a special guest to tell them what she had learned. Afterwards, it was suggested at Braven's that she run in the next election. She said she would keep it in mind.

One week, the news broke that Earl Smith had been the one to smash the crypt, and that he was nowhere to be found, but the story made only a small ripple of interest as the pirate's tomb played such a small role in anyone's life these days. In fact, the whole idea of pirate's treasure had fallen into disfavor. Maybe it would stay that way for another fifty years.

Recently she had an interview in Portland with an export company. The job was a poorly masked sales position, but things were skittering along the bottom.

She had even sent resumes out of state. She had thought she might be able to take a job away from Maine. Then one day when she got a nibble from halfway across the continent in Milwaukee, Wisconsin, she realized that was not going to happen. If they wanted her to leave Maine again, they were going to have to haul her out in her final resting box because if she were alive, she'd fight, like a Mainer...

Edwin Beaudin had returned two weeks after he'd left. He had found out, he thought the way she had. Pine box or nothing. As lovely as it may be, the state of Florida taught him what age and experience had not.

Today was the third Monday in May. Mia sat on the window seat of her living room window sipping coffee and watching the cars go by on Church Street as it met Blueberry Avenue. If construction had started that day she found the notice tacked to her door she'd be opening Pirate's Roost to anyone brave enough to come and try it out.

Monique had totally recovered with Lenny at her side all the way. If fact, she had recovered enough to be able to wear a great big rock on her engagement-ring finger. Her friend was dreamily, ecstatically happy, until she saw her poor old broke unemployed friend. Well, Mia wasn't totally unemployed. She filled in at Mandrel's, stocked shelves and operated the cash register at the drug store and kept books for a couple of the fishermen who seemed to be totally numbers challenged.

Her phone chimed in her pocket and she pulled it out to see Monique's smiling face on the caller ID screen.

"Mia, you need to get down to Pirate's Roost. There's something going on down there."

"How do you know, Monique?"

"Just a second, Mrs. Carmody. Just get down there, Mia."

Like she had anything else to do. Maybe Dr. Donovan had brought real dogs and ponies this time.

She hiked down the street and as she got closer, she could see the police tape was gone. The notice no longer hung on the door, and if she wasn't mistaken Daniel Mac-Carey's car sat parked at the far end of the block.

"Get in here." He held the door of the Roost open as she approached.

As she passed him, she refused to let herself even breathe. He was here for some reason and she was certain it was not for her. Whatever it was, she'd cope. There would probably be a few tears after he left, but she'd survive.

Everything looked just as it had been left, except the big hammer had been returned and Daniel MacCarey was now standing in the middle of the room looking as annoyingly delectable as he always had. Today he had on a dark brown sweater with flecks of blue in it.

"Why are you standing in my building grinning?"

"Before you say no to this…"

"No. You have a new sweater. I like it."

"Before you say no to this…"

"No and no."

He pulled her against his chest and put his fingers over her mouth so she couldn't speak. She tried anyway.

"Mnnkll."

He lifted his fingers from her mouth.

"Uncle."

"I will put up the money."

"No." This time she spun away. "I can't let you do that."

"Why not?"

"I—um— Well, because it's yours. You'll need it someday."

"Great-Aunt Margaret would always tell me, if I ever wanted money, I just needed to ask her. I guess I should have." He looked all sad when he said that and it made her want to hug him, but she kept her distance. "I never thought I needed anything from her, but it might have given her more pleasure if I had taken some while she was alive. And she had a boatload, Mia. I had no idea. She'd be really happy if you took some of it."

"Well, I can't take it."

"You realize if you don't take it, I'll have to leave it to my cats."

"You don't have cats."

"Then I'll leave it to the university, or maybe Heather's museum."

"Daniel, if I had all the money in the world— Well, maybe if I had that much."

He shook his head. "Great-Aunt Margaret only left me half that much."

"There aren't enough workers to get the job done, even if they hadn't repossessed all my building supplies and equipment."

"Except for that stupid hammer," he added very unhelpfully.

"Except for that stupid hammer and my orange buckets."

From one rear pocket he pulled a handful of bright shiny nails and from the other, a hammer.

He held them up.

"Thanks. That's sweet." Tears tried to push into her eyes and she pushed back. "Maybe I can save up nails and someday afford lumber and drywall...if I had a building to use them on."

He took hold of her shoulders and turned her to face him. "You are such a pessimist all of a sudden."

"I think I always was, a pessimist who was fooling herself."

He walked over to the door of the building and pulled it open by its shiny old brass handle. She couldn't believe he was just going to walk away.

Then people started filing in one by one. Men, women, kids, parents, grandparents. Faces she knew and loved, and a few faces she didn't know at all, each one carrying a hammer, a saw, a sawhorse, a power tool, an extension cord. The little ones carried boxes of screws and nails. She greeted them all, most of them by name. Her parents came in empty-handed but they were there and they were together.

One little girl hurried up to her and handed her a bunch of well-squeezed flowers and then scooted away to her mother.

She looked into the faces of these people. She loved this town. Each and every one of them was a treasure she had not totally appreciated until she started talking to them about the things that were important to them.

When Monique came in carrying a plaque that read "Pirate's Roost, the final resting place of the pirate Liam Bailey," the crowd clapped and cheered and tears flooded Mia's eyes and tumbled onto the buttons of her yellow Henley.

"Monique," she whispered. "What am I supposed to do, to say? I have nothing for them to work on. I've no…"

Monique grinned and Mia saw why. Lenny was out in the street directing traffic as a big-box-store truck lumbered past her building and stopped. Monique moved people aside so they could get to the window. The first truck made room for a second. When the second truck stopped Lenny waved traffic on and then he waved to Monique. When she waved back, her diamond flashed and sparkled.

Henry Markham, the contractor who had told her he could get her back on the schedule in eight or nine months, if she was ready, pulled up in his big white pickup truck, and then shortly afterwards there were pickups parking up both sides of the street and twice that many men and women wearing hats and shirts bearing the blue-and-orange Markham Construction logos.

She grabbed Monique's arm. "Monique, what's going on? Quick, before I wake up and I'm in the poorhouse and this is all just a nightmare."

"Daniel did it, and they helped him."

She looked up at Daniel who was surrounded by several of the town's older folk. They were laughing and teasing him. He looked up at her and smiled from amongst his fellow conspirators.

She saw for the first time that the fatigue had fled from his face. He looked like a man who knew what he wanted.

*Too bad it isn't you,* her new pessimistic side informed her.

He shed the crowd and came over to where she stood. "I figured that it would be easier to apologize afterwards than to get permission from you beforehand. I did insist you be here before the first screw went into place."

She looked at him steadily.

"I should certainly hope so." She grinned to see the innuendo hit its mark.

"If I thought you knew how to behave," he said when he recovered, "I'd tell you to do so."

Four Markham people with clipboards, pencils, tape measurers and cameras marched in with a purpose in their step and dispersed inside the building.

Henry Markham entered and walked up to Mia. "I can't tell you how glad I am to be back here. My sister-in-law wouldn't speak to me after, as she put it, I left you in the lurch."

"Well, I'm so glad you're back. I'll make sure Maxine knows it wasn't your fault."

Markham went off on a building tour with one of the clipboard people, and Harley and Millie Davies stepped in to congratulate her, and then the Schroeders and the Finns.

Mia smiled her happiness for them as the Carmodys, the widow and the brother-in-law, came in shoulder-to-shoulder to congratulate her.

People kept doing that, and it was kind of strange because it seemed like all she'd done was get up this morning.

Monique came up and slugged her on the arm. "You are playing the unworthy melody inside your head, I can hear it spilling out your ears. Suck it up and not to worry. These will be the same people who will one day complain the food is not warm enough and too salty."

When Monique went out to greet Lenny, Mia walked up to Daniel and nudged him. "You are going to owe me the biggest apology ever for not asking for permission to do this, and on top of that, I intend to pay you back."

"You don't ever have to pay me back, but I won't try to

convince you of that. This—" he swept his hand around the room at all the people "—is the least I could do."

"You didn't have to do anything."

He brought her face around to look at him. "I did it because I could. Please, let me."

Just then Heather Loch entered through the front door and the crowd parted. When she marched toward Daniel and her, two of the old guys stood up to block her.

"I've come to see the boy," she said as she stepped up to them.

Mia snickered as Daniel put a thumb to his chest and raised his eyebrows.

He put his hands on the shoulders of the men and they separated. Then as the crowd watched, he stepped up to the older woman and put his arms around her. She wiggled and squirmed to get away but he held on to her.

"I'm all you got, Heather—" he paused and looked directly at Mia "—and I'm not going anywhere."

The air completely left the room and she grabbed Monique's arm for support.

When Heather quieted he let her go. The older woman looked at him with longing, the way a mother might look at a long-lost son. He took a step away and reached into his pocket. Mia thought Heather might flee until Daniel pulled out her buttons.

"I'm glad I found you, Cousin Heather."

She took her pouch and solemnly opened her hand and held his pouch up on her palm. He took it and tucked it into his pocket.

"I knew all along Liam Bailey had a treasure." Her chin jutted and Mia thought she might be close to a tear. "I just didn't know it would be so precious."

Everyone watched as she stepped up to Daniel and returned the hug he had given her.

That exchange left many scratching their heads. Mia assumed it meant the remains of Liam Bailey now had provenance that would withstand the strongest scrutiny and that two of his descendents had found each other.

As the food came out, as it always did when a big crowd gathered in Bailey's Cove, more people arrived, among them Chief Montcalm, Officer Doyle and other police officers, some on duty and some off. With each new face, Mia felt more humble.

Daniel escorted a skittish-looking Heather out the door and down the street in the direction of the museum.

"He's not really back, is he?" Mia said to Monique who had come up and stood shoulder-to-shoulder with her.

"I'm so sorry, honey. I wish I could tell you different. He's so in awe when he speaks of you. He'd do almost anything you asked of him. Did he ever tell you?"

Mia nodded.

"It didn't help, did it?"

This time she shook her head.

## CHAPTER TWENTY-TWO

MIA STOOD IN the middle of the new and gleaming Pirate's Roost. Every distressed wood table had chairs and one special Captain's Chair. Oil and acrylic renditions of ships, and even one of South Harbor, hung on the wall. One painting of a ship's captain, based on the computer image and era of Liam Bailey, took center stage on the wall behind the counter. Melissa Long had painted it masterfully. She would not be the receptionist at the police station for long.

A pair of shoppers stopped and stood, hands shading their brows so they could see inside. She recognized two of tonight's dinner guests, Millie Davies and Francine Erickson, the wives of a tavern goer and the tavern owner. When she waved, they waved back and moved on.

Her fingernails flashed red. She'd had a manicure for this very special occasion. Not the restaurant opening, but the occasion that through all this she had not chewed off a single nail.

The stools had been installed at the gleaming oak counter. The bakery display case awaited pastries, most of which she had only seen in pictures, but the ones she had tasted were each a delightful treat. Monique would never tell her she was too skinny again.

The kitchen had the space and equipment to lure a pair of recent culinary school graduates, who had wined and dined her to prove their worth. Monique and Lenny particularly enjoyed these meals, as did her parents. The pair of chefs were grateful to be given such a chance to prove themselves and Mia was willing to let them. They would all grow together.

A building extension had been added to the stairs, and the new elevator, leading to the hotel portion of the building could be segregated from the restaurant. Daniel had insisted the rest of Mia's plans be carried out along with the restaurant. It was all breathtaking and as lovely as she had ever hoped it would be.

She even had a full staff.

The ex-vandal Mickey Thompson worked there on weekends and he actually seemed to enjoy something besides truancy. He and Edwin Beaudin had struck up a friendship because Mr. Beaudin had become the procurer of fresh seafood for the Roost and often delivered product himself.

Charlie, Rufus and Stella all had positions with Pirate's Roost, even though they admitted to digging the hole in the root cellar... Well, Charlie had dug while the two of them encouraged him. As a condition of employment, they did promise to perpetrate no more destruction on the premises of Pirate's Roost. That left the rest of Bailey's Cove and it seemed a fair and adequate bargain for all involved.

In the area that had been the center wall, in between the load-bearing columns of two-hundred-year-old lumber was a three-foot-high partition. On the partition was a monument to the love story of Liam Bailey and Colleen Fletcher.

On the town's new website and in all the official literature, only a minor reference had been made to Bailey's previous job experience and but a handful of treasure hunters had come so far.

Liam Bailey had been interred in the old Sacred Heart Church cemetery next to Colleen Fletcher McClure. His tomb had been given to the Bailey's Cove museum where Heather painstakingly reassembled it and restored the rose to the vibrant color it had been two hundred years ago.

Heather Loch didn't seem to be afraid of the people of Bailey's Cove anymore, nor they of her.

Was there a treasure buried somewhere in town? No one knew. All they knew for sure was the pirate did not take his money and run. What most assumed is that Archibald Fletcher stole the treasure when he took the pirate's life.

Mia strode over and ran her hand over the shining surface of the counter.

Was it shiny enough?

She took the always-present rag from her pocket and began to polish.

The Pirate's Roost staff would be arriving in a couple hours to begin preparation for the first public serving of food, a single buffet seating of VIPs. The guest list included the likes of the denizens of Braven's tavern, several police officers, one chief of police, the mayor, who had finally returned to town, and the members of the town council who had promised to run the town like the democracy it was always intended to be. Invited also were Dr. Daniel MacCarey, Monique, Heather Loch and the people in town who had done their best to make sure the Roost came to be. She loved each and every one of these people and one in particular...

She couldn't wait to have these Very Important People fill the dining room and spill out onto the gorgeous patio behind. The decorative paving and plantings would help make up for the lack of a harbor view back there. Tonight it would be lit with tea-light candles and twinkle lights.

All the guests were expected to roam the premises as they drank cocktails and tested the appetizer menu. Then a slightly altered menu, one designed to withstand the rigors of a buffet would be served, including dessert, of course. The food would be a test of the two new chefs, who reminded Mia of Monique and her at age twenty-two. Friends forever, then and now, they had a chance at always.

For the past two days, the staff had been there until late, prepping food and practicing the dance of serving and keeping guests happy. She had told them all not to show up until noon today.

Daniel hadn't come to town often and the last two times he understood when she was too busy for more than a hello. Today he was stopping in to see her at ten o'clock—in two minutes. He said he needed to speak with her alone before the staff arrived.

She stopped polishing the counter when she noticed a black Cadillac convertible pull up in front of the Roost. The car Daniel's great-aunt Margaret had left him. The car was immediately surrounded by people. She watched as he started getting hugs even before he got out of the car.

He'd be inside in a few moments.

She turned and fled into the kitchen. In there she could freak out for a minute before he got away from the crowd and none of those who peeked in the windows would see her. She leaned over the stainless-steel counter and let the cool of the metal ground her.

She could do this.

He'd most likely come to discuss something about the opening.

Or he probably wanted to deliver a grand bouquet of flowers personally. That would be just like him. Make sure they got there and found a place to be displayed without causing her any inconvenience. Ah-yuh. No inconvenience to see Daniel MacCarey. Only heartache. Of one thing she was sure, she could not die of a broken heart. Alas.

She heard the door open and let in the street sounds and then it closed again and everything was quiet except the hum of the refrigeration equipment. She was never ready enough to see Daniel's face, hadn't prepared herself enough to withstand the storm of loss that would follow when he left.

A second later, the kitchen door swung open and he stood in the doorway.

No flowers.

She refused to worry. It didn't have to mean anything except the flowers would be delivered. Maybe they would arrive any minute and then she would have something to do with her hands, because now she had to tuck them into her pockets because she couldn't find anything to clean.

"Daniel, I'm not sure I have the time right now." *Or the courage.*

"I know I am responsible for the scared look on your face."

"Don't be silly. I have a restaurant opening, unless you've forgotten. That's pretty scary."

"So you're ready to sell great seafood and a passable hamburger to the tourists?"

"You heard me say that? I thought you were too busy checking out the granite pieces after Earl trashed the site."

"I have heard every word you have ever said to me."

She had no idea why that took her breath away, but she pulled out the stool from under the stainless-steel counter and took a seat.

He sat next to her. Then he took hold of her stool and pulled her closer to him. He looked happier than she had ever seen him.

The change had begun subtly the day he rescued Pirate's Roost when Heather Loch, his cousin many generations separated, quieted in his arms. If Heather was responsible for the change in Daniel, Mia was grateful.

Mia got that he didn't need her for this transformation, that he had reconciled himself to the solo life. It seemed to be going well for him.

She smiled at him. "Hey, you said you weren't sure how going over Dr. Donovan's head to get Pirate's Roost freed up would turn out. Do you still have a job?" She tried to make her words sound light but concerned.

"I'm no longer an assistant professor at the university."

"Oh, Daniel, where will you go? Positions for an anthropologist in the state of Maine are few and far between."

"Thin on the ground, Mrs. Wahl would say."

The dread that began to clench her insides when he arrived with no flowers started to bloom in her chest.

"You're pretty casual about your future."

"Apparently, Dr. Donovan had been doing some creative billing of expenses over the last few years and was hoping to use the treasure of Liam Bailey as a get-out-of-jail-free card with the university. That's why he was so adamant about keeping Pirate's Roost. It was for himself, not the university."

"Oh, my, what does that mean?"

"It means he has a lot to pay back and now he is free to seek another job to do so."

"They fired him? And they gave his job to you?"

"They fired him, and they gave the job to a very deserving woman who has been a professor there for several years."

"Stop teasing me. I still care what happens to you."

"They promoted me to full professor and gave me tenure."

"Oh, Daniel." She hugged him. "That's wonderful."

"I have something else to tell you."

"You're off to Guatemala?"

"I'm staying right in Maine for as long as I need to be here."

"Okay, I'm not guessing anymore. What else do you have to tell me?" She knew it made no difference where he worked or lived or traveled for his job, it would not affect her much—yet she felt a sense of relief knowing he wouldn't be in another country.

"Are you ready?"

"Not yet." She pointed at his boots. "You had them fixed. You had those old boots you wore the first day fixed. They look great."

"Aunt Margaret gave them to me. Said they would give me a good *understanding* as I pursued my dreams. I couldn't part with them."

Mia swallowed the lump of gratitude in her throat. Daniel had found his way. He'd go on with his life and he'd do it well. "Okay, now I'm ready. What else do you have to tell me?"

"Heather Loch came to see me at the university. She had some very important things to say to me."

Mia didn't move. She breathed only a few molecules at a time. She was afraid if she breathed more, she might disturb the fragile healing that had begun in Daniel. "What did she say?"

"She said in fifty years I'd be her."

"That you'd have bushy white hair?"

He nudged her gently. They both leaned against the stainless-steel counter and stared face out toward the large hooded grill. Thanks to him, the kitchen was everything she had dreamed of.

"She didn't promise that."

"Then I don't know what that means," she managed to say.

"She said she felt as I did when she was my age and look where it got her. She said she stopped taking real life chances, stopped letting people get close to her, and she missed out on a lot, which she now regrets."

Mia tried to stay calm. The words he spoke changed nothing.

"Then she asked me what my wife would have done if she found out a child of ours might die. Would she have married me or not? I thought I knew the answer to that, but Heather wouldn't let me tell her. She said the answer was not for her, but for me. That I should think about it and not to be selfish when I did."

He took hold of her hand. Mia wasn't even sure he realized he had done it. She sat quietly.

"And then she told me I was an idiot."

A laugh burst from Mia. "An idiot? When was the last time someone called you an idiot?"

"Never happened before." He squeezed her hand. "Have I burned every bridge between us?"

She looked into his eyes, searching for a hint of hope that this was anything but more of the same. "I don't know. Why did Heather call you an idiot?"

"The first time she called me an idiot..." He let her chuckle about that and then continued. "She said if I got into a relationship thinking there were guarantees, I needed to take my head out of the sand. Only she didn't say out of the sand. She was more anatomical."

"She said that to you?"

He nodded slowly.

"I might—have kept one or two bridges hidden from you."

He leaned in and kissed her on the lips.

It was a wonderful, long kiss, but she'd been here before. Exactly here. What if this was goodbye?

She broke the kiss and started to get up, but he stopped her and pulled her back down onto the stool.

He kissed her again and this time the contact paralyzed her. He put a hand behind her head and deepened the kiss, and then pulled back.

"I'm desperately searching for that bridge here."

"I thought..."

He pulled her against him and kissed her until she put her arms around his neck and kissed him back.

She broke away and panted before she spoke. "I can't let myself dream about us anymore, Daniel. I can't."

"MIA…"

"I lost you, Daniel. I had lost you forever. I could never get used to that." There was still fear in her voice and he wanted to make that go away.

"I'm here now."

She remained still, stayed where she was. He hadn't planned this very well today. He just knew he had to find her, make her believe in him again. If he could just figure out the words to make things better.

"I could not see any other way that seemed fair," he said at last.

"That's part of what makes you who you are. Funny, no matter how much I hurt, I could never hate you."

"I would like to make it up to you for my being the idiot."

She turned toward him and reached out her hand. Her gentle tentative touch on his face gave him hope. She couldn't hate him and that gave him hope, too. She was his friend. She loved him as a friend. That was a start.

He took her hand in both of his and kissed each fingertip.

She stiffened, but didn't pull away.

"I was alone in my office when Heather burst in looking less frazzled and purely determined. Every time she called me an idiot, she made it sound as if she were doing me a favor."

The expression on her face didn't change and that made him hurry on before she bolted.

"She said I should take a chance on happily ever after, another chance. And for the first time in years, I felt free."

She stared at him, her eyes widened.

"I love you, Mia."

"Daniel, I—"

"I know I'm not doing a very good job with this. Maybe I am an idiot." A tiny smile curled the corners of her mouth. "But please, if you will still have me, I'm yours."

"What about—"

"What about my past? That's where I want to leave it. Otherwise I'd be an…"

"Idiot." She grinned and his heart soared.

"Yes, and I don't like that status much. Even before Heather, Aunt Margaret pleaded with me to find somebody to spend my life with. She would be ecstatic to know I feel I can do that now." He wanted her to throw herself at him, wind her arms around his neck and never let go, but he wasn't sure she had that to give anymore. He looked into her blue eyes and searched for the answer. If she rejected him, he'd leave for good this time and let her get on with her life.

She didn't say anything, she just stared at him. Unshed tears glistened in her eyes.

"I hope I have found someone. I hope you will have me after all I've done to discourage you." He kissed the palm of her hand and she curled her fingers around the kiss as if she wanted to keep it forever.

"I love you, Daniel." Her voice was low and sweet. "I think I have ever since you didn't rat me out to the chief that first day. And I have never found a way to stop."

Wild joy shot through him. "Mia, I want you in my life forever. I love you."

Just then the room seemed to burst into color as the sun came out from behind the clouds and the light from the skylights flooded the gleaming kitchen.

"Fireworks!" she exclaimed.

He was sure that must have some special meaning to her.

"Monique said when a guy told me he loved me, fireworks should go off and the world should suddenly seem brighter."

He brought her mouth to his and she kissed him eagerly, putting her arms around him, giving him what he had wanted all along but was afraid to accept.

He pulled back and smoothed her hair away from her face.

"If I asked you to marry me, would you think I've gone too far in the other direction?"

"No. No, I would not. I'd accept, but I have one condition."

He laughed. She made him laugh and he knew she always would. "Really? A condition? Already?"

"Yes."

"Okay. I deserve that. You name it."

It was a while before she could name anything, but fireworks went off over and over.

# *EPILOGUE*

THE BRIDES AND the grooms and their immediate families were all that fit in the tiny old wooden church for the double wedding ceremony. On the brides' side were Mia's parents, Monique's grandfather and Chief Montcalm. On the grooms' side were Heather Loch, Mrs. and Mr. Gardner and Lenny's partner, Officer Doyle.

Waiting, eagerly, at the Pirate's Roost for the wedding reception were more fishermen and women and townsfolk from the Braven's gatherings than could be counted on the fingers and toes of both brides and their spouses. There were on- and off-duty police officers, dry cleaning customers and the owner of said store, a contractor without his blue shirt but with his lovely wife and several of his crew. Also in attendance were four distinguished-looking women and their mates, some university types. There were even a few teenagers, but they didn't stay past the food.

Tending to the guests were the most wonderful bunch of workers, none of whom had been found digging for treasure anywhere in town.

\* \* \* \* \*

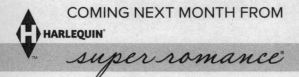

# COMING NEXT MONTH FROM

**HARLEQUIN**®

*super romance*®

## Available December 3, 2013

### #1890 CAUGHT UP IN YOU • *In Shady Grove*
### by Beth Andrews

Eddie Montesano does what's best for his son. No way does he want his kid in special classes, regardless of what the teacher says. So Eddie will stand up to her...even if the teacher is one very sexy Harper Kavanagh!

### #1891 A TEXAS CHILD • *Willow Creek, Texas*
### by Linda Warren

Years ago, Assistant D.A. Myra Delgado betrayed Levi Coyote—but now she desperately needs his help. Will working together just make them relive past heartaches? Or will their commitment to finding a missing child bring them together?

### #1892 THE RANCH SHE LEFT BEHIND
*The Sisters of Bell River Ranch* • by Kathleen O'Brien

Penny Wright has always lived up to other people's labels. But no more. She won't live on the family ranch, even if she's come home to help. Her little house in town is perfect for her...and so is the gorgeous man next door, Max Thorpe!

### #1893 SLEEPLESS IN LAS VEGAS by Colleen Collins

Private investigator Drake Morgan would rather work with anyone than Val LeRoy. She's nothing but trouble. Still, he's learning to appreciate her *unusual* approach to investigating. Now all he has to do is control his attraction to her.

### #1894 A VALLEY RIDGE CHRISTMAS by Holly Jacobs

Aaron Holder doesn't mean to sound like old man Scrooge. But Maeve Buchanan's bubbly holiday cheer brings it out in him. It's a sudden act of Christmas kindness that finally draws them together, though will they admit their true feelings even when they meet under the mistletoe?

### #1895 THE SWEETEST HOURS by Cathryn Parry

Kristin Hart has romantic notions of Scotland, but she doesn't expect to find a real-life Scotsman in her Vermont hometown. Turns out Malcolm MacDowell isn't exactly Prince Charming when he closes the factory. To save her town she must go confront him...and maybe find a little magic along the way.

---

This might be the best Robbie Burns' Day ever
for Kristin Hart. Why? Because the gorgeous
consultant, George, who her company hired
joined her at her family's celebrations. And now,
the night is coming to a close.... Read on for an
exciting excerpt of the upcoming book

# The Sweetest Hours

### By Cathryn Parry

"I hope that you got all you need from us today," Kristin said,
as she walked George out.

He turned and smiled at her, descending two steps lower
than her on the stairs. His eyes now level to hers. "I did."

His hand touched hers, warm from the dinner table inside.
His fingers brushed her knuckles. Kristin was glad she hadn't
put on mittens.

"Kristin," he said in a low voice.

She waited, barely daring to breathe. Involuntarily, she shivered and he opened his coat, enveloping her in his warmth. It
was a chivalrous response, protective and special.

"Is it bad that I don't want this day to end?" she whispered.

"No." His voice was throaty. The gruff…Scottishness of it
seeped into her.

His eyes held hers. And as she swallowed, he angled his head and…and then he kissed her. He was tender. His lips molded gently over hers, moving with sweetness, as if to remember her fully, once he was gone.

The car at the end of the drive flashed its lights at them.

He straightened and drew back. Taking the warmth of his coat with him.

"I have to go." He looked toward the car. "Maybe some day I can tempt you away. To Scotland."

Maybe if she were a different person, in a braver place, she would dare to follow him and kiss him again…. But she wasn't that fearless.

"Goodbye, George," she whispered, touching his hand one last time.

"Kristin?" His voice caught. "I hope you find your castle."

And then he was off, into the winter night, the snow swirling quietly in the lamplight.

**After this magical night, will George tempt her to Scotland? And if he does, what will Kristin find there? Find out in THE SWEETEST HOURS by Cathryn Parry, available December 2013 from Harlequin® Superromance®.**